"What's wrong? And, damn it, don't try to tell me it's nothing,"

he growled before she could open her mouth.

If she hadn't been so shattered, Sarah would have laughed at the stubborn set of Dugan's square chin. She didn't doubt for a minute that he was a man who came through on his promises. Just like the man on the phone. She shuddered at the comparison, the hysterical urge to giggle threatening to turn into a watery sob, frightening her. She saw Dugan's eyes narrow, saw him take another step toward her, and she wanted to cry, "Don't!" He'd slipped past barriers that she'd thought were carved in stone, and she was too raw, too vulnerable, to suffer his nearness now with any degree of composure.

Jerkily, she gestured to the notes scribbled on the paper in front of her. "I—I think I just got a call from the r-rapist...."

Dear Reader,

There's so much excitement going on this month that I hardly know where to begin. First of all, you've no doubt noticed that instead of the four Silhouette Intimate Moments novels you usually see, this month there are six. That increase—an increase you'll see every month from now on—is a direct result of your enthusiasm for this line, an enthusiasm you've demonstrated by your support right where it counts: at the bookstore or by your membership in our reader service. So from me—and all our authors—to you, *thank you!* And here's to the future, a future filled with more great reading here at Silhouette Intimate Moments.

And speaking of great reading, how about this month's author lineup? Heather Graham Pozzessere, Barbara Faith, Linda Turner, Rachel Lee and Peggy Webb, making her Intimate Moments debut. And I haven't even mentioned Linda Howard yet, but she's here, too, with *Mackenzie's Mission,* one of the most-requested books of all time. For all of you who asked, for all of you who've waited as eagerly as I have, here is Joe "Breed" Mackenzie's story. This is a man to die for (though not literally, of course), to sigh for, cry for and—since he's a pilot—fly for. And he's all yours as of now, so don't let him pass you by. And in honor of our increase to six books, and because Joe and some of the other heroes I have in store for you are so special, we've decided to inaugurate a special program as part of the line: American Heroes. Every month one especially strong and sexy hero is going to be highlighted for you within the line, and believe me, you won't want to miss his story!

Finally, I hope you've noticed our bold new cover design. We think it captures the sense of excitement that has always been the hallmark of Silhouette Intimate Moments, and I hope you do, too.

In the months to come, expect only the best from us. With authors like Kathleen Eagle, Emilie Richards, Dallas Schulze and Kathleen Korbel coming your way, how can the future be anything but bright?

Leslie Wainger
Senior Editor and Editorial Coordinator

THE LOVE OF
DUGAN
MAGEE

Linda
Turner

Silhouette®
INTIMATE MOMENTS®
Published by Silhouette Books New York
America's Publisher of Contemporary Romance

SILHOUETTE BOOKS
300 East 42nd St., New York, N.Y. 10017

THE LOVE OF DUGAN MAGEE

ISBN: 0-373-07448-4

First Silhouette Books printing September 1992

All the characters in this book have no existence outside the imagination of the author and have no relation whatsoever to anyone bearing the same name or names. They are not even distantly inspired by any individual known or unknown to the author, and all incidents are pure invention.

Printed in the U.S.A.

Books by Linda Turner

Silhouette Desire

A Glimpse of Heaven #220
Wild Texas Rose #653
Philly and the Playboy #701

Silhouette Intimate Moments

The Echo of Thunder #238
Crosscurrents #263
An Unsuspecting Heart #298
Flirting with Danger #316
Moonlight and Lace #354
The Love of Dugan Magee #448

Silhouette Special Edition

Shadows in the Night #350

LINDA TURNER

began reading romances in high school and began writing them one night when she had nothing else to read. She's been writing ever since. Single and living in Texas, she travels every chance she gets, scouting locales for her books.

This book would have been very difficult to do without the help of Polly Jeter, the coordinator of the Temple, Texas, Crime Stoppers, and Brian Peters of the SAPD. Thank you both for your help and patience. I would also like to thank my cousin, Sheri Whiteley, for taking me to work with her at Crime Stoppers and giving me the opportunity to see how the program works firsthand. Thanks for all your help and input, Sheri.

Prologue

"Attention all units in the vicinity of Blanco and Jackson Keller. Code 211 in progress at 781 Blanco, Harry's Hot Dog Stand. Possible 10-71. Suspect armed with sawed-off shotgun. Repeat. Attention all units—"

A robbery in progress and a possible shooting. Detective Dugan Magee snatched up the mike of his radio and responded to the call, quickly giving his location. Seconds later he grabbed the portable flashing red light he carried in his unmarked car and slapped it on the roof at the same time that he hit the gas. He was off duty and on his way home after an incredibly frustrating day, but he was only three blocks from the scene and would probably be there before a black and white. Adrenaline pumping through his veins and sharpening his reflexes, he raced down Blanco with siren blaring. In his rearview mirror he caught the whirling lights of a backup unit more than a mile down the road behind him. Tires screeching, he shot into the poorly lit parking lot of the hot dog stand and hit the brakes, his eyes locked on the scene before him.

Four customers lay face-down on the pavement, their hands locked behind their heads, unmoving. Standing over them brandishing the sawed-off shotgun was a giant of a man, fury etching his face, daring anyone to move. No one did.

Swearing, Dugan turned the wheel sharply and set his car skidding to an abrupt stop thirty yards from the gunman. Before it had shuddered to a complete standstill, he was out of the vehicle, his gun in his hands as he took up a crouching position behind the front end. "Police!" he yelled as his backup came screaming into view. "Drop it!"

"No! Stop! My God, what are you doing?"

Startled, Dugan's eyes swung to the woman who rushed out of the shadows at one side of the parking lot, frantically waving her arms as she stepped right into the line of fire of his drawn gun. "What the hell . . . Lady, get out of the way!"

"No, no!" she cried, standing her ground. "You don't understand. It's not real. There's no robbery. We're taping a reenactment for Crime Watchers. Oh, God, you're ruining everything and we were just getting it right!"

The roaring sirens of two more arriving patrol cars drowned out Dugan's curse as he finally spotted the camera, nearly lost in the darkness, recording everything. Uncomfortable color flooded his neck and cheeks. Crime Watchers, he thought with a groan. She was with Crime Watchers, which meant she had to be Sarah Jane Haywood, the new director of the program. And the chief's goddaughter.

"Great," he muttered to himself. "Just great." He couldn't have found a better way to cap off a bitch of a Friday. Frustrated, anger gleaming in his smoky gray eyes, he glared at her. "Damn it, lady, don't you know better than to step in front of someone holding a gun? You could have gotten your head shot off! And why the hell didn't you notify the department of your taping schedule? Someone could have been seriously hurt here!"

Sarah stiffened, her own glare glacial. She'd instinctively stepped in front of him so that just such a mishap *wouldn't* happen, but she had no intention of explaining herself to such an infuriating man. "If you'll check the bulletin board downtown, you'll see a posted notice of tonight's shoot," she said coldly. "I believe that's standard procedure."

"Next time send a memo out," he snapped, jamming his piece back into his shoulder harness. "Not everyone reads the bulletin board." Without giving her a chance to respond, he whirled to face the uniformed officers surrounding the hot dog stand like it was under siege. "False alarm, guys," he called in a voice that was still tight with fury. "Put away your guns. Looks like we busted up Crime Watchers."

The tension snapped; a chuckle floated on the night air. In the shadowed light Dugan caught the glint of grins as the other officers reholstered their weapons. He knew from past experience that the whole force would be laughing itself silly over this incident by Monday morning. Normally he would have been, too. But the scene had looked too real when he'd driven up, too dangerous. If the actor holding the shotgun had unwittingly made one wrong move, he didn't like to think what he might have done. Swearing, he shot Sarah Haywood a hostile look and turned toward his car. He drove out of the parking lot with a squealing of tires that said louder than words that he was not amused.

Chapter 1

The note Sarah Haywood found in her In box after lunch was short and to the point. *Chief Fletcher wants to see you.* Staring at it, Sarah felt a grin tug at one corner of her mouth. There was nothing intimidating about the message itself, yet Sarah knew if she'd received the command a week ago, she would have been more than a little worried. Being Russell Fletcher's goddaughter wouldn't have saved her if the chief had been in one of his moods when he'd heard about the fiasco at Harry's Hot Dog Stand. And she didn't doubt that he had heard about it. He ran a tight ship and knew everything that went on at the SAPD. The fact that he hadn't called her in before now could only mean that he'd been as amused as the rest of the force had. God, wouldn't the jokes ever end? It had been over a week!

Hurrying upstairs to his office, she gave his door a perfunctory knock at a nod from his secretary and swept inside. She intended to tease Russ about calling her on the carpet when she'd been on the job little more than a month, but the words died in her throat when she found him standing at the window. His back was half turned to her and a dark frown etched his weathered face as he stared at the red rocked Bexar County Courthouse down the street. The weight of the world seemed to rest on his shoulders.

Surprised, she stopped just inside the door. He wasn't a man who normally brooded. "What's wrong?" she asked bluntly, dispensing with a greeting.

He turned at the sound of her voice, affection pushing aside the shadows darkening his deep-set blue eyes. He'd never had a child of his own, but if he'd had, he would have wanted a daughter just like Sarah. Dressed for success in a green and white spring suit that tried and failed to conceal a figure that was model slim, she appeared at first glance to be one of those frightfully competent career women who could play hardball with any man stupid enough to get in her way in her climb to the top. But a second, closer look revealed a mouth that was soft and vulnerable, and large, wide-set eyes that were windows to a tenderhearted soul. As a child she'd cried over one-eyed teddy bears and puppies caught in the rain. At twenty-seven, she could get suspiciously bright-eyed over sentimental telephone commercials, though she tried her best to hide that weakness from the world. To a large extent she had succeeded. Only he and her family knew just how close she had come to the breaking point over the last three years.

Which made what he had to tell her all the more difficult to say. Stalling for time, he moved to his desk, scowling at her with twinkling eyes. "Can't an old man have his goddaughter in to chat for a few minutes without everyone making a federal case out of it?" he blustered. "Have a seat and tell me how you like the new job. You want some coffee? A soda? And don't tell me you're watching your weight. You're too thin as it is."

Truly alarmed now, Sarah stubbornly remained where she was. From the moment he'd hired her as the head of the San Antonio Police Department's Crime Watchers Program a month ago, they'd both been careful to keep their relationship at the station strictly professional. Everyone knew she was his goddaughter, but there'd been no chitchats in his office, no contact with him at all on the clock unless her job called for it, which it hadn't thus far. It was the detectives and captains she worked with, not the chief.

Don't jump to conclusions, a voice in her head admonished, but it was suddenly painfully clear to her why he was beating around the bush. Her spine ramrod straight, she looked him right in the eye. "You called me in here to fire me, didn't you?"

He couldn't have been more surprised had she asked him if he was having an affair with the mayor's wife. "Good Lord, no! Why would you even think such a thing?"

"Because you look like you've got some bad news to tell me and you don't quite know how to say it. I didn't think you'd be so upset about a little mixup."

Russ lifted a graying brow at that. "A *little* mixup?"

"Okay, so one detective and three squad cars might be stretching 'little,' but it turned out all right. No one was hurt."

"Honey, this isn't about the hot dog stand." He sighed heavily. "Sit down," he said quietly, his mouth compressed into a grim line as he stepped around his desk and perched on the edge of it. "We need to talk."

She would have preferred to stand, but something in his tone warned her that whatever he had to discuss was something she would take better sitting down. Outwardly composed, she sank into the chair in front of his desk. "Okay, I'm sitting," she said, curling her fingers around the arms of the chair as she unconsciously braced herself. "Just give it to me straight and let's get it over with. What's wrong?"

His eyes trapped hers. "There's been another rape."

The words were softly, reluctantly spoken, but for a split second Sarah recoiled as if he'd struck her. *Rape.* Memories, stark and brutal in their clarity, lashed at her. A dark night three years ago. A small car with power locks she couldn't reach. A date who refused to take no for an answer.

Suddenly cold, she shivered, the action abruptly bringing her back to her surroundings. From across the width of the desk, she could feel Russ's concern and love, his frustration at his inability to shield her from memories of a night that was better off forgotten. She'd felt the same mix of emotions from her parents, seen the same sadness in their eyes. Hating it, yet loving them all, she'd learned to hide the fear she fought daily to keep locked away.

Forcing her fingers to relax their fierce grip on the chair, she asked huskily, "When?"

"Early this morning. Same M.O. as the other two."

Sarah didn't have to ask what that was—only someone who lived in a cave could have missed what had been going on in the city for the last two weeks. Ten nights ago a masked man, who spoke with what was obviously a phony English accent, dragged a student nurse off to a remote area, where he viciously violated her. It wasn't until three nights after that, when a cleaning woman was grabbed as she left the office building where she worked, that the police began to suspect they had a serial rapist on their hands. This latest rape only confirmed those suspicions.

Fighting the need to hug herself, she sat frozen in her chair. "Did the crime scene turn up any clues this time?"

He hesitated, but there was no protecting her from the truth. "No," he said flatly. "Nothing. The only thing we've got to go on is a bad accent and a blue ski mask that could have been purchased at any discount store in town."

So the detectives handling the case had no clues, no suspects, and not even a hint of where to look for either, while a madman freely moved about the city in the shadows of the night, picking his victims at his leisure, as elusive as a bad dream. Suddenly the need for this meeting and her godfather's reluctance to get right to the point became clear. "You want me to do a reenactment of one of the rapes for Crime Watchers."

Russ winced at the flat, unemotional cadence of her words. He'd have given anything if she'd just flash those brown eyes of hers at him and demand to know how he could ask such a thing of her! The Sarah he'd watched grow from toddler to gawky teenager to beautiful young woman had always moved through life like a whirlwind, spontaneous and free, catching up family and friends in her laughter and tears, her emotions there on her face for all the world to see. Then a sorry excuse for a man had date raped her and gotten off scot-free because of lack of evidence. He'd left Houston soon after that, flaunting his freedom, and she'd never been the same since. Oh, she'd gotten on with her life, acting as if that awful night had never happened, but she guarded her emotions carefully, refusing to let anyone, including those who loved her the most, get too close.

In the last three years the wall of reserve she'd constructed around herself had cracked only once—last month when her rapist returned to Houston. Knowing she was terrified of running into the man face to face, Russ had offered her the job as head of the Crime Watchers Program in San Antonio. With her years of experience in community theater and skills as an executive secretary, she was more than qualified for the position. She'd jumped at the chance to get out of Houston.

When he'd made the offer, Russ never dreamed he'd be forced to ask this of her. But he had no other choice. There'd been three rapes too many. Someone somewhere in the city had to have seen *something*. If they were too scared to come forward, the five-thousand-dollar reward offered by Crime Watchers just might tempt them to call in.

Unable to bear the haunted look that darkened her brown eyes with a fear she wouldn't even admit to, he started to reach for her. "Honey, I'm sorry. You know I wouldn't ask this of you if I thought there was any other way—"

"No, don't!" She stopped him with nothing more than a sharp, jerky movement of her hand, then could have bitten off her tongue when she saw the hurt that flashed in his eyes. She knew he was only trying to help her, to protect her from a past that refused to stay buried. She loved him dearly, but sympathy from someone she loved was so much harder to handle than that of strangers. One touch, one hug, and her control would start to crumble. And that was something she couldn't allow to happen. She wouldn't, *couldn't* feel. Because if she didn't let herself feel anything, she couldn't hurt.

Her eyes silently pleading with him for understanding, she said, "Don't apologize for asking me to do my job. My past has no bearing on today." Not giving him the chance to point out that she wouldn't even be in San Antonio having to deal with this if it hadn't been for her own rape, she deliberately pushed the memories back into the dark little corner where she kept them locked away. Squaring her shoulders, she lifted her chin. "How soon do you need the reenactment taped?"

In the blink of an eye she was all business. Russ could have hugged her, he was so proud of her. Instead he rose and stepped back behind his desk. "Tomorrow if possible. If not, then the day after that."

"Tomorrow!" she gasped. "You can't be serious! It usually takes me a week to put one together."

"We haven't got that kind of time," he retorted. "Fiesta's only a little more than a month away. Think about it. Think of all the partying that goes on around town during that week. All the tourists who don't know about the city's program, Park and Ride, who drive to the different events then have to park in out-of-the-way places, blocks from where they want to be. They'll stagger back to their cars in groups of twos and threes. Some of them will even be alone. More than a few will be drunk and totally unaware of their surroundings. If this rapist is still on the loose, he's going to have a field day."

The images his words stirred sent sick dread coiling through her stomach. He was right. They didn't have any time to waste. Agitatedly she rose to her feet. "I'll call Freddy at the station and see if he's free to do the taping tomorrow night, then see what I can track down. We can have it ready for the twelve o'clock news on Thursday, but I'll need to meet with the detectives handling the case to work out the script—"

"They should be right outside." Leaning across his desk, he pressed the intercom button that connected him to his secretary. "Mrs. Trask, are Detectives Roberts and Magee here yet?"

"Yes, sir."

"Good. You can send them in now, please."

Slouched in the chair across from the secretary's desk, Dugan heard the chief's order and pushed to his feet, his hard-edged face etched with a scowl that showed every sign of being permanent. Twenty minutes, he thought in disgust. The old man had kept him and Buck cooling their heels for twenty damn minutes just so he could personally introduce them to his precious goddaughter.

For two cents Dugan would have told Fletcher he wanted nothing more to do with Sarah Haywood. He hadn't seen much of her in the dark at that damn hot dog stand the other night, but he knew all about her. Who didn't? For the last month she'd been the favorite subject of conversation in the locker room. Class, legs, and a smile that would freeze ice on an Eskimo's buns. From the first day she'd stepped foot in the station, she'd had men falling all over themselves to ask her out. According to the gossip mill, she'd coldly turned them all down flat, thereby earning herself the title of Ice Princess. If Dugan had had his way, he would have avoided her like the plague. Instead he and Buck now had to work with her. Sometimes, life could be nasty.

At his side, Buck grinned crookedly. "I've never worked with a princess before. Is she really as cold as everyone says? Maybe I should have worn my thermal underwear."

Shooting him a quelling look, Dugan reached for the handle to the chief's door. "Stuff it, Roberts. I've had it up to *here* about Sarah Haywood!"

Buck's blue eyes danced with devilment. "Touchy, touchy. The way I heard it, you're the only one who's been able to get a rise out of the princess. Course, afterward, the word is she almost froze your—"

"Buck, I'm warning you—"

"—Off," he finished triumphantly. "Who knows, man, she may be just the woman you've been waiting for. She'll shake you up a little."

"Don't even think it," Dugan retorted, and pushed open the door to the chief's office.

His long legs carried him halfway into the room before he saw her standing by the window with the light behind her, her red hair highlighted like a Madonna's. Surprise stopped him in his tracks. At their previous meeting he'd been too infuriated to take a really good look at the lady, but rumor had it that she was one of those women who exuded sex appeal with every breath she took, sending out signals that any man with blood in his veins would find difficult to ignore. But the woman who stood before him was anything but a seductress.

She could have been Miss America beautiful—she certainly had the bone structure for it. Nature had graced her delicately angled face with the high cheek bones and perfect skin of a model, then added large, expressive brown eyes and a wide, sensuous mouth for good measure. But instead of drawing attention to her prettiness by accentuating her assets, she seemed to have done everything possible to detract from them by wearing only the barest trace of makeup and no lipstick at all. The green and white suit that covered her willow-slim figure was attractive enough, but it concealed rather than flattered, hiding her long, slender legs all the way to mid calf. Even the rich, wild glory of her auburn hair was confined, gathered in a thick braid that kept all but a few rebellious strands off her neck.

Yet for all that, she was gorgeous in a way Dugan didn't want to notice. Quietly, innocently, breath-stealingly gorgeous. Deep in his gut, he felt heat stir when his eyes met hers, and suddenly he knew why most of the available men on the force—and a few that weren't—had made a play for her. It wasn't knowledge he wanted to have.

Sarah's eyes widened in recognition the minute she met his hostile gaze. *Oh, no!* He couldn't be one of the detectives she had to work with! Fate couldn't be so cruel.

"Sarah, I'd like you to meet Detectives Dugan Magee and Buck Roberts," Russ said, motioning to the tall, antagonistic man in front of her and then to his smaller, blond partner who followed him into the office. "I'm sure you recognize Magee," he teased, "but I wasn't sure if he took time to introduce himself when he rushed to your rescue the other night. He and Roberts are investigating the rapes and will be working with you on the reenactment."

Buck Roberts stuck out his hand, a boyish smile transforming his plain, angular face. "Nice to meet you, Ms. Haywood. I've seen your segments for Crime Watchers. You do good work."

For the last three years she'd made it a point to avoid contact of any kind with any man who wasn't a member of her family, but she sensed immediately that Buck Roberts was the type of man who would never be a threat to a woman. It was his partner she was worried about. Unable to hold back a smile, Sarah gave Buck's hand a quick, firm shake. "Thank you. But please, call me Sarah."

He nodded, releasing her hand, and she had no choice but to offer it to the man at his side. She braced herself for what should have been nothing more than a simple formality, but the second his long, strong fingers closed over hers, nothing was simple. Heat. It surrounded her, seeping from his palm to hers, slipping under her skin and shooting up her arm like an unexpected streak of summer lightning in a clear sky. Stunned, she stared down at their joined fingers and felt time come to a jarring halt. Somewhere in the back of her mind the voice of reason tried to

tell her that his handshake was no different from his partner's, but suddenly she felt as if he had stepped closer,
crowding her, stealing her breath. Startled, her gaze flew
to his.

He was the kind of man she now made it a point to
avoid, the kind who strode into a room and took charge
with his very presence, the kind who exuded a raw sexu-
ality with nothing more than a lift of a brow. Instinct told
her to back away from him before he destroyed the peace
of mind she'd worked so hard to regain since moving to
San Antonio, but her leaden feet refused to obey the command.

Dressed in scuffed cowboy boots and a charcoal-gray
suit that only seemed to emphasize the long, lean line of
him, he towered over her, topping her own five foot seven
by nearly half a foot. All angles and planes and rough
edges, his face was no softer in daylight than it had been
at night. Stubbornness—it was there in the square, un-
compromising line of his jaw, in the intimidating knot of
his dark brows, in the unyielding set of his granite chin. He
might have been made of stone but for the shock of thick,
coffee-colored hair that fell over his forehead and the sensuous curve of his unsmiling mouth. His frown still fierce,
he watched her with an unblinking intensity, his probing
gray eyes seeming to delve into her very soul.

Her heart lurching in her breast, Sarah jerked her hand
free and took a quick, involuntary step back, out of reach.
She saw his eyes sharpen in surprise, saw a dark brow lift
in mocking inquiry, and wanted to crawl into the nearest
hole. Instead she ignored the warm tide of color that
surged into her pale cheeks and coolly stood her ground.
"Detective Magee."

She acknowledged the introduction as regally as a queen
looking down her aristocratic little nose on a peon who'd

had the audacity to spit at her feet. He'd be damned if he was going to let her get away with it! "Make that Dugan," he said smoothly. "I'm not much on titles. How about you?"

Her expression didn't change by so much as a flicker of an eyelash, but inside, Sarah wanted to cringe in mortification. She didn't have to ask what title he was referring to, the knowledge was there in his steely gray eyes, mocking her. The police station had a grapevine that could put Ma Bell in the shade, and gossip about her had spread like wildfire from her first day on the job. *Ice Princess.* No one had had the nerve to call her that directly to her face, but she'd heard the whispers, and they hurt. Yet she couldn't bring herself to do the one thing that would deflate all the gossip about her—accept a date. If rumors that she was frigid kept men like Dugan Magee from asking her out, then she could live with the gossip.

"I suppose there's a time and place for them," she retorted, looking him right in the eye. "Some people need them to feel superior."

Hidden meanings fairly crackled in the air. Caught off guard by the sudden tension, the chief looked at Sarah questioningly, but the reserve she usually hid behind whenever a man got too close was firmly in place. Reluctantly he turned his attention to Dugan and Buck and the matter at hand. "I know you've done everything you can with the little you've had to work with," he said, "so the decision to film a reenactment at this point in the investigation is in no way a reflection on you. But Fiesta's right around the corner and we're running out of time. I want the bastard caught."

"Nobody wants to nail his ass to the wall any more than we do," Buck assured him, his blue eyes now as hard as diamonds. "We'll do whatever it takes to catch him."

The older man nodded. He'd never doubted it. "Good. Sarah's assured me she can have a reenactment put together for the noon news on Thursday. That doesn't give her much time, so I know you two will help her as much as you can."

Dugan's mouth flattened into a thin line of disgust. That's what this meeting was all about? The chief wanted them to baby-sit his hoity-toity goddaughter and protect her from the ugly realities of the case. He should have known. The last thing the Ice Princess would want to deal with would be rape. "When do you want to work on the script?"

His tone was coolly civil, his gaze clearly irritated. Annoyed in spite of the tight control she held on her own emotions, Sarah bit back the urge to tell him she didn't want to work with *him* at all. "This afternoon if you're free. We can hammer out a rough draft and I'll polish it up at home tonight. We'll tape tomorrow night."

"Once the segment airs, Sarah will report back to you on any response it generates," the chief added. "I want all calls followed up, regardless of how insignificant they may seem. It may take something as trivial as a caller's unwarranted suspicions of a neighbor to break this case wide open."

"And if we don't get any calls?" Dugan said, voicing the thought in all their minds. "Then what?"

The chief sighed heavily. "Then Fiesta's going to be one long nightmare I don't even want to think about. I suggest we do everything we can to make sure that doesn't happen."

At his desk two hours later Dugan scowled down at the report he was finishing on the latest rape, his eyes blindly focused on the unfinished sentence he'd been mulling over for the past ten minutes. Pandemonium reigned around him unnoticed. Phones rang, someone cursed the sludge that passed for coffee in the coffee machine in the corner, and members of two rival gangs yelled at each other in the hallway as they were hauled in for questioning about a shooting in a downtown housing project.

From his own desk three feet away Buck watched him with rueful eyes, a grin twitching at his mouth. "You know, I don't think I've ever seen you put so much time in on a report before. You sick, or what? You hate paperwork."

Dugan didn't even look up. "I still hate it. But it's got to be done."

"Oh." Leaning back to prop his feet up on the corner of his desk, Buck made himself comfortable and prepared to enjoy himself. Gazing thoughtfully at his nails, he said, "I thought this newfound dedication might have something to do with the princess."

Slowly, carefully, Dugan lifted his head until he had his too innocent friend caught in the trap of his dangerously narrowed eyes. "And why would you think that?"

Another man might have started backpedaling at the sound of the silkily spoken question, but Buck only gazed back at him with laughing eyes. He'd worked with Dugan for too long to be so easily intimidated. "Because you almost dropped your teeth when you saw her. Any time a man does that the *second* time he meets up with a woman, he's in trouble. She knocked you for a loop, Magee, and you know it."

A muscle jumped along Dugan's jaw. "In case you've forgotten, I'm not looking for a woman. And the princess obviously isn't looking for a man, so this discussion is pointless. Shut your yap, Roberts."

But Buck only crossed one booted ankle over the other and jauntily tapped the air with one foot. "If you *were* looking for a woman, you probably couldn't go wrong with a woman like Sarah Haywood. She's one classy lady. And discriminating. Any woman who has the good sense to refuse a date with Mark Evers and Steven Rodriguez is no dummy. You could do worse."

"Damn it, Buck—"

The phone on his desk rang, cutting off his impatient retort. Snatching it up, Dugan glared at his grinning partner and growled, "Detective Magee."

"Daddy?"

At the sound of his fourteen-year-old daughter's tentative greeting, Buck and the coming meeting with the chief's goddaughter were forgotten. Alarm snaked through him. Tory called him at least once a week from California, where she lived with her mother, but never at this time of day. "Tory? What's wrong?"

"I . . . I just needed to talk to you."

He thought he heard her swallow a sob, but couldn't be sure. His fingers bit into the phone. "What about, sweetheart? C'mon, tell your old dad what's wrong," he urged softly when she hesitated. "You know I'll fix it if I can."

Once, long ago when they'd both still believed in fairy tales, he wouldn't have added any restrictions to what he could fix for her. But the last six years had taught them both that while his love for her was limitless, what he could do for her was not. Some things were out of his control.

"Mom and Joe had another fight," she sniffed finally. "It was awful."

Dugan swallowed a curse. If he'd been a vindictive man, he could have found a lot of satisfaction in the fact that the man his ex-wife, Laura, had divorced him to marry had turned out to be less than ideal husband material. But any feelings he had for Laura had died a long time ago. His only concern now was for Tory. Damn it, what the hell was Laura doing? Couldn't she see her constant fights with her husband were turning his daughter's home into a battlefield?

"I'm sorry, sweetheart. I know it's not easy for you, but summer will be here before you know it, then you can spend some time with me."

"Can't I come now, Daddy? *Pleeeease?*" she begged before he could say no. "If you'd just talk to Mom, I know you could talk her into it. You're good at that kind of thing. All you have to do is remind her she's had me all to herself for six years. It's your turn now."

If he'd thought that argument would have done any good, he'd have been on the phone to Laura the minute Tory hung up. He wanted his daughter, and he'd made damn sure that Laura knew it. He'd fought her tooth and nail for joint custody when they divorced, but he hadn't stood a chance with a judge who believed an eight-year-old little girl belonged with her mother. Then Laura had dragged Tory off to L.A. with her—in spite of the fact that Tory had thrown a fit to stay with him—and his bitterness had nearly destroyed him. Frustrated and disillusioned, he'd gradually come to realize that the only way he would ever have a chance of convincing his ex-wife to let Tory live with him was to make peace with her. He had, but she still refused to budge on changing—or even sharing—custody.

Wishing he had Laura there before him now to shake some sense into her, he said regretfully, "Honey, you know it won't do any good—"

"I hate it here, Daddy," she choked in a voice thick with tears. "You don't know what it's like. I don't even like to go home anymore. Please . . ."

Her unhappiness struck him right in the heart. "All right, honey," he soothed gruffly. "I'll call her tonight. Okay? It can't hurt to ask. But don't you nag her about it. That'll only make her dig in her heels more."

She gave a watery giggle. "I won't say a word. I promise. Thanks, Daddy."

"There's nothing to thank me for, sweetheart. I love you." Hanging up with her "Luv you" ringing in his ears, he frowned down at the phone and wished he had as much faith in himself as she did.

"Damn!"

The softly spoken curse drew his eyes to Buck, who had just hung up his own phone and was quickly shrugging into his suit coat, the wicked amusement that had lighted his eyes only moments before replaced by worry. Dugan straightened. "Problem?"

He nodded. "The nurse from Bryan's school just called. He fell during recess and gashed his head open. She thinks he needs stitches and she can't find Cathy. I've got to take him to the emergency room and get him patched up. I don't know when I'll be back."

"Don't worry about it," Dugan told him. "I can handle anything that crops up around here. You just take care of your son."

"Thanks, man. I owe you."

Looking more harried than Dugan had ever seen him, Buck hurried out the door. It wasn't until he was out of sight that Dugan remembered Sarah Haywood and swore. It was turning out to be a hell of a day.

When the knock came at her office door, Sarah stiffened. Refusing to allow herself to dwell on the subject of this week's reenactment, she'd spent the past two hours setting up the shoot and already had Freddy and his camera lined up for tomorrow night. Before the meeting in the chief's office had broken up, they'd decided to focus the public's attention on the first rape. The possibility of someone having seen something was greater than in the other two rapes because the victim had been snatched right out of a hospital parking lot. As usual Sarah's biggest headache had been finding actors to play the parts. There were any number of aspiring Oscar winners out there only too anxious for television exposure, but their eagerness to do the job usually dive-bombed when they learned there was no pay and, worse yet, no screen credit. Luckily she'd been able to track down two college drama students who felt the experience itself more than compensated for the lack of pay.

Now her only problem was finding a way to work with Dugan Magee. She didn't kid herself into thinking it would be easy—there was something about the man that made the air back up in her lungs. He disturbed her more than she cared to admit, and after the way she had jerked her hand out of his, she didn't doubt that he knew it.

Thank God, Buck Roberts would be there to act as a buffer between them, she told herself as she called out, "Come in."

But when the door opened, there was only Dugan standing there, larger than life, already filling her office though he'd done nothing more than step across the threshold. Unconsciously, her fingers tightened on the pencil she held as her heart began to pound. Unable to stop herself, she looked past him to the empty hallway. "Where's Buck?"

She looked as cool as a cucumber sitting there behind her desk, the lift of her delicately arched brow showing only the mildest curiosity. For a fleeting moment, however, Dugan would have sworn that something that looked uncomfortably like apprehension had flashed in her eyes. But what did she have to be apprehensive about? Frowning, he strode toward her, his eyes searching the mask of composure she hid behind. Damn it, what was she thinking? "He had a family emergency," he said, explaining the situation. "He won't be back today."

So it was just the two of them. Alone. Her throat went dry at the thought.

Call it off! a desperate voice ordered in her head. *There's no reason why you have to do this now. You can wait until Buck gets back tomorrow so you won't have to work with Dugan alone.*

For the span of a heartbeat she was tempted to jump at the suggestion. He had done nothing more than walk further into her office and take the chair across from her desk, but she already felt as if he was too close, too big, too masculine. She didn't want to be aware of him as a man; she didn't want to be aware of the breadth and strength of his shoulders, the animal grace with which he moved, the measuring way he watched her. But she couldn't stop herself, and that terrified her.

But she still couldn't call off this meeting. The hard glint in his eyes told her that was exactly what he expected her to do, and she'd be damned if she'd give him the satisfaction. "Then we might as well get started on the script," she said calmly. "Since there's little likelihood that there were any witnesses to the rape itself, we'll focus on the abduction of the victim from the hospital parking lot." All business, she turned to the computer monitor on her desk. "I'll need all the pertinent details—location, time, the clothes both parties were wearing, any conversation, or identifying mannerisms the victim was able to report."

For a long, tense moment he didn't do anything but give her a hard stare. Though she never took her gaze from the monitor in front of her, Sarah felt the touch of his eyes all the way down to her toes before he finally jerked a small notebook out of his pocket and surveyed his notes.

"The victim, a twenty-one-year-old student nurse, works the late shift at Westfield Hospital," he said flatly. "On the night of March 27, she developed a migraine and took sick leave. She walked out of the hospital at 3:05 a.m. and headed for her car, which was parked in the southeast corner of the parking lot. Just as she was unlocking her car a man wearing a blue ski mask, black pants and a black turtleneck, grabbed her from behind, put a knife to her throat and forced her to walk with him into the woods across the street. In a bad English accent, he told her he wouldn't hurt her if she didn't fight him. He then raped her, tied her to a tree with her panty hose, and left her to get free the best way she could."

Sarah stared down at her fingers, which had begun to tremble on the keys, and thickly swallowed the coppery taste of fear that welled up in her throat. With ruthless disregard for the price it cost her, she turned a blind eye to the words she was typing into the computer and deliberately shut down her emotions. "Did she give you any description of the rapist? Height? Weight?"

Dugan's mouth tightened. There wasn't an ounce of pity or caring in her voice, not a flicker of sympathy on her expressionless face. No wonder she'd been nicknamed Ice Princess. She had to be the most unfeeling woman he'd ever met in his life!

"He's a small man," he said coldly. "Five-eight, one hundred and fifty pounds. He never took the mask off, but there's a possibility his eyes are brown. It was dark and the victim couldn't be sure."

Somewhere in the coldness that enveloped her, Sarah heard the disapproval in his voice, but she didn't even flinch. What he thought of her didn't matter. She just had to get through this as quickly as possible. "Did she say anything to dissuade him? Try to fight him in any way? I'd like to keep the dialogue as accurate as possible."

"She begged him not to hurt her."

The words went through Sarah like a lance, the memory of that same plea falling from her own lips echoing in her head like a litany from hell. With fingers that stumbled, she finished the rough draft and sent the information to the printer with a push of a key. Seconds later she handed the hard copy to Dugan. "That should be a fair reenactment of what happened."

He read it as dispassionately as she had typed it and reluctantly admitted to himself that she did damn good work. She had depicted not only the details of the abduction in what would only be a thirty-second spot, but also the horror. From the coolness with which she'd written it, he wouldn't have thought there was that much emotion in her.

Giving credit where credit was due, he said, "Actually, it's more than fair. It's excellent."

He'd made no attempt to hide his surprise. Or his dislike. Considering the panic he stirred in her just with his presence, she thought it was time they lay their cards on the table. Her eyes locked with his. "You don't like me, do you, Detective Magee?"

If she hoped to unsettle him, she was disappointed. He merely lifted a brow. "Do I have to like you to work with you?"

"No."

"Then what difference does it make?" Rising to his feet, he headed for the door. "Since we're finished here, I have other things to do. I'll see you at the taping tomorrow night."

He walked out without a backward glance, leaving Sarah sitting at her desk, staring after him. After tomorrow night there would be no reason for them to work together again unless a call came in once the reenactment was aired. Disturbed by the tingling awareness his presence had wrought and she still felt, even after he was gone, Sarah could only see that as a blessing.

Chapter 2

The sky was dark and clear, the warm spring air sweetly scented with the mountain laurel that grew in small islands in the parking lot of Westfield Hospital. It was a night for stargazers and daydreamers, but Sarah was in no mood to appreciate its beauty. She just wanted to get the taping over with and go home. From the look of things, she wasn't going to be able to do either of those anytime soon. Darcy Fredricks, the college student who had agreed just yesterday to play the victim in the reenactment, was more than twenty minutes late. Sarah had a sinking feeling she wasn't going to show.

This wouldn't be the first time an actor had failed to show up, of course. No-shows weren't uncommon, considering the fact that no pay was involved, but finding a replacement at the last minute was often a nightmare. She'd been known to pull off-duty officers right out of the station when she was shorthanded, and she'd even played a few parts herself when she was desperate. But she liked to keep her on-screen involvement to a minimum whenever possible. Since she introduced herself at the beginning of each segment and gave the lead-in information, she wasn't protected by anonymity as the other actors were. She hadn't had any problems so far, but her home number was restricted and patrols on her street were increased whenever she stepped in as a last-minute replacement.

In spite of that, this was one part she didn't want to play. Just thinking about it made her blood run cold.

Quelling the urge to pace, she stared at the entrance to the parking lot, willing Darcy to appear. But there wasn't a car in sight, only an arriving ambulance that took the corner on what looked like two wheels and disappeared from view, its red lights whirling and siren blaring as it shot toward the emergency entrance at the back of the hospital.

Then there was only silence again . . . the peaceful silence of the night. The eery, hushed silence that emanated from the thick woods that rose like an impenetrable wall in the darkness across the street. Without quite knowing how her gaze came to be trained there, Sarah couldn't drag her eyes away from the black, concealing shadows where the rapist had brutally attacked his first victim. A shiver of revulsion slid down her spine, chilling her, urging her to flee.

"How much longer we gonna wait? I ain't got all night, you know. I gotta date."

The complaint, grumbled for the fifth time in as many minutes, came from Jason Tyler, the student she'd lined up to play the rapist. He'd arrived late, then done nothing but complain when he learned Sarah intended to wait for Darcy. Tired of his self-centeredness, she said firmly, "We'll wait another few minutes. She may have gotten the time mixed up or had car trouble or something."

When he only snorted at that, she turned away, only to stop when Dugan's voice rumbled out. "And if she doesn't show? Then what?"

She didn't want to think about that. She didn't want to think about *him*. But he gave her no choice. He'd already been on the scene when she and Freddy arrived with the camera and lighting equipment, sitting in his unmarked car in the southeast corner of the parking lot, watching everything that moved. Including her.

Unnerved by the way she could almost feel his eyes touching her, she'd tried to ignore him as she and Freddy set up everything for the taping. But Dugan Magee wasn't a man who was easily ignored. Even with her back turned to him most of the time, she was aware of the way the light from the nearby streetlights deepened the angles and planes of his face and shadowed his eyes as he casually leaned against his car. He never made a move toward her, or did a single thing to draw her gaze, yet she could have described in detail the way his blue-gray knit shirt clung to the hard muscles of his chest. And she didn't even want to think about the way his snug-fitting, obviously well-loved faded jeans hugged his lean hips and long legs.

Praying that he couldn't see the heat climbing into her cheeks in the poor lighting, she shrugged. "We could always postpone until tomorrow night."

But the words were hardly out of her mouth before Freddy Sanchez, the camera man, was shaking his head. "Sorry, Sarah, but I'm booked up the rest of the week. If we don't get this done tonight, we'll have to wait until next week."

Since that was out of the question, they had no choice but to do the shoot tonight. Her stomach churning with growing dread, she once again checked the entrance to the parking lot.

Dugan wasn't sure, but he could swear that Sarah's usually enigmatic brown eyes were dark with desperation. "It looks like she's not coming," he said quietly, guessing her thoughts. "Why don't you play the victim? You've got the same build, your hair's just redder. No one will even notice in the dark."

She almost cringed at his words, denial tearing at her throat. No! She wouldn't do this. She couldn't. No one, knowing her history, could blame her for refusing to put herself in a position that would open up a Pandora's box of heinous memories. There had to be another way... someone else...

But the street that ran in front of the hospital remained frustratingly empty.

Her back to the wall, she accepted the inevitable. She had no choice, she told herself hollowly. Do it, get it over with, and go home and forget it. That was what she had to do. As long as she didn't let herself feel, she could handle it.

Her face carefully blank, her voice even, she said quietly, "I have a nurse's uniform in the car I brought along for Darcy to wear. It should fit. Give me a minute to change, then we can begin."

Later she never remembered walking into the hospital to change in the rest room, or returning to the parking lot where the men were waiting for her. Concentrating strictly on the mechanics of the shoot, she lined up what she had to do in her head and refused to allow herself to think of anything else. It should have been easy. For a while, it was.

Like a marine drill instructor working with new enlistees, she took charge. "All right, Freddy, are you ready? Let's try to get this in one take. Have you got the prop knife, Jason?" When he held it up for her inspection, she nodded. "Remember to make sure Freddy gets a good shot of it when you first grab me. You do know your lines, don't you?''

As there weren't but a few of them and he'd had almost half an hour to memorize them, she couldn't really blame him for huffing indignantly. For the first time since she'd put on the nurse's uniform, she smiled. ''Sorry, of course you do.'' She handed him the ski mask she'd brought along with the prop knife. ''Time to get this show on the road then. Put this on and let's get started.''

Without a word he did as she asked. That was when everything changed.

In the blink of an eye the air turned cooler, the night darker, more threatening. Sarah told herself the young man standing before her was the same one who'd spent the past half hour grumbling and pacing like a frustrated four-year-old. He wasn't a threat to her. She was perfectly safe. But she couldn't drag her gaze away from the mask and the eyes that gleamed behind it. The past, like a tiger waiting to pounce, crept closer. She'd been date raped, she reasoned as her skin started to crawl. The man who'd forced himself on her had been a friend who hadn't bothered to disguise his features in any way. Yet she only had to look at the masked figure before her to hear automatic door locks snapping shut like the slamming of a cage door. Without closing her eyes, she could feel strong male hands groping for her, forcing her...

Suddenly realizing just how close she stood to the edge of her own personal nightmare, she pulled herself sharply back to reality, horrified. Dear God, had the others seen? Could they hear her heart thundering with panic? Had they seen her fingers shaking in reaction before she'd buried them in the pockets of the nurse's uniform she wore?

''So what do we do first?'' Jason asked. ''Where do you want me?''

Thankful he hadn't noticed her distress, Sarah almost wilted in relief before she quickly pulled herself together and went to work. "Freddy, where do you want to start?"

Chewing on his bottom lip, he surveyed the scene, framing it in his mind. "How about a front shot of you walking toward your car with the hospital in the background. Then I want to get you from the back as you're walking between the rows of cars, so the viewers will feel as if they're right there with you. Then Jason's going to slip in behind you, that way we see him before you do. Okay?"

She nodded, her face impassive. "Sounds good. Let's do it."

Standing well out of camera range, Dugan watched Sarah walk back toward the hospital until Freddy had the distance he wanted. Turning, she started forward toward the spot where Jason would grab her, changing, from one heartbeat to another, into a nurse wearily making her way toward her car, her mouth drawn with pain as she rubbed at the migraine that held her head in a vise. Stunned by the transformation, Dugan couldn't take his eyes off her. Totally wrapped up in her role, she didn't even glance at Freddy as he zoomed in for a close-up. Yet for all her concentration, Dugan couldn't ignore the niggling feeling that something wasn't quite right.

He tried telling himself he was crazy. Sarah Haywood handled herself like a seasoned actress and obviously knew what she was doing. There was no reason for him to think she was in any kind of trouble. Hell, he hardly knew the woman. He couldn't possibly know what she was feeling and didn't want to. If his gut knotted when Jason started to sneak up on her, it was because the rapist was still out there, stalking innocent women for his own twisted enjoyment. The bastard's days were numbered; he just didn't know it yet.

You can do this. You can do this. The words echoed in Sarah's head like a mantra as she approached Freddy's small compact, which was identical to the victim's car. She could feel Jason drawing closer on silent feet, his breath hardly more than a whisper on the still night air. Her heart tripped, then picked up speed, and it took every ounce of her self-control not to look behind her. Deep down, where no one could see, she braced herself. But still he hesitated. Dear God, was there anything worse than this waiting? she wondered, fighting back a sob. Why didn't he just grab her and get it over with?

Suddenly he was directly behind her, a devil slipping out of the night to grab her, his chest pressed to her back, the bands of his arms surrounding her, the knife at her throat. On one level of consciousness her mind registered the fact that the knife was nothing but a prop and Jason was so nervous he was shaking. But the fear crawling under her skin had nothing to do with logic. She wanted to run, to scream, to give in to the panic choking her and lash out. But all she could manage was a startled gasp as her hands flew to the arm wedged under her chin, the blade of the knife resting just below her ear. "No, please..."

Her hoarsely whispered cry was straight out of the script, but she couldn't be sure later whether she was speaking her lines or denying what was about to happen. Her vision blurred, the present becoming less clear as the past tauntingly pushed beyond the lines of her control. Another night raised its ugly head, another man lunged at her, another terror, older and infinitely more horrible, tried to force itself upon her.

No! she screamed silently, her nails sinking into the arm that choked her. *Not again!* This time she would fight!

"Do as I say and I won't hurt you."

Caught up in the nightmare, it was several long moments before the gruffly spoken words came to her like a hand through the fog. She blinked, awareness flooding her. It was Jason who held her, Jason whose voice rose slightly in surprised alarm when she began to deviate from the script. The fingers gripping his arm had started to shake. He must have thought she was losing her mind!

The fight went out of her so quickly her knees almost buckled. But the camera was still rolling and she didn't allow the terror she knew was etched on her face to alter by so much as a flicker of an eyelash. Her eyes wide with fright and her breath tearing through her lungs, she managed what looked like a thick swallow and whispered hoarsely, "Y-yes. Whatever y-you s-say."

The relief that flashed in his eyes was almost comical, but he didn't break character. With a grunt of satisfaction, he urged her toward the woods that waited in the darkness across the street.

Sarah lost track of the number of times they repeated certain parts of the scene so Freddy could tape it from different angles. Once the lighting wasn't quite right; another time Jason forgot to make sure the knife was prominently displayed. An hour passed, then another. She never noticed. When Freddy was finally satisfied with the footage he'd gotten, she still wasn't finished for the night. Drawing herself up to her full five foot seven inches, her smile as easy as if she'd spent the past few hours reading a good book instead of struggling with a would-be rapist, she stood in front of the hospital, faced the camera and gave her lead-in information. The only thing left to do after that was the sign-off. Placing her back to the sinister woods, she urged anyone who might have seen or heard anything the night the nurse was raped to please call Crime Watchers. The five-thousand-dollar reward would be good for one week only.

"Okay, that's a wrap."

She uttered the words with a weary relief that seemed to come from the bottom of her soul. The camera clicked off, her shoulders drooped. For the first time since she'd pulled on the nurse's uniform, Sarah realized what the past few hours had cost her. Shaken, her nerves frayed and her knees trembling as if they could no longer support her weight, she gave serious consideration to sinking right down to the ground.

"That was a damn fine performance," Freddy congratulated her as he began to collect his equipment. "You had me convinced you were terrified."

"Yeah, you were really into it," Jason added. Taking off the ski mask, he ruffled his flattened hair and grinned, a mixture of awe and excitement dancing in his eyes. "It's like you just flipped a switch, and suddenly you had this look of horror on your face. I've never seen anything like it in my life! Why aren't you in Hollywood? You're good, lady!"

Sarah would have laughed at his boyish enthusiasm, but her nerves were too raw, the unexpected need to cry too close to the surface. "Thanks," she whispered, blinking rapidly. "I guess I was just...inspired tonight."

Still standing in the background, Dugan wasn't at all sure that inspiration had anything to do with the terror he'd seen on her face and heard in her voice. Even now, when the effects of the taping should have had time to gradually wear off, she was pale and drawn, her guard down. But it was the lost look in her soul-deep brown eyes that pulled at him. The last thing he'd expected from the Ice Princess was vulnerability.

Disturbed, he felt concern stir in him and bit back a curse. He wasn't going to fall into the trap of wondering who or what had put those shadows in her eyes, he thought irritably. He knew his weaknesses, and beautiful women were low on the list. A good puzzle, on the other hand, was hard to resist. And Sarah Haywood, with her cool, expressionless face and haunted eyes, was a definite puzzle. If he wasn't careful he'd find it all too easy to forget that her ghosts, whatever they were, were none of his business. She might appear to be in distress right now, but from what he had seen of the lady, she could take care of herself.

That should have ended the matter right there, but those damn wounded eyes of hers continued to tug at him, destroying all his fine intentions. Before he realized what he was doing, he stepped toward her. "Are you okay?"

Sarah's head snapped up as the quiet timbre of his words wrapped around her, offering a grudging comfort that completely unnerved her. Although she hadn't looked at him once the taping had started, she'd been aware of his presence on the sidelines, his arms crossed over his chest, his expression almost bored as his gaze had shifted from the scene being played out before him to their dark, shadowy surroundings and the danger that might be lurking there. Had she been a gambling woman, she would have bet he was too preoccupied to see the lingering fear that Freddy and Jason had missed even though they'd been watching her every move. Obviously she would have lost hands down. He'd seen it all.

Suddenly feeling as if he'd stripped her bare with nothing more than his eyes, revealing secret hurts that she never let anyone get too close to, she knew she couldn't take any more. Dragging the tattered remnants of her control around her weary figure, she gave him a look intended to make the most persistent man back off. "I'm fine," she said evenly. "But it's been a long day, and I'm sure you're all anxious to go home." Turning to include Jason and Freddy in her statement of appreciation, she continued quietly, "You were all great tonight. I couldn't have done it without you. Thanks."

The mask of reserve she hid behind was safely in place, the No Trespassing sign clearly posted in her eyes. Disgusted, Dugan was tempted to keep pushing her, just to see how far it would get him. He didn't want her gratitude; he wanted to know what the devil was wrong. But she wasn't going to give him a chance to find out. Not tonight, at least. Before he could do more than shrug off the thankyou, she was turning toward her car. Moments later she was gone, her taillights winking at him as she disappeared into the night. If he didn't know better, Dugan would swear she'd fled as if the hounds of hell were after her.

"If you know anything that could lead to the arrest and conviction of this man, please call 55-WATCH. You need not give your name. Crime Watchers is offering a reward of five thousand dollars for one week only—"

The tape ended abruptly, the cool, professional tones of the woman's voice spinning into static as the screen shifted suddenly to black and white emptiness. With a languid push of a button on the VCR remote control, the man sitting in the dark in the sparsely furnished apartment rewound the tape to the beginning. Seconds later he sent the Crime Watchers segment in motion again. And again. And again. Since he'd seen it at noon, then taped it at five, he'd lost track of the number of times he'd watched it. But it didn't matter. Nothing mattered but the woman on the screen.

"This is Sarah Jane Haywood, Coordinator of San Antonio Crime Watchers, with this week's Crime of the Week. On the night of March 27 of this year..."

She gave the details of his crime, but he knew the words by heart now and they hardly registered on his consciousness. Impatiently he waited for the scene to change. Tall and graceful and pale with fear, she began to struggle with a man who had the gall to pretend to be him. By now he knew every move before she made it, every plea before she whispered it. Fascinated, his body tightening with anticipation, his eyes as black as sin, one corner of his mouth twisted up into a cold, malevolent smile. Yes, this was what he'd waited for, he thought in satisfaction. *She* was what he'd waited for.

Up until now his victims had all been nameless women plucked out of the night to assuage the burning rage that took possession of him more and more often with the setting of the sun. Why hadn't he realized that there was no satisfaction in that? No challenge? It wasn't just any woman he wanted to make pay for the wrongs done to him. No, it was the women who had looked down on him all his life, the women who had pulled away from his touch as if he were filth, the women who thought they were too good for the likes of him. Women, he thought with a feral gleam in his eyes, like Sarah Jane Haywood.

He would have her.

The thought came to him swiftly, sharp and clear, the details already beginning to work themselves out in his mind. This would be no impulsive move dictated by blind rage. Not this time. No, he was going to savor every delicious moment of anticipation, taunt her with *his* superiority, staying just out of reach until she couldn't close her eyes at night without worrying that he was out there somewhere in the dark, watching. She would be the one to feel the impotence this time, the frustration, the anger that ate like a cancer in the gut. Only then, when he was ready, would he end the sweet torture and allow himself the satisfaction of taking Sarah Jane Haywood.

Five minutes, Sarah promised herself as she tried to rub out the headache that pounded in her temple. All she had to do was last five more minutes, then she could walk out of her office and close the door on what had been an awful week. The minute she got home, she was going to collapse in a tub of hot, scented water and forget the world. Maybe then when she closed her eyes at night, she'd see something other than Dugan's steel-gray eyes staring back at her, seeing too much. Maybe then when she finally drifted into sleep, her dreams would be free of the nightly terror that waited for her in the dark, jumping out at her the minute her guard was down. Maybe then, for the first time since she'd driven away from Westfield Hospital three nights ago, she could rest.

Glancing at the clock again, she sighed. Four minutes and counting. With sure, unhurried movements, she locked away the tip sheets from the calls she'd taken that day and began to clear her desk.

She was reaching for her purse in the bottom drawer of the filing cabinet when the phone rang, shattering the silence. Startled, she jumped, but made no move to answer it. No one she wanted to talk to would call at two minutes to five on a Friday afternoon, she reasoned. All she had to do was forward the call to the Public Service Office and someone there would take over for her, just as they did whenever she was out of the office. Once that was done she could leave a few minutes early.

But instead of locking the filing cabinet and heading for the door, she turned back to her desk with a weary sigh of defeat. For all she knew, the caller could be an informant with a tip that would break one of the detectives' numerous dead-end cases wide open. There was also the chance that it could be someone who would speak only to her. If she didn't take the call, whoever was on the other end of the line might never work up the nerve to call back.

Sinking into the chair behind her desk, she quickly pulled pad and pencil from the top drawer and reached for the phone. "Crime Watchers. May I help you?"

She held the pencil poised to write, adrenaline rushing through her system just as it always did whenever she answered the hot line. There was no recording made of the call, nothing that would link the caller with whatever crime he called in about except the handwritten notes she took. She couldn't afford to miss anything.

The silence that followed her greeting was a familiar one. Turning in a friend or family member—or even an enemy, for that matter—was not a step anyone took lightly. Sometimes it was done for the money, often for revenge, occasionally to get a dangerous criminal off the streets. But to do that the caller had to betray a trust, take a chance. Only a fool wouldn't have hesitated.

Forcing herself to relax, Sarah repeated, "Crime Watchers. May I help you?"

For a moment she thought whoever was at the other end of the line was going to quietly hang up. Then a gravelly voice rasped, "I saw the rape."

She had to strain to catch the words which came out of the silence like a nearly unintelligible whisper from the devil and sent an icy chill sliding down her spine. The pencil she held tumbled from her fingers. She knew she should have been elated. At the very least, pleased that the reenactment had generated a response so quickly. After all, that was the whole purpose of her job. But all she wanted to do was slam the phone down as if the caller had said something obscene and walk away.

That wasn't an option. Picking up her pencil again, she gathered her self-possession around her as if it were a shield that would protect from the details she knew she didn't want to hear. If her fingers weren't quite steady when she drew the pad in front of her to take notes, there was no one there to see but her. "Which rape, sir?" she asked calmly. "What did you see?"

"The one with you on TV. The one by the hospital."

There was something in his low, strangely accented words—a smugness, a purring satisfaction—that repulsed her. Hit again with the urge to hang up, she ignored his reference to the part she played in the reenactment and deliberately steered the conversation away from herself. "You were at the hospital the night of March 28?"

"Her hair wasn't as red as yours," he whispered thickly, ignoring her question. "And she didn't wear it up. If you're going to play the part, you should do it right."

Jotting down his ramblings in an abbreviated code that was decipherable to no one but herself, she felt something that was very close to revulsion snake through her. He sounded as if he'd seen the victim up close. What had he done? Stood in the shadows and watched without ever lifting a finger to come to her aid? "What can you tell me about the rapist?"

"She dropped her purse the minute she felt the knife at her throat," he continued as if she hadn't spoken. "I like knives. They're so much safer than guns. Quieter. And a woman respects a blade in a way she doesn't a gun."

He offered that confidence in a soft murmur that conjured up images of a man at a phone, slowly caressing a razor-sharp knife, stroking it as he would a lover. Sarah never felt her fingers tighten their grip on the phone. Why did the weirdos always call at quitting time on Friday afternoon? "Sir, you must have seen the rapist. I know he was masked, but did he have any discernible features? Any visible tattoos or scars? Any noticeable oddities that would help identify him?"

"She didn't struggle as much as you did with that fool that held you. None of them did. They were too scared of me."

The hand recording the conversation jerked to a stop, the garbled accent echoing in her ears suddenly crystalizing into a bad imitation of an Englishman. Horrified, Sarah stared at what she had written and tried to tell herself she must have misunderstood. The caller couldn't have said what she thought he had. He couldn't have admitted—

"You won't struggle with me."

The softly spoken promise was little more than a whisper, but it drove every drop of blood from Sarah's face. "Who is this?" she demanded.

"The others were nothing," he assured her in what sounded bizarrely like an apology. "Mistakes. I should have realized they weren't right at all. But I didn't know then I was looking for you. I'll find you, Sarah," he promised huskily. "I'll find you, and then I'll make you pay. It's the only way."

He was a copycat talking madness, she thought, swallowing a sob. He had to be! She should hang up and just file her notes of the call in the crackpot file. But he sounded so vengeful, so sure of himself, like a man who had every intention of doing exactly as he promised. And his accent was just as bad as the victims said it was.

A chill shuddered down her spine. "Make me pay for what?" she cried harshly, her fingers gripping her pencil so hard she almost snapped it in two. "What do you think I've done to you? *Who are you?*"

Her only answer was a mocking click as he hung up.

He hadn't seen her since the night of the reenactment.
Standing outside her closed office door, Dugan told himself that he hadn't been deliberately avoiding her. After all,
it wasn't as if he sat around all day with his feet up and a
margarita in his hand. The weather was turning warm,
heating up the streets in a portent of what was to come. If
something wasn't done soon to curb the crime wave that
seemed to be escalating with the rising thermometer, the
city would be a war zone by the time the long, sultry days
of summer arrived.

He had his hands full just keeping his head above water, he rationalized. And if that wasn't enough of a load,
he'd floundered badly when he'd tried to negotiate peace
between his daughter and his ex-wife. Laura had flatly refused to even consider letting Tory live with him for a
while. She'd been outraged—and if the truth were told,
embarrassed—that Tory had told him of her marital dif-
ficulties and had ended the discussion before it had even
begun. He'd been on the verge of destroying the fragile
truce between them by telling her exactly what he thought
of her selfishness when she'd hung up on him.

Considering all that, he shouldn't have had time to give
Sarah Haywood a second thought. But the minute he relaxed, the second he let his thoughts wander, she drifted
into his head, images of her flashing before his mind's eye,
refusing to leave him in peace. Whether he wanted to or
not, he saw her dark, impassive eyes, the smile he'd rarely
seen her gift anyone with but her godfather, the lightning
flash of real fear on her face that no one else had seemed
to notice. The memory of the latter had the uncanny ability to disturb his sleep at night.

Which was why he was here, he reminded himself with a scowl. He wasn't going to spend the weekend brooding about Sarah Haywood. Five minutes with her—hell, probably even two minutes—would be more than enough to remind his overactive imagination that the lady was as tough and self-assured as her reputation said she was.

Giving her door a perfunctory knock, he pushed it open and stepped inside, promising himself he was going to keep this short and sweet. But the minute he saw her sitting behind her desk, he knew that wasn't going to be possible. She was as white as a sheet, her large brown eyes unguarded and tortured, just as they had been the night they'd taped the reenactment. He'd never seen a woman look so stricken in his life, and before he could stop himself, he was halfway across the room, the protectiveness he'd sworn only moments ago she didn't need from any man stirring to life. Damn it, how did she pull that emotion from him so easily when he'd never had a problem with it before? It wasn't like him to want to slay dragons for a woman he hardly knew!

"What's wrong? And, damn it, don't try to tell me it's nothing, the way you did the other night," he growled before she could open her mouth. "I'm not blind. You look like you've just been scared out of your wits, and I'm not leaving this office until you tell me what's happened."

If she hadn't been so shattered, Sarah would have laughed at the stubborn set of Dugan's square chin and the fighting light in his gray eyes. She didn't doubt for a minute that he was a man who came through on his promises. Just like the man on the phone. She shuddered at the comparison, the hysterical urge to giggle threatening to turn into a watery sob, frightening her. She saw Dugan's eyes narrow, saw him take another step toward her and wanted to cry "Don't!" He'd slipped past barriers that she'd thought were carved in stone; and she was too raw, too vulnerable, to suffer his nearness now with any degree of composure.

Jerkily she gestured to the notes scribbled on the paper in front of her. "I . . . I think I just got a call from the r-rapist."

He stiffened. "What do you mean you *think?* What did he say?"

"He had an English accent...a bad one. And the things he said..." Her voice cracked as a shudder rippled through her.

A break. They finally had a damn break! Dugan thought, and waited for the surge of adrenaline he always experienced when he knew he was finally on the right track. But for one tense, timeless moment all he could think of was that the bastard must have said something vile to Sarah to affect her so. That's when Dugan knew Buck was right. He was in trouble. Her notes were there, right within reach, and he couldn't take his eyes from her face!

Muttering a curse he snatched up the yellow notepad and scowled down at what looked to be chicken scratchings. He glanced back sharply at her. "What the hell is this?"

She blinked. His tone was cold, accusing, impatient. The man who looked as if he'd been ready to ride to her rescue only moments before was long gone, and that was just the way she wanted it, she told herself. She could handle Dugan Magee when he was hostile. It was the softer, human side she instinctively knew he resented showing that she had trouble dealing with.

She lifted her chin, thankful that her insides were no longer quivering with fear. "My notes of the call."

He pushed it back across the desk at her and sat down in a chair, watching her closely. "Read them."

She would have rather walked through fire, but there was a glint in his eyes that dared her to object. Fuming, she wondered what it was about this man that always challenged her. Grabbing the legal pad, she began to read. Her temper, rarely stirred, especially during the last three years, carried her through most of the task. But then the horror of those awful moments when the caller's oily voice had whispered in her ear washed over her, and the fingers holding the notes began to tremble. By the time she finished reciting the last twisted threat, her knuckles were white from the strain of trying to hold the paper steady enough to read.

Silence hung in the air, ringing with the echo of her words. Watching her through hard, implacable eyes, Dugan's gut clenched. He'd never wanted to reach for a woman so badly in his life, and he didn't like it. He didn't like it at all, damn it! He hadn't been kidding when he'd told Buck he wasn't looking for a woman. He'd been kicked in the teeth once already. Once was enough.

Surging to his feet, he turned away from the sight of her pale face and restlessly paced the confines of her office. "I want a copy of the transcript of the call," he said gruffly, "but I doubt you talked to the real rapist. Some pervert probably saw the reenactment and considered this his chance to get off on terrifying you."

"But he had the accent," she argued. "And he knew things that weren't in the segment or the papers. Like the hair color. The victim's picture was never shown. How could he know my hair was redder than hers if he wasn't there?"

It could have been a lucky guess, but Dugan doubted she'd buy that any more than he did. "Any number of ways," he replied. "For all we know, he could be a confidant of the real rapist, someone the lowlife just had to brag to. And anyone can fake an accent. Just to play it safe, though, I'll put a tap on the hot line. If he calls back, we'll trace the call and find out just where the hell he's getting his information."

"No!"

Her denial caught him flat-footed. Stunned, he whirled from his pacing and looked at her as if she'd lost her mind. "*No?* What do you mean, *no?*"

He never raised his voice; he didn't have to. His tone could have intimidated a hardened criminal, but this was something Sarah knew she couldn't give in on. Rising to her feet, she met his gaze unflinchingly. "Just what I said," she said quietly. "The whole purpose of Crime Watchers is to make sure the caller has the protection of anonymity. If I let you tap the line, it could jeopardize the integrity of the whole program. I'm sorry, but it's out of the question."

"Sorry?" he echoed furiously. "We've got a serial rapist on the loose and right now you're the only one in town who has a lead on him, and all you can say is you're 'sorry'? My God, what if that really was him on the phone? He threatened you! For all you know, you could be next on his list. Any other woman would be demanding that we tap the line!"

He'd unknowingly hit on the one argument that could sway her. She flinched. "No one wants this man caught more than I do," she whispered. "But I can't let you do this. I can't take the chance that some defense attorney will question how you became suspicious of the rapist when you had no clues to track him down. That's all it would take. One question, and people that are depending on this program to get drug dealers and thugs off their streets would be afraid to call in. I can't let you do that to the program. You'll have to find another way."

She made it sound so simple. Ignore the one lead you have after weeks of having nothing to work with. And in the meantime, the bastard who had just threatened her would still be walking the streets! Grinding his teeth, he took a step toward her, not even sure what he was going to do short of shaking some sense into her. But even with the desk between them, she felt the need to retreat a step. That one single action stopped him in his tracks. Damn it, why was she always acting as if *he* was a threat to her?

"Forget it. Just forget the whole damn thing!" he snarled, and stormed out of the door before he could do something stupid. Like ignore her wariness of him and reach for her.

Chapter 3

Hours later he was still fuming. Throwing a frozen dinner into the microwave, he started the timer with a jab of his finger, but what he really wanted to do was grab a certain leggy redhead and make her see what should have been obvious to her. She had to be the stubbornnest, most bullheaded, irritating woman he'd ever met! A man had threatened her, damn it, and all she could think of was protecting the integrity of the Crime Watchers program. Grinding his teeth on an oath, he glared unseeingly at the microwave. Had she even stopped to consider what she was going to do if the pervert tried to carry through on his promises? he raged. Granted, the call had probably been nothing more than a prank by a sicko who'd seen her in the reenactment and decided to take advantage of the situation, but what if he wasn't? What if he was the rapist he'd claimed to be?

If that was the case, then he had to figure out how the hell he was going to place a tracer on the line without Sarah's cooperation. But instead, it was the image of Sarah that filled his head, the same image of her that had haunted him ever since he'd stormed out of her office hours ago. Sarah, standing straight and tall before him, calmly facing his outrage, stubbornly refusing to budge. Sarah, meeting his look head-on, her brown eyes turbulent with a dark fear that went beyond distress, her mouth flattened into a thin line to stop its trembling. Sarah, as he doubted few people ever saw her—shaken and afraid.

It was a side of her that he would give anything not to have seen. Because when he looked at her from now on, he wouldn't see a proud, touch-me-not Ice Princess, but a woman badly in need of a man to hold and protect her. The fact that he had to tell himself he didn't want to be that man scared the hell out of him. He shouldn't need the reminder.

The wall phone next to the microwave rang suddenly, ripping through his uncomfortable thoughts. Snatching it up in relief, he barked, "Hello."

"I hope you didn't have any plans for tonight," Buck said grimly in his ear. "We've got trouble. There's been another rape."

Dugan swore, his unwanted attraction for Sarah forgotten. "What happened?"

"The victim's a history teacher at St. Andrew's College. Somebody grabbed her from behind and dragged her into a broom closet. If he was wearing a mask, she didn't have time to see it."

"What about an accent?"

"A cheap imitation of a British noble," Buck replied.

They both knew the accent alone didn't signify anything. With all the press coverage the rapes had generated, copycat rapists were bound to start coming out of the closet. "And here I thought it was going to be another boring Friday night," Dugan drawled. "I'll meet you at St. Andrews in twenty minutes. What about the victim? Is she still at the rape crises center or has she already gone home?"

"Neither," Buck said flatly. "She's in the hospital. Our boy didn't like it when she decided to scream for help. He cut her throat."

On the verge of hanging up, Dugan felt his blood turn to ice. The game had turned from ugly to vicious with nothing more than a slice of a knife. He knew from experience that a man who had cut a woman once wouldn't hesitate to do it again.

The uneasiness gripping him only increased as he and Buck arrived at the crime scene. Just as in the previous rapes, there were no clues, no telltale pieces of evidence left behind to lead them to the rapist. He had planned the attack brilliantly, slipping into the nearly deserted building at a time when most teachers and students were leaving the campus as fast as possible—late in the afternoon on Friday. The only reason Gail Bowman had been there was that she'd had a meeting with a student worried about his grade. While she was waiting for him to arrive, she'd made the mistake of walking down the hall to the lounge for a soda. She never made it.

Up until that point the rape fit the M.O. of all the others. It was the knife that nagged at Dugan, the knife that signaled an important change that he couldn't for the life of him find a reason for. This wasn't the first time the rapist had held a knife to his victim's throat. This wasn't the first time the victim had instinctively cried out for help. But always before, the rapist had found another way to silence the women—a hand across the mouth, a squeeze of the throat, a threatening jerk of the knife that stopped just short of penetrating vulnerable skin.

So what happened? Dugan wondered in growing frustration. Why did the bastard use the knife on Gail Bowman when he hadn't used it on his other victims? What was it about her that pushed him over the edge?

It wasn't until hours later that Dugan had his answer. Walking with Buck down the long, sterile hallway of the hospital, they cautiously entered Gail Bowman's private room. At his side, Dugan felt Buck stiffen, his gaze on the woman in the bed. Dugan didn't have to read his mind to know that his thoughts had jumped back to the conversation they'd had at the college less than thirty minutes ago, when Dugan had filled him in on the threatening phone call Sarah had gotten from a man claiming to be the rapist. Unable to take his gaze off the latest victim, Dugan had a sudden sick feeling that Sarah's caller was just who he'd claimed to be.

Gail Bowman was a small, pretty woman with delicate features. She lay propped up in the hospital bed, her head half turned away from them, the dark circles of pain under her eyes standing out in sharp relief against the paleness of her skin. At her throat was a bandage that was the only outward sign of the obscene injury done to her. But it wasn't her ivory skin or petite build or even the wound at her throat that held Dugan motionless in the doorway. It was her hair. A deep, dark auburn, it spilled onto the pillow behind her in a mass of wild curls that glinted with red and gold highlights.

Feeling as if he'd taken a blow to the solar plexus, Dugan could only stare at her as ugly suspicions started to form in his mind. There could be any number of reasons why the rapist had singled Gail out as his next victim, any number of reasons why he'd used his knife for the first time. But Dugan had a horrible feeling all those reasons had something to do with the color of her hair. And Sarah.

* * *

The last place Sarah had expected to be bright and early on a Saturday morning was her godfather's office at the police station. But when he'd called before eight o'clock and asked her to meet him there, the request had been more in the tone of a command, and she'd known something was seriously wrong. Scrambling into jeans, a white cotton blouse and tennis shoes, she'd only taken time to throw on a bare minimum of makeup, pull her hair back in a ponytail and brush her teeth before hurrying out to her car.

Now, rushing into his office, she found that he'd also summoned Dugan and Buck. All three men stood at her entrance, their faces seemingly carved in stone. Hit by a feeling of déjà vu, she felt sick dread spill into her stomach. They had only one reason to meet with the chief at such an early hour on their day off. Her eyes unconsciously shifted from her godfather to Dugan for confirmation. "There's been another rape, hasn't there?"

He nodded grimly. "Early last evening. A teacher at St. Andrew's."

Her godfather saw her stiffen and came forward to slip an arm around her slim shoulders. "That's why I called you in, Sarah," he said quietly. "The case has taken a turn in the past twenty-four hours that we need to discuss. Sit down, honey."

But she stood her ground, her eyes flying to Dugan's. "You told him."

He didn't bat an eye at her accusing tone. The minute he'd realized the implications of last night's rape, he'd known he had no choice but to relay the information to his captain. Dugan hadn't been surprised when his superior called the chief. After all, Sarah was the old man's goddaughter, and the captain had his own butt to cover.

"He needed to know," Dugan retorted. "I was just doing my job."

"That's right," the older man agreed, scolding her gently. "You should have told me yourself."

She'd thought about it; she'd even picked up the phone a few times to call him, only to hang up again. She couldn't go running to him every time she got scared, every time something happened in her work to dredge up the past. Up until three years ago she'd prided herself on her independence, her ability to stand on her own two feet no matter what life threw at her. The night Trent Kingston forced himself on her, he'd stolen that away from her, along with so many other things she'd taken for granted. Somehow, someway, she had to get it back, and that meant fighting her own battles.

"I didn't want to worry you about a stupid prank call—"

"It wasn't a prank," he cut in gravely. "After last night's rape, we have reason to believe that you really did speak to the rapist yesterday." At her startled look, his arm tightened around her shoulders. "Honey, the victim's hair is red. Like yours."

She wanted to ask what that had to do with anything, but deep inside she already knew. In spite of that, she insisted, "That could just be coincidence. There must be thousands of redheads in a city this size."

"There's no such thing as coincidence in a case like this one, Sarah," Buck told her grimly. "Less than three hours after the man promised he was going to get you, he attacked a woman whose hair is the same color as yours. There's no question that he did it deliberately, if for no other reason than to let you know he was deadly serious."

"But—"

"He used the knife," Dugan added, his face carved in harsh lines. "Not enough to kill, but enough to get his point across."

He saw the blood drain from her face and suddenly wished it was his arm circling her shoulders, offering her comfort, offering her safety. He'd lost his mind, he thought, stunned. He wanted to touch her, to hold her, to assure her she was perfectly safe. Where the hell had that come from? He wasn't a man who believed in wrapping the truth in candy coating to make it more acceptable. She wasn't his to protect, and she sure as hell wasn't safe. Damn it, what was she doing to him?

"We believe he was striking out at you," he continued, giving her the cold, unvarnished truth. "It may only be a one time thing, just to get your attention, or make a statement, or whatever. Who the hell knows? Or it may be the beginning of a pattern . . . striking out at other women until he gets what he wants. You."

"But why?" she cried. "I don't even know this man. What have I ever done to him?"

"You created a reenactment that hopefully will lead to his capture," the chief replied grimly. "I hate like hell that I ever asked you to do it, but there was no way any of us could have known that he would react this way once he saw it." Urging her to one of the chairs in front of his desk, he waited for her to sit before hitting her with the decision he'd made. "I want you to take some time off till we catch this nut. Just in case. I may be overreacting, but I'd rather play it safe. I'll get someone in to man the phones and pull some old reenactments on cases that are still open. There's no reason for you to even come in."

"No!"

"You can't be serious!" Dugan protested indignantly, drowning out Sarah's startled cry of dismay. "This is the first break we've had in the case. You take Sarah out of Crime Watchers now, and it may be weeks, even months, before we get another chance at catching this dirtbag.''

The chief pinned him to the carpet with eyes that were as hard as forged metal. ''I hope you're not suggesting we use Sarah as a guinea pig, Magee. I'm not placing her in any more danger than she's already in just to close a case.''

Did the old man actually think that was what he wanted? To use Sarah, to hold her out before the rapist like a red flag before a bull? Damn it, just the thought of that slimeball calling her, threatening her, made him want to wrap his fingers around the worm's bony throat. He tried to tell himself he'd feel the same way about any woman who'd been threatened, but he never could lie to himself worth a damn. How the hell had this woman gotten under his skin so fast?

Scowling, he said flatly, ''I don't want that, either, but yanking her out of Crime Watchers at this late date isn't going to accomplish a damn thing except place her in more danger if this creep really has developed a fixation on her. Placing her on leave now will only put her at home all day by herself. Don't you think she'd be a hell of a lot safer here at the station? This guy may be brazen, but even he's not stupid enough to try to get to her here, where she's protected by the entire department.''

''The real danger to her is when she goes home at night,'' Buck added. When he saw Sarah pale, he said, ''Sorry, Sarah, but you might as well know what you're up against. We're dealing with an unpredictable nut case here, and there's no telling what he might do. You need to be prepared for just about anything.''

''Which is exactly why she needs to keep a low profile,'' the chief argued, scowling. ''If she's not going to be safe at home, then she can go back to Houston for a while, visit her parents—"

"No!" She was *not* running. Not this time! Tired of being discussed as if she had no say in the matter, she jumped to her feet to confront the three men. "You're all acting as if it's a given that the rapist saw me in the reenactment and immediately developed this unnatural interest in me. Maybe that's not the case at all. Maybe he's just trying to scare me so I'll back off. If I take some leave, get out of town for a while, I'll be playing right into his hands."

She knew by the look on their faces that she'd made her point. But her godfather wasn't convinced. The worry clouding his eyes told her more clearly than words he was afraid that this would only make it more difficult for her to put the past behind her.

"Running is not the answer," she told him quietly. "I just can't let him manipulate me that way."

"Sometimes it's better to cut your losses than stand and fight," he argued. "Are you sure you don't want to take some time and think this over?"

No, she wasn't sure of anything. Just knowing that there was a rapist out there who *might* try to track her down made her want to hide. But how could she, knowing that would only delay his capture? The longer he was free, the more women he would terrorize.

Her knees shaking, she ignored the wild thundering of her heart and lifted her chin. "I'm sure."

He could still have overruled her, but she would have never forgiven him. "All right," he sighed heavily. "You can stay on Crime Watchers, but I want security increased anytime you're out in the field. And your on-screen participation in the reenactments will be limited to the lead-ins from now on." When she opened her mouth to object, he immediately threw up his hand, stopping her. "I mean it, Sarah," he warned. "No more acting. At least for the present."

She knew that stubborn look of his, that dogged, determined set to his jaw that warned he had given as much ground as he was going to give. She nodded grudgingly. "All right. No acting. *For now.*"

He smiled at her intimation that this was only a temporary situation, but when he turned his attention back to Dugan and Buck, he was the picture of grim determination. "I want nightly patrols on her street increased. If these threats continue, put a plainclothesman at the end of the block whenever she's home. There's a good possibility this bastard's just blowing hot air, but we're not taking any chances. You'd better set up an escort to and from work, as well," he added. "Just in case he takes it into his head to follow her home from work."

"It'd probably be just as easy for her to ride in with one of us," Buck said, glancing toward Sarah. "Where do you live?"

"Off West Avenue. Outside the loop."

Dugan just barely swallowed a groan. Fate had a nasty little way of playing tricks on a man just when he thought he had everything under control. From the beginning, he hadn't wanted to work with Sarah, hadn't wanted to be so aware of her scent, the tantalizing length of her long legs, the tempting, wild beauty of her hair. He'd told himself all he had to do was ignore her, remember the painful lessons Laura had taught him and steer clear of Sarah. So much for his well laid plans, he thought in disgust. He couldn't very well steer clear of her when she was going to be right there beside him in his car every morning and afternoon on the way to and from work.

Grudgingly accepting defeat, he said, "That's not too far from me. I'll follow you home after we're through here, then pick you up Monday morning."

It was the only practical solution, but when Sarah looked at Dugan, it wasn't practicality she thought of. It was the width and breadth of his shoulders, the probing intensity of his eyes, the sheer size of him. Trapped in a car with him, she'd be even more aware of him...and the jumbled emotions that destroyed her hard won composure whenever he got within six feet of her.

Her throat suddenly as dry as dust, she swallowed. "F-fine." She almost winced at the hoarseness of her voice, but when she glanced back at her godfather, she somehow managed to regain her cool. With her hands half buried in the pockets of her jeans, no one but she knew that her fingers were starting to tremble. "*Now* will you stop worrying?" she teased, forcing a smile. "You've got me surrounded by S.A.'s finest at work and at home. I won't be able to sneeze without you hearing about it."

"Good," he retorted. "Your parents would never forgive me if I let something happen to you. Now get out of here before I change my mind and make you take some leave. And if you get any more threatening phone calls, I want to hear about it directly from you," he called after her as she headed for the door. "Understand?"

"You'll be the first to know," she promised. But as she slipped out into the hall and headed for the parking lot, it wasn't the rapist she worried about. It was Dugan Magee. He followed her out to her car like a shadow, then tailed her all the way home. Every time she looked in her rear-view mirror, he was there, right behind her, his eyes meeting hers in the mirror, setting her heart thumping madly. She didn't want to think what his nearness would do to her blood pressure once they were actually in the same car together.

After that, the rest of her weekend was ruined. Sarah told herself the extra precautions taken to protect her were temporary necessities that she would just have to suffer through. But within minutes after she arrived home after the meeting in her godfather's office, a plainclothesman was stationed at the end of the block in a dark-windowed, unmarked car. As soon as his shift was over, he was replaced by another officer, then another. By the time Dugan arrived Monday morning to pick Sarah up for work, she felt like a prisoner in her own home.

The situation only worsened on the drive to work. Just as she had feared, she was achingly aware of every move Dugan made, every sideways glance he shot her. In the silence that enveloped them, she was sure he could hear the wild pounding of her heart. Mortified, she jumped into a conversation about the weather, the controversial crime bill currently being debated in both houses of Congress, anything to distract her from her preoccupation with the man at her side. It worked for all of five minutes. Then her eyes inadvertently shifted to his side of the car and she found him watching her with eyes that gleamed with amusement. She wanted to die right then and there. She was acting like a sixteen-year-old who had suddenly found herself in a car with Tom Cruise. This had to stop! Her cheeks burning with color, she shut her mouth with a nearly audible snap and stared out the window for the rest of the ride downtown.

Arriving at work should have been a relief. But the minute she stepped through her office door, the phone rang. She froze, the nervousness she'd experienced in Dugan's company was nothing compared to the dread that now spilled into her stomach. What if it was the rapist calling her to let her know he hadn't forgotten her over the weekend? Horrified, she stared at the ringing phone for what seemed like an eternity before she suddenly realized what she was doing.

"Snap out of it, Sarah!" she ordered herself fiercely. She couldn't just ignore the phone all day. What if the caller was an informant with news of the rapist?

Stalking across the office on legs that were suddenly as stiff as wood, she snatched up the receiver. It wasn't until she recognized the voice of a detective who had recently approached her about doing a reenactment of a convenience store holdup that she realized she was holding her breath. Sighing in relief, she sank down into the chair behind her desk and got down to work.

For the next three days her heart jumped in her chest every time the phone rang, but the caller was never the rapist. Her nerves stretched to the breaking point, Sarah felt as if she were on an emotional roller coaster of unexpected dips and blind curves. She knew she was being paranoid, but she couldn't seem to stop herself. She found herself searching faces in crowds on the street and constantly looking over her shoulder whenever she left the station. Half expecting to find someone following her, she didn't know if she was disappointed or relieved when no one seemed to pay her the least mind. The waiting for something to happen was driving her right up the wall!

Ironically the only time she was able to forget the threats was when she rode to and from work with Dugan everyday. Then she found it impossible to think of anyone but the man at her side. He handled the car with deceptively lazy skill, always taking a different route to her house each afternoon in case they were followed, the sudden, sharp turns he would make without warning often catching her by surprise. Before she could even begin to brace herself, she would find herself thrown against him, her shoulder rubbing his, the spicy scent of his after-shave teasing her senses. At those times she would quickly pull back and act as if nothing had happened, but when her eyes met his, she was sure that he knew what his nearness did to her. Tension curled between them, filling the car like a thickening fog.

Then on Thursday afternoon Dugan braked to a stop in her driveway and announced, "We're pulling the suit."

Her eyes immediately flew to the side mirror, but the black sedan that usually pulled up at the corner across the street only moments after she got home every day was nowhere in sight. She wasn't really surprised. No more threats had been made against her; no one had tried to get close enough to harm her. She might be the chief's goddaughter, but she could hardly expect the protection of a plainclothesman indefinitely.

Torn between relief that she would no longer be watched like a parolee in a halfway house and alarm that she was now on her own in a fight with a particularly vicious wolf, she watched him put the car in park before saying quietly, "I know the department can't just put someone on the corner until something happens. But what about the increased patrols in this area? Are those being stopped, as well?"

"No."

"So there's a possibility that I'm still in danger. Just because the rapist hasn't come after me yet doesn't mean he won't eventually."

Her voice was as flat and emotionless as a telephone recording of the time, but Dugan wasn't fooled. The last four days had given him plenty of opportunities to study her, and he'd noticed things he hadn't wanted to. Like the way she pretended being escorted to work was nothing out of the ordinary, yet her fingers unconsciously bit into her purse whenever another car came unexpectedly close. She was constantly on the lookout for the slightest hint of danger, her dark, somber eyes always moving, always searching. He went home at night haunted by the memory of those eyes.

Staring at her now, he knew tonight would be no different than the past three. Swearing under his breath, he said, "I didn't say that, but you know as well as I do that it's a possibility. But when you're talking possibilities, you can't limit yourself to just the most likely scenarios. You have to consider everything. All the publicity that has surrounded the rapes may have convinced his next victim to carry a gun in her purse. She could put an end once and for all to any possibility of his ever coming after you."

"But what if that never happens?" she persisted. "You've been on this case from the beginning. You and Buck have studied the rapist's behavior more than anyone. Do you think he was making an idle threat just to scare me? Or is he capable of planning and carrying out a premeditated rape?"

Dugan stared down at her and wondered how he could give her the guarantees she wanted. He knew from experience that there wasn't any such thing—in life, in love, in anything. The fact that he intended to somehow find the right words anyway warned him he was headed for a trouble he wanted no part of—woman trouble.

"I think we're dealing with a coward," he said gruffly. "This isn't a man who ever takes a chance. He hides in the dark, covers his face and waits until he finds a victim in a deserted place before he climbs out from under his rock. Even when he called and threatened you, it's a safe bet he did it from the security of a phone booth somewhere. I don't think a man like that's going to risk getting caught by coming after a woman who's surrounded by cops during the day and neighbor's at night—unless he feels cornered. Then there's no telling what he'll do.''

"So in other words, you're saying there's probably no immediate danger, but don't do anything stupid,'' she summed up. "Don't go anywhere alone.''

He nodded. "That's basically about it. Right now all we can do is wait for him to make a mistake. And hope there's someone out there who knows what he's done and has the guts to turn him in for the reward.''

It wasn't an unreasonable hope, but the reenactment had aired days ago, and the few calls they'd had had turned up absolutely nothing. They both knew that the odds of getting a legitimate tip diminished with every passing day.

And she had never been very good at waiting, she thought with a grimace. She just wanted it over and done with so she didn't have to live any longer with this sick fear that seemed to have taken up permanent residence in her stomach. Gathering her things together, she reached for the door handle and forced a smile. "Then I guess it's a good thing I brought some work home with me. Hopefully it'll take my mind off the waiting.''

Reminding her that he would pick her up in the morning as usual, he waited while she unlocked her front door and slipped inside before backing out of her driveway. He didn't have to hear the dead bolt on her front door sliding into place to know that she had locked herself in. As she'd stepped out of his car, her eyes had held the haunted look of a woman who was determined to put on a brave front regardless of the circumstances. But he knew she was scared and it tore at his gut.

The minute Sarah stepped into the house and locked the front door, she stepped out of her shoes and turned on the stereo. The mellow sounds of soft jazz immediately engulfed her, filling the empty silence that surrounded her. Kneading the tense muscles at the back of her neck, she headed for her bedroom to change into an old, ragged, well-loved pair of jeans and a T-shirt. Ten minutes later she was in the kitchen chopping vegetables for chicken stir-fry, determined not to think about the plainclothesman who was no longer parked at the corner and the rapist who might even now be plotting to take advantage of his absence.

But it wasn't either of those men who tramped through her thoughts, distracting her from her task. It was Dugan. The knife still in her hand, she found herself bombarded with images of him. Dugan in the morning when he picked her up, his hard jaw freshly shaven, the scent of soap and man and cologne assaulting her the minute she slipped into the car. Dugan glancing at her from the corner of his eye while he drove, always seeming to watch her, as if he were trying to figure her out. Dugan only inches away from her in the front seat, so close she could almost feel his heat reaching out to her, seducing her.

Before she could stop herself, she found herself wondering what it would be like to be held by him. Kissed by him. Made love to by him. She'd seen his intensity when he was working on a case, his single-minded determination. What would it feel like to have the full force of his concentration turned on her, to know that she had his undivided attention? If he set his mind to destroying a woman's inhibitions with pleasure, he wouldn't stop until he'd succeeded.

A shiver rippled down her spine, bringing her back to her surroundings. She dropped the knife numbly, her hands flying to her suddenly scorching cheeks. Dear God, what was she doing? she wondered, dismayed. She couldn't be fantasizing about Dugan! About any man! Hadn't she learned the danger of trusting too easily, of letting her emotions overrule her judgment? It would be a long time—if ever—before she trusted a man again, and it wouldn't be someone like Dugan. He was too big, too sexy, too sure of himself, too overpoweringly male. Just the thought of placing herself in his hands made her tremble.

"Work," she said hoarsely. She needed to work...to forget another man's hands, another man's strength, another man's single-minded determination. Abruptly throwing the vegetables she'd chopped into a stock pot, she decided to make soup instead. Adding chicken, water and spices, she set it on a burner to boil, then cleared the counter. Moments later the tantalizing scent of yeast filled the kitchen as she began to make homemade bread. She'd made her first loaf three years ago when she discovered, quite by accident, that mixing and kneading the dough offered her an outlet for her frustrating, tortured thoughts. She'd been baking bread ever since.

By the time she turned out the kitchen light hours later, there were two loaves of bread on the counter and a pot of soup in the refrigerator. Pleasantly exhausted, she took a quick shower and climbed into bed. Her head barely touched the pillow before she was tumbling into a deep, dreamless sleep.

It could have been hours, or maybe only minutes, after that when she heard the noise. Still asleep, the small thump at the front of the house hardly registered on her subconscious. She shifted into a more comfortable position without even opening her eyes. Three houses down, a dog barked, shattering the stillness of the night.

In spite of that, it was several long moments before the thought that something was wrong nudged her awake. Lying with her cheek pressed against her pillow, she frowned as the dog's steady barking turned sporadic, then slowly dwindled off altogether, as if whatever had disturbed it was now gone. For reasons she could not begin to explain, her heart jumped in her breast and started to race. Bolting upright, the sheet clutched to her chest, she sat wide-eyed in the dark and listened.

Only the thunder of her heart echoed in her ears.

She tried to tell herself there was nothing to be worried about. The dog had probably just been barking at a leaf blowing in the breeze and the only noise she'd heard was in her head. But she knew she wouldn't be able to go back to sleep unless she got up and made sure everything was okay. Throwing back the sheet, she rose to her feet and padded barefoot down the night-shadowed hall.

The kitchen was as she'd left it, the foil-wrapped loaves of bread she'd made earlier gleaming in the darkness. As silent as a wraith, she glided over to the back door and checked the lock, then glanced out the window into her small backyard. Nothing moved.

With a sigh of relief, she turned toward the living room. Here, too, it was dark and quiet, the only light was that that spilled through the windows from the streetlight on the corner. Everything appeared to be as she'd left it; even her shoes lay drunkenly just inside the door, where she'd stepped out of them earlier.

"Your imagination's working overtime tonight, Sarah," she whispered as she crossed to her shoes and picked them up. "You were just dreaming."

But just to be safe, she checked the door and, finding it safely locked, glanced out the front window. She'd already started to turn away when she saw something on the porch. She froze, every ounce of blood in her body seeming to congeal at the sight of the small package lying on the porch.

Her heart slamming against her ribs, she tried to tell herself there was nothing to be alarmed about. It was just a small, oblong box, hardly bigger than four by twenty-four inches. But it hadn't been there when she'd gotten home from work, and even U.P.S. didn't deliver in the middle of the night.

Her eyes flew to the street out front, to all the dark shadows cast by trees and bushes where whoever had delivered the box could even now be hiding. But the neighborhood slept as soundly as the dead and there wasn't a sign of life anywhere. Even the Wilson's dog had gone back to bed, and he was notorious for not giving up the bark until whatever had disturbed him was at least three blocks away.

Her gaze once again on the box, Sarah hesitated. Common sense told her to call the station and report the incident. A patrol car could be there in a matter of minutes. But she'd feel like a fool if the box turned out to be nothing but a joke instigated by one of the neighborhood kids.

Torn, she glanced at the empty street again, then back at the box. Making a snap decision, she gripped one of her shoes like a hammer, the high heel pointed outward, and unlocked the door. Not giving herself time to think about the danger she was placing herself in, she jerked open the door and darted out onto the porch. Seconds later, the box in her hands, she ran back inside and slammed and locked the door behind her.

For what seemed like an eternity, she leaned back against the closed door, waiting for her pulse to steady. Her knees still too unsteady to make the trip across the room to the couch, she flipped on the ceiling light and stared down at the object gripped tightly in her left hand. It was white, a little battered, possibly from being thrown on the porch, and had no identifying marks on it. It's contents, whatever they were, were as light as a feather.

So open it, a voice in her head ordered. Or are we going to stand here all night and guess what's inside?

Her heart in her throat, she slowly lifted the lid. A gasp of terror nearly strangled her. A dead rose, its petals all withered and brown, lay mockingly on a sheet of tissue paper. Whimpering, Sarah dropped the box and backed up against the door. The rose fell to the floor and scattered its dead petals near her feet. But it was the note, which landed face-up directly in front of her, its message written in large bold letters, that drew her horrified eyes.

I'M WATCHING YOU, SARAH. AND WAITING. OUR TIME WILL COME.

Chapter 4

The phone rang shrilly in the darkness, fracturing the sleep it had taken Dugan hours to find. Opening one eye to glare at the clock on the nightstand, he swore when he saw it was only three in the morning. He'd been asleep little more than an hour. Snatching up the phone, he growled through his teeth, "This better be good!"

"That you, Magee?"

Recognizing the irritatingly cheerful voice of Raul Martinez, one of the night detectives, Dugan almost hung up. No call in the middle of the night was good news, and whatever Martinez had to say, he didn't want to hear it. "If you were expecting Santa Claus, you've got the wrong number," he snapped. "Of course it's me. What the hell do you want?"

Martinez clicked his tongue reprovingly. "You day people are always so damn touchy after midnight. I just don't understand it." No longer teasing, he said, "This is serious, man. It looks like there's another twist in your rape case. A call came in a few minutes ago from the chief's goddaughter."

Every muscle in Dugan's body seemed to turn to ice. "Is she all right?" he demanded harshly. "What happened? Damn it, if that scum touched her—"

"Slow down, man," Martinez cut in. "He never even laid a finger on her. In fact, she didn't even see him. But she knows he was there. He left a package for her on the front porch—a dead rose with a note promising her he would get her. A black and white's already out there investigating."

Dugan didn't have to close his eyes to imagine Sarah's reaction when she realized that while she slept, the rapist had been right on her front porch. Swearing under his breath, he swung his legs over the side of the bed and reached for his pants. "Thanks for the call, Raul. I'm on my way."

"Just doing the lady a favor," the other man said. "When she called in, she asked that we notify you. She didn't have your number."

Less than two minutes after he hung up, Dugan was in his car and speeding toward Sarah's place. His jaw clenched, his gray eyes as hard as granite, he squealed around a corner, his blood running cold at the thought of Sarah facing the rapist alone. The bastard had been right there on her porch! he thought furiously. Almost within touching distance... within hurting distance. His hands tightening on the steering wheel, Dugan pressed down harder on the accelerator.

The porch light was on when he braked to a screeching halt in her driveway, the black and white still parked at the curb. Slamming his door, he took the porch steps in two long strides and walked into her living room without bothering to knock.

During the short drive to her house, he'd convinced himself that it was fury that sent him racing to her side. The slimy little cockroach thought he could thumb his nose at the police and get away with it, but this time he had made a mistake. He'd left a clue. And come hell or high water, Dugan was going to use it to catch him.

But when he saw Sarah sitting on the couch, quietly talking to a uniformed policeman, he came face-to-face with the truth. He hadn't shot over to her house like a madman because of a damn clue. He'd come for Sarah. Because he had to see for himself that she was okay. Because she might need him.

Stunned, he stopped halfway across the living room, unable to do anything but stare at her. She was pale but composed, her shoulders stiff under the green cotton robe she wore demurely buttoned at her throat, her hair unbound and rippling like dark red fire halfway down her back. At first glance he had no reason to think she couldn't handle this new threat, but then his gaze dropped to her hands. Her slender fingers were clutched in her lap, the knuckles white with strain.

Something twisted in the region of his heart. The uniformed officer, who looked hardly old enough to shave, stood to greet him, but Dugan had eyes only for Sarah. "Are you all right?"

Two seconds ago Sarah had been sure that she had a tight grip on her emotions and was holding her own. But the minute she looked up to see him charging through the door, tears welled in her throat and burned her eyes. He'd obviously just jumped out of bed and thrown on the first clothes he could find—faded jeans and a wrinkled T-shirt. With his hair only finger-combed and his square jaw shadowed and unshaven, he fairly oozed the type of intimidating virility Sarah had gone out of her way to avoid the last three years. To her amazement, she realized that no longer seemed to matter. Given the least encouragement, she would have walked right into his arms and cried her eyes out.

This couldn't be happening, she thought, forcing back a sob. She knew the danger of trusting too easily, the risks that could befall her if she let a man she hardly knew get too close. Dugan Magee might be as safe and honorable as the pope's brother, but she couldn't take a chance with him or any other man. Trent Kingston had made certain of that.

Pulling herself together, she called on the strength that had gotten her through the nightmare of the last three years and tried not to think of how tired she was of always having to be strong. "I'm fine," she finally managed huskily. "He didn't even try to get in the house."

Because the dirtbag was taunting her, Dugan thought furiously. He was playing with her like a cat teased a wounded bird, drawing out the torture until he was ready to pounce. And whether she would admit it or not, Sarah knew that. He could see the knowledge in brown eyes that were nearly black with a distress she was trying her damnedest to hide. She was scared. Anyone in their right mind would be, but he knew she would bite off her tongue before admitting such a thing. Anger flared in him. Who had taught her she always had to be so damn self-sufficient? So strong? It wasn't a weakness to need someone once in a while.

Frustrated by the confusing battery of emotions she stirred in him, his tone was harsh when he turned to the young cop, who was discreetly watching the interplay between them. "What have you got?"

"Just the package and its contents," he replied, indicating the items he'd slipped into an evidence bag. "Ms.

Haywood was awakened by the sound of the package hitting the porch and a dog barking. By the time she got to the front door, there wasn't a soul stirring.''

Dugan's gaze dropped to the note that had accompanied the flower, its large print clearly readable through the plastic of the evidence bag. A muscle rippling along his granite-hard jaw, he sent Sarah an equally hard glare of disbelief. ''You opened the door at three in the morning without calling for protection? Damn it, Sarah, what the hell were you thinking of? What if he'd still been out there?''

She flushed. ''He wasn't. The Wilson's dog is better than an electronic security system. He'd already gone back to bed, so I knew I was safe.''

Dugan only snorted at that. ''You aren't safe as long as this sleeze is loose.'' Turning back to the younger man, he said, ''The neighbors will have to be questioned in the morning to see if they heard or saw anything. If you want to go on and get that down to the lab, I'll finish up here.''

The minute the front door closed behind the other man, Dugan said, ''Pack yourself a bag. You can't stay here now that the rapist knows where you live. I'll take you to the chief's.''

''No.''

Nonplussed, Dugan blinked, as if she'd just told him to stand on his head. ''What?''

''No, I'm not going to Uncle Russ's,'' she repeated stubbornly.

''Why the hell not? He's expecting you.''

''You called him?''

His brows snapped together at her horrified tone. ''What the hell did you expect me to do? Damn it, he's your godfather! He'd have my head on a platter if he heard about this through the grapevine.''

He was right, of course, but that didn't change anything. She couldn't stay with Russ. He was as protective as her parents and had already done enough for her by offering her a way out of Houston. She was desperately trying to get on with her life. She couldn't do that by running to her godfather every time she got scared. "I'm not going to Russ's," she said tightly.

Dugan didn't even bat an eye. "Then you're coming home with me."

Home with him? she thought wildly, her heart jumping into her throat. She couldn't possibly! "Oh, no," she gasped. "I can't!"

Annoyance grooved his brow. She didn't have to look so horrified at the idea! "You haven't got a hell of a lot of choice here, lady, not if you want to stay safe," he said flatly. "You can't stay here alone. Sure, we can put someone outside again," he continued, forestalling the argument she was about to throw at him. "Hell, we can even put someone in the house with you. But so far, this slimeball has been damn clever at outsmarting us. We can surround you with cops, but can you honestly say you'll be able to sleep at night knowing that the pervert knows where you are?"

The mere thought of that man standing outside her house, staring at her windows, raised goose bumps on her skin. Suddenly cold, she hugged herself. "No, but I don't see how I'll be any safer at your house. If he found out where I live, what's to keep him from tracking me down at your place?"

"Me," he retorted grimly. "He doesn't know I'm in charge of the case, and my phone number's unlisted. I know yours is, too, so the only way he could have found out your address was to follow you home one day after work. Since there was no way he could have tailed us once

I started escorting you to and from work, he had to do it sometime between the day the reenactment aired and the day of the rape at St. Andrew's."

Three days, she thought, stricken. He could have been following her for three days, watching her every move like a hunter watches a doe in his sight, and she hadn't even suspected it.

Dugan saw her eyes widen with realization, and could almost read her thoughts. It was sinking in, the danger she was in, a danger that would grow more terrifying with each passing day as the rapist used time itself as a weapon. Staring at her ashen cheeks, Dugan wanted to swear until the air turned blue with curses, to condemn the man who was doing this to her to the deepest bowels of hell, to hold her until she realized she wasn't alone. But it wasn't his job to hold her, just to protect her. Why did he find it so difficult to remember that lately?

"If you think about it, you'll realize my place is the best place for you," he said grimly. "The rapist won't have any idea you're staying with me, and I'll make damn sure it stays that way. He won't be able to get to you without going through me first."

Safety. He held it out to her like a lure, tempting her to forget the painful lessons of the past and trust in him. Part of her already did. But old, unhealed wounds still throbbed, reminding her she'd made the mistake of trusting once before and was still paying the price. Torn, she studied him with tortured eyes, wishing in vain that a voice from the heavens would tell her what to do. But all she had to guide her was the instinct that led her to ask for him when she'd called 911 an hour ago, so scared she couldn't do anything but shake. She knew now she hadn't asked for him because he was in charge of the case, but because he was the first man in a long time who could make her feel safe.

"Give me a few minutes to get my things together and I'll be ready," she said quietly.

Dugan reached for the phone to call the chief.

She followed him back to his house in her car, her gaze glued to his taillights as he executed the same sharp, unexpected turns he made when he drove her home from work each day. She knew she was being foolish, taking her car even though she wouldn't be going anywhere by herself until the rapist was caught, but she refused to be completely dependent on Dugan. She already owed him more than she was comfortable with.

Sparing a quick glance for the rearview mirror, she saw nothing but blackness behind her. They weren't being followed. She should have been relieved, but she was too busy reassuring herself she was doing the right thing. Dugan was doing his job above and beyond the call of duty. He would have done the same thing for anyone else at the station who happened to find themselves in similar circumstances. There was nothing personal between them; from what she could tell, he didn't even like her. There was no reason for her to be nervous. He was offering her shelter and protection, nothing more.

But when he opened his front door and motioned for her to precede him, her heart jerked out of its smooth rhythm, then pounded against her ribs at what seemed like a thousand beats per minute. She hesitated, fighting the need to **bolt**, while her common sense sternly ordered her not to be an idiot. He wasn't going to hurt her. Deep down inside, she knew that, but even so, she couldn't stop herself from shying clear of him as she hurried inside.

She heard him shut the door and follow her into the living room, but she kept her eyes determinedly on her surroundings. It was common knowledge that he'd been divorced for years, and she'd halfway expected him to bring her to a bachelor pad that would only increase her anxiety. But his modest two-story home was anything but that.

Surprised, her eyes darted around the living room, noting the comfortable red and brown plaid early American furniture piled with pillows, the braided rug and rocker, the fireplace that looked well used. Every place she looked, there were the homey touches usually supplied by a woman—knickknacks and pictures and several treasures on the mantel Sarah would love to examine more closely, including an antique pewter replica of a square-rigger and a picture of a pretty, dark-haired teenager in a crystal frame.

Noticing where her gaze lingered, Dugan moved to her side and said, "That's my daughter, Tory. She did most of the decorating around here." In a flat voice that didn't encourage questions, he added, "She lives in California with her mother and stepfather."

And he hated it, she thought, her eyes unconsciously searching his. His face was carefully blank, revealing nothing of his emotions, but Sarah somehow knew he hated the idea of being separated from his daughter by a thousand or more miles, that he resented like hell the idea of another man raising her.

Disturbed by the insight, she realized she'd made a mistake by coming to his home and allowing herself to see a more private side of him. She didn't want to know what he was thinking or feeling behind that tough cop image he showed to the world. As long as she didn't think of him as anything but a co-worker, a professional protecting her, she could cling to the belief that she was secure from the feelings he stirred in her without even touching her. She couldn't let herself sympathize with him, she couldn't let herself like him. She couldn't, *wouldn't* let herself care. But she had a sinking feeling that it was already too late.

Alarmed by her wayward thoughts, she suddenly couldn't breathe for the thundering in her heart. He was too close, the house too intimate, bathed in shadows but for the small lamp he'd turned on when they'd first arrived. Needing space, even if it was only inches, she unobtrusively skittered away from him.

Dugan's eyes narrowed at her obvious uneasiness. After everything that had happened tonight, any woman would be more than a little jumpy. She had a serial rapist stalking her, he knew where she lived, and she had every right to be scared out of her mind. But not of him, damn it! He knew his size could be intimidating and had always been careful not to give any woman reason to shy away from him. Surely Sarah knew he wouldn't harm a hair on her head. Didn't she?

Puzzled, he frowned at the dark secrets that were back in her eyes. "Are you sure you're okay?"

Heat bloomed in her cheeks. Dear God, had he read her mind? "Yes! I'm j-just tired. It's been a long day."

It was more than that, but he was in no mood to drag the truth out of her tonight. And even if he could have, he wasn't sure he wanted to. He was already too intrigued by the lady, too damn aware of her for his own good. The less he knew about her and her past, the better.

"You can use Tory's room while you're here," he said, heading for the stairs with her suitcase in hand. "I've turned the other bedroom upstairs into a weight room. The master bedroom is downstairs off the living room."

So she would have the whole upstairs to herself and not have to worry about running into him in the middle of the night if she had to get up for any reason. Relief almost made her weak-kneed and she had to hurry to catch up with him.

"If you need something you can't find, just ask," he continued as he reached his daughter's bedroom and set Sarah's suitcase down right by the door. "The bathroom's—"

Close on his heels, Sarah didn't see him stop until it was too late. He turned, his arm extended to gesture in the general direction of the bathroom down the hall, and almost caught her on the chin with his knuckles. "Oh!"

Later, she couldn't say who moved the fastest. She gasped in surprise and stumbled back, forgetting the stairs were directly behind her. Lightning quick, Dugan reached for her, his hands clamping down on her shoulders, steadying her.

Their eyes met, and time ground to a screeching halt as the awareness that had tugged at them from the moment they'd met set the night air throbbing. Sarah could feel the beat of it in her ears, in the wild rhythm of her pulse, in the very core of her. He made no move to pull her toward him, but she felt as if she was falling into his arms. *Run!* The warning echoed through her, his spicy scent, like the smell of smoke before a fire, warning her of danger. But she couldn't think, couldn't move, couldn't do anything but stare up into the intense, churning gray depths of his eyes.

Dugan's common sense shut down the instant he touched her. Why couldn't he summon any defenses against the delicate fineness of her bones? he mused, staring down at her in wonder. Under his hands he could feel the sweet sloop of her shoulders, the daintiness of her, the fragility that hit him right in the gut. Before they'd left her house, she'd changed from her gown and robe into a sweatshirt and jeans, but the heavier clothes did nothing to disguise her supple curves. She was tall for a woman and would, he knew, fit perfectly in his arms. All he had to do was tighten his fingers ever so slightly, and he could have her right where he wanted her, her breasts pressed to his chest, every beautiful inch of her long legs molded to his. Lord, he ached to hold her.

The thought had barely entered his head before his hands were tightening on her shoulders, pulling her...

What the hell do you think you're doing, Magee?

The voice in his head stopped him cold. What *was* he doing? Sarah Haywood was there in his home, in his life, for only one reason, and it wasn't to play house. Which sat just fine with him. He'd tried that once and watched another man walk away with what was his. It wasn't something he cared to repeat. Yanking his hands away from her as if she'd scalded him, he took a quick step back and said harshly, "The bathroom's halfway down the hall. Towels are underneath the vanity. Did you bring an alarm clock, or do I need to wake you in the morning?"

"N-no. I brought my own."

"Then I'll see you in the morning. Good night."

He was gone before Sarah could even recover her breath, disappearing down the stairs without a backward glance. His bedroom door slammed shut, the sound reverberating through the house. Feeling as if she had just stumbled over the edge of a cliff, she stared at the empty stairwell for a long, timeless moment before she finally turned into Tory's bedroom.

It was a typical teenager's bedroom, a world caught between childhood and adulthood. The walls and ceiling were splashed with posters of teenage heartthrobs and long-haired rock bands, while the bed was covered with a tattered menagerie of stuffed animals that had managed to survive years of loving from childish arms.

Picking up a one-eyed teddy bear, Sarah gave it a tender pat before placing it and the others in the wide window seat that overlooked the front of the house. She changed back into her nightgown and turned out the light. Silence settled around her in the darkness as she crawled into Tory Magee's narrow twin bed. Downstairs something creaked and stilled, strange noises in a strange house. But it wasn't the house, or the noises, or the young girl whose bed she lay in that Sarah thought of as she stared up at the shadowed ceiling. It was Dugan and the fire of desire burning in his eyes when he had, just for a moment, started to pull her into his arms.

Clutching the sheet to her breast, she tried to block out the image, but the memory was indelibly etched in her head and she could still feel the heat from his eyes, his touch. Her heart pounded and her throat went dry as she realized just how close he had come to kissing her. She wanted to believe the emotion still dancing along her nerves was a residue of fear, but she couldn't lie to herself in the dark when there was no one else to see. It wasn't fear but disappointment that had surged through her when he'd abruptly released her and walked away.

She'd wanted him to kiss her!

The thought hit her like a sudden, unexpected earthquake, jarring her to the core. No! She couldn't want him. She wouldn't! Because wanting could only lead to things she wanted no part of, things like touching, holding, kissing. And taking, she thought, choking back a sob. Dear God, she couldn't forget the taking and the vulnerability that had accompanied it, the helplessness that had left her defenseless in the hands of a man bent on getting what he wanted with or without her cooperation. She wouldn't go through that again! Not with Dugan or any other man, she promised herself.

Satisfied that all her defenses were firmly in place, she buried her face in the pillow and willed herself to relax. But it was a long time before she was finally able to go to sleep. And when she did, Dugan slipped uninvited into her dreams.

When his alarm clock went off the next morning, Dugan was half tempted to throw it across the room. Bleary-eyed, he stared at the time and cursed: 6:00 a.m. He might have gotten one good hour's sleep if he was lucky, and it was all Sarah's fault. He hadn't been able to put the damn woman out of his head from the moment he'd left her last night. Every time he closed his eyes, every time he started to relax enough to slip into sleep, she came into his thoughts, taunting him, making his body burn.

Throwing back the covers with a savage oath, he walked naked into the connecting bathroom and stepped into the shower. Hot water pounded on his back, but the steady, pulsing beat only seemed to increase the tension that tied his muscles in knots. Soaping his body with quick, terse movements, he reminded himself that the only women he'd had any dealings with since his divorce were forgotten as soon as they left his bed. And that was just the way he intended to keep it. If he'd needed any proof that Sarah wasn't that kind of woman, last night had given it to him. She hadn't even been in his bed yet—hell, he hadn't so much as kissed her—and she could still make him ache in the night. It had to stop!

But as the steam rose around him like smoke, the heat in his loins made a mockery of his musings. Angrily he switched the water to cold. It didn't help.

By the time he stalked into the kitchen fifteen minutes later, his mood hadn't improved. He was dressed for work in a blue suit, white shirt, and flowered tie that Tory had given him for Christmas. He'd half convinced himself that if he just thought of Sarah as a civilian in danger, he could deal with her presence in his home. All he had to do was stick to business. But at the sight of her standing at his stove, cooking breakfast for the two of them as if she'd done it for years, he knew that wasn't going to be possible.

No woman had a right to look so pretty the morning after she'd been terrorized during the night, he thought, unable to drag his gaze away from her. She'd dressed conservatively in black slacks and a black and white print blouse, yet the simple classic lines only seemed to emphasize her femininity. Tall and graceful, her hair neatly arranged in an intricate braid, she couldn't have been any more breathtaking if she'd been decked out in satin and diamonds.

Suddenly the tie that had been tied just right only moments before was too tight. Scowling, Dugan jerked at it. "Good morning."

Her eyes on the bacon she was frying, Sarah jumped, startled. The composure she'd been able to regain only after hours of stern lecturing crumbled the minute her eyes flew to his. Just that quickly, the memory of his hands on her shoulders, pulling her toward him, sent heat climbing into her cheeks.

"Good m-morning." Looking anywhere but at him, she gestured to the food she'd already cooked. "I hope you don't mind..."

Mind? he thought mockingly. Hell, yes, he minded. He'd never be able to smell bacon again without thinking of her here, in his kitchen, cozily cooking for him. "You didn't have to go to all this trouble," he said stiffly. "We could have stopped on the way downtown and picked up a breakfast taco or something."

She shrugged. "It was no bother. I've been up for hours."

His eyes sharpened on her face. "Because of what happened last night?"

For a wild, heart-stopping moment, she thought he was referring to the sparks that had flown between them outside Tory's bedroom. But there was nothing personal in the hard, probing look he gave her, and she knew he had to be talking about the rapist. What had she expected? According to the department scuttlebutt, Dugan wasn't a man who had difficulty getting a woman when he needed one. His nearness last night may have rocked her on her heels, but she doubted that he'd given the innocent encounter a second thought after he'd walked away from her.

"Partly," she said honestly. "I'm not used to the sounds of your house, and I kept listening for someone who wasn't there."

If he'd have kissed her instead of walking away, he wouldn't have given her time to think of anyone but him.

The thought teased him, pricking him like a stinging mosquito until he swore in frustration. He wouldn't let her distract him this way! His mouth tightening into a flat line, he stepped past her to the refrigerator for the pitcher of breakfast juice always kept there. "I'm going to put a tap on the Crime Watcher's hot line," he said in a voice that dared her to argue with him. "The slimeball's not through toying with you, so it's only a matter of time before he calls you again. When he does, we'll be ready for him."

Sarah would have given anything to meekly go along with whatever he wanted to do. All she had to do was nod her head and close her eyes to the fact that she would be selling Crime Watchers out to protect herself. But she couldn't do it.

Carefully removing the last of the bacon from the pan to drain on paper towels, she switched the burner off and turned to face Dugan. Bracing herself, she said quietly, "No, we won't. Because I still can't let you tap the line."

Dugan stared at her, unable to believe his ears. After last night, after the fear he'd seen in her eyes when he'd arrived at her house, he expected her to leap at the chance to catch the creep who was terrifying her. She couldn't be serious!

But one look at the stubborn tilt of her chin convinced him she was. Muttering a string of curses, he slammed the pitcher he held down on the counter and stepped toward her. "Do I have to remind you the rapist was right outside your house last night?" he growled. "Damn it, what more does it take to convince you you're in serious danger? Do you actually need to have his hands on you before you'll believe he isn't making idle threats?"

She paled, nauseated by the thought, but she stood her ground. "No, of course not. But I can't let you do this, Dugan. Don't you see? It's my responsibility to protect the program, not destroy it. If I let you tap the line and that somehow came out in court, no one would ever trust Crime Watchers again."

"To hell with Crime Watchers!" he roared, incensed. He was fed up with hearing about the damn program when she was the one in danger! "What about you? You're the one in danger here. You're the one taking a chance."

"But I have you to protect me."

She said it so simply, yet the faith implicit in her words drove the air right out of his lungs. Stunned, he stared at her, wanting to tell her that he wasn't Superman; he couldn't be with her twenty-four hours of the day; he couldn't predict where someone as diabolical as a serial rapist would strike next. But he knew she'd already made up her mind that she was safe and nothing he could say would convince her otherwise. So frustrated he couldn't think straight, he reached for her, determined to shake some sense into her. But the minute his hands closed over her shoulders, something just seemed to snap. Before he even realized his intentions, he hauled her up against his chest and swooped down to cover her mouth with his.

He knew immediately that he'd made a mistake—he'd made enough in his lifetime to know one when he tasted it. She was too sweet, too soft, too *right* in his arms. If he'd had any sense, he would have put her from him the minute his mouth touched hers and his heart started to thud in his chest. But it seemed as if he'd been aching to sink into her softness forever. A few more minutes, he promised himself. That was all he wanted. Just enough time to tap the desire he knew lay hidden just beneath the cool exterior she presented to the world. Groaning low in his throat, he dragged her closer, lost to everything but the need clawing at him.

He pulled her to him so fast, Sarah never had a chance to throw up any defenses. Suddenly she was caught up in a vortex of desire so overwhelming, she couldn't do anything but feel. Pleasure. It rippled through her in waves, warming her, melting her bones, surprising her with its intensity. Her head spinning and her knees buckling, she felt herself sinking and couldn't find the strength to care. More, she thought, whimpering as she clutched at the lapels of Dugan's suit coat. She wanted, *needed* more.

But then his arms closed around her and everything changed. Dark images flashed behind her closed eyelids, and from out of the past, large, rough hands reached out to grab her. The sweet sting of passion turned abruptly into panic. Too tight, she thought in growing agitation. The arms banding around her were like steel, cutting off her air, pressing her down into an inky blackness where she knew terror lurked, waiting for her. Gasping, she couldn't taste anything but the acrid tang of fear, couldn't feel anything but the hard male body that pressed against her like her worst nightmare.

"No!"

Trapped in the terror that held her in its viselike grip, she never heard her strangled cry. Sobbing, she struck out blindly. "No! Stop! *Let go of me!*"

Stunned, Dugan hardly had time to blink before he found his arms suddenly full of scratching, clawing wildcat. "What the hell!" Swearing, he caught the hand that swung toward his face inches from his jaw. "Damn it to hell, woman, what's the matter with you?" he thundered, shaking her. "Stop that! What the hell's gotten into you?"

It was his roar of bewilderment that finally penetrated the cloying fog of fear that engulfed her. She froze, her eyes focusing in growing horror on the scratch she'd managed to inflict high on his cheek before he'd managed to subdue her. The one hand he hadn't been able to capture flew to her mouth. Oh, God, what had she done?

Shuddering, she slammed her eyes shut against the sudden rush of hot tears. "I'm sorry," she whispered. "Please . . . let me go."

Dugan hesitated, but if there was any fight left in her, he couldn't see it. Her cheeks were as red as her hair, her shoulders slumped in defeat, and slow, silent tears seeped out from beneath her tightly closed eyes. His jaw clenched at the sight of those tears, and it was all he could do to release her. Slowly, reluctantly, he let go of her. Before he could take a single, calming breath, she'd put half the distance of the kitchen between them.

She was scared of him!

He immediately rejected the idea—he'd never hurt a woman in his life! But there was no denying that he'd seen real terror on her face when she'd fought her way out of his arms. His dark brows knit in a frown, he stepped toward her. "Sarah—"

"Don't touch me!"

The shakily whispered plea cut through him like a knife. She really was afraid of him! he thought incredulously. "All right, I won't touch you. I promise," he assured her, holding up his hands to signify he was backing off. "But I would like to know what the hell's going on here. You have to know I would never hurt you, honey."

The endearment flowed over her like a caress, but nothing could dispel the coldness that chilled her from the inside out. Of course she knew he wouldn't hurt her, but she'd learned the hard way that reason had nothing to do with fear. Hugging herself, she stared blindly out the kitchen window to the back yard. "I...I don't like to be...manhandled."

If any other woman had accused him of that, he'd have been furious, but instinct warned him that it would take little more than a curse from him to shatter her. "It was just a simple kiss," he said quietly, watching her carefully. "I wasn't forcing you into something you didn't want. You kissed me back."

She had, she couldn't deny it. And for one wild, sweet moment, she'd been lost to everything but the wonder of being in his arms. Then the nightmare had intruded, pressing down on her, suffocating her. "I know. It wasn't you—"

"Then what the hell was it? There's no one here but me and you."

She winced. She hadn't meant to admit that. "It doesn't matter," she said huskily. "Forget it. It's getting late and we've got to get to work."

But she wasn't putting him off so easily. Stepping in front of the kitchen door, he blocked her path. "You might as well tell me, Sarah. We're not leaving here until you do."

Her heart lurched in alarm. "There's nothing to tell."

"Oh, really? So you always react this way when a man kisses you, is that it?"

"No, I—"

"Then it *is* me. I only wanted to kiss you, but somehow I frightened you. What did I do? Come on, Sarah, I've got a right to know. I've never had a woman fight her way out of my arms before, and damn it, I don't like it! Tell me!"

"I was raped!"

She hadn't meant to say the words, let alone scream them at him, but suddenly they were echoing off the kitchen walls. Appalled, she saw the shock register in his eyes, but now that the truth had come tumbling out, there was no holding back the rest of the story. All the pain and heartache, the frustration and anger that coiled in her gut when her attacker had managed to elude prosecution, came spilling out in disjointed, jerky sentences. "In Houston...three years ago. A date rape. Trent Kingston. I thought I knew him. We'd worked together. Somehow I should have known," she said numbly. "So fast. It happened so fast."

She looked up in bewilderment at Dugan, as if *she* were the one at fault for showing poor judgment, and it was all he could do not to reach for her. The bastard had forced her. Horror washed over him, along with a rage that nearly choked him. Sickened by the images that sprang to mind, he swore savagely. No wonder she never dated or let anyone get too close. She was coping the best way she knew how, and now she had a serial rapist stalking her, bringing back the terror of the past with his sick threats. After everything that had happened to her, Dugan wouldn't have blamed her if she'd screamed the minute he'd touched her.

No, grabbed her, he silently amended, thickly swallowing the bitter taste of regret. He'd grabbed her. And terrified her. Aching to comfort her, he rasped, "I'm sorry. I wouldn't have grabbed you if I'd known. It won't happen again."

She couldn't doubt his sincerity. No, it wouldn't happen again, she thought sadly, fighting back tears. Dugan Magee was a man a woman could trust to keep his word. Why couldn't she have met him before Trent Kingston had made it impossible for her to enjoy this honest man's touch?

Chapter 5

How she managed to sit down to breakfast with Dugan and act as if nothing had happened, Sarah never knew. Seated directly across from him, she found her eyes straying to him every time she looked up from her plate. She'd wanted him. For one crazy, unthinking moment, she'd had no past, no painful memories, and she'd lost herself in the taste of him on her tongue, the feel of him against her, hard and sure. The wonder of it still had the power to fascinate her. He'd shown her that in spite of everything that had happened to her, she could feel desire for a man again. But she couldn't have him. Heaven and hell, she thought, fighting tears. That was all she could hope to find in his arms.

This wasn't going to work, Dugan thought, watching her through narrowed eyes. He'd had a hard enough time keeping his hands off her before he'd touched her, before he'd kissed her, before he'd learned why she retreated behind a wall of ice every time a man got too close. Now he couldn't look at her without thinking about some faceless sleeze forcing her, hurting her. God, he wanted to hold her! Just hold her and promise nothing was ever going to hurt her again.

He was, a voice in his head murmured, losing his mind. A sane man didn't make that kind of promise to any woman, let alone one like Sarah.

She didn't want to be touched, was terrified of intimacy. Those types of problems couldn't be fixed with a spoonful of sugar and a kiss on the forehead. If a man was foolish enough to let himself want her, he was setting himself up for nothing but frustration. Dugan told himself he wasn't a masochist. She was not only in trouble, she *was* trouble, the kind that could haunt him in the darkest part of the night and leave him wanting. And he would go on wanting. If he had any sense, he'd find somebody else to baby-sit her, someone else to worry about her. Before he did something stupid. Like fall for her.

But he hadn't been thinking straight from the moment he'd met her. And there was no way in hell he was walking away from her now. He couldn't fight her demons for her, but he wouldn't rest until he hunted down the slimeball terrorizing her. Then he'd get out of her life while he still could. Maybe once he only had to see her at work when they happened to pass each other in the hall, he'd be able to forget what it felt like to hold her. He didn't fool himself into thinking that would be easy. No woman, not even his ex-wife, had ever felt so damn good in his arms.

His appetite nonexistent, he set down his coffee cup with a snap and looked at his watch. "We'd better get moving, or we're going to be late for work," he said tersely.

Sarah was only too ready to comply. At least she could put some space between them at the station. Here, even when she was upstairs and he was not, she was constantly aware of the fact that she was in his home, surrounded by his things, and she only had to raise her voice to have him at her side. Rising quickly to her feet, she carried both their plates to the sink, rinsed, then placed them in the dishwater. Drying her hands, she picked up her purse, which she'd left on the counter earlier. "All right, I'm ready. Let's go."

They rode to work in his car just as they had every morning that week. But leaving from his house somehow changed things. They could have been an old married couple caught up in a daily routine they performed by rote—she cleared the breakfast table, he followed her out to the car after locking the front door behind him, he started the car while she switched on the radio to listen to the morning traffic report.

It was all so ordinary, so... intimate.

Caught up in the stop-again, start-again motion of the morning rush hour, Dugan was thinking the same thing and trying to ignore the intoxicating scent of Sarah's perfume. In self-defense, he turned his thought to the investigation. Six cars ahead a truck driver suddenly slammed on his brakes, starting a chain reaction. Tires screeched, a horn blared and Dugan swore, somehow just managing to miss the bumper in front of his. "Idiot," he muttered, glaring at the truck in the distance. Without missing a beat, he added in a challenging tone, "You're going to have to reconsider letting us trace the hot line. There's no other way."

Her heart still in her throat from the near accident, her eyes whipped to his. "Damn it, Dugan, we've already been through this twice! The answer is still no."

"Then just get prepared to go through it again because this isn't settled, sweetheart. Not by a long shot." The traffic started to move, and he eased forward, his eyes trained on the unpredictable movements of the car in front of them. "In case you hadn't noticed," he reminded her, "the cops are the good guys here. You don't need to protect the program from us. We aren't threatening it. Or you."

"But—"

"No buts," he cut in. "Think about it. The only one threatening you and using Crime Watchers to his advantage is the rapist. By refusing to allow the trace, you're protecting him. Is that what you want?"

"No, of course not!" she replied, stung. How could he even think that after what she'd told him last night?

"Then let us put a tracer on the line. And that doesn't mean we'd trace every incoming call," he said before she could protest. "We're not interested in your informants. Hell, they're calling in to help us, so why would we want to jeopardize the program? The only calls we need to trace are the rapists's, and I'm pretty sure the phone company could rig it so that you could activate the trace yourself. That way, *you* would be in control of the operation. No one would have to know about it but you, me, Buck and the chief."

She stared at him, desperately wanting to believe that justifying the break in the security of the program could be that easy. "Okay, I'll think about it," she finally said. "But I'm not making any promises."

It wasn't the answer he wanted, but it wasn't another outright no, either. For the moment, it would have to do. "Fine," he said, exiting from the freeway as they reached downtown. "Let me know what you decide."

Sarah half expected him to take up the argument again once they reached the station, but the minute they stepped out of the elevator onto the second floor, he headed for the detective unit, which was in the opposite direction of the administrative wing, where her small niche of an office was located. Watching him stride away from her, she was hit with an almost overwhelming need to call him back, but she couldn't even say for what. To hold her? To tell her everything was going to be all right? It wasn't, and she didn't know if it ever would be again.

Fumbling in her purse for the keys to her office, she found them just as the phone started to ring inside. Muttering under her breath, she finally got the door open and hurried over to her desk. Snatching up the phone on the fifth ring, she balanced it between her shoulder and ear as she dropped her purse to reach for pen and paper. "Crime Watchers," she said breathlessly.

"I saw you leave last night."

The harsh, accented voice was colder than hell when it froze over and all too familiar. Sarah stiffened, the instant fear that seized her by the throat infuriating her. She would not let him scare her! she thought fiercely. Not this time. She'd be damned if she'd give him the satisfaction!

Gripping the phone tightly, she said icily, "You didn't see anything. You couldn't have. The neighbor's dog—"

"Took a nice long nap," he finished mockingly. "Surely you didn't think a dog could protect you from me, Sarah? I'm much too smart for that."

Repulsed by the sound of her name on his lips, she snapped, "You're lying." He had to be. If the dog had been drugged, she'd have heard by now.

"Am I?"

Her fingers started to shake. He sounded so smug, so confident. Could he be telling the truth? Last night when she'd unlocked her door and darted onto her porch for the package, could he have really been out there in the dark watching her?

"You were wearing a pale robe," he said silkily, guessing her thoughts. "You changed into a sweatshirt and jeans before you left."

Hang up! a voice in her head ordered, but instead she choked, *"Leave me alone!* You have to leave me alone!"

Sinister laughter echoed in her ears. "Who's going to make me, Sarah? Hmm? The detective you left with last night? I don't think so. Nobody will be able to save you when I come for you, pretty lady. Nobody," he promised, and quietly hung up.

"No!"

Sarah never knew how long she stood there, still as death, while the dial tone buzzed in her ear. There were footsteps in the hall outside, a call of greeting, the sound of a door being shut. She blinked, suddenly realizing she was still holding the receiver to her ear. With a strangled sound of abhorrence, she quickly dropped it back into its cradle.

He'd seen her leave with Dugan.

Like a thief in the night, the thought slipped past the shock that gripped her and turned her blood to ice. Horrified, she gasped. No! He couldn't have already tracked her down at Dugan's.

Snatching up the notes she'd made even in her terror, she read them, her eyes racing over her unorthodox shorthand. But there wasn't a single hint that he'd followed her after she'd left the house, only that he'd seen her leave with him. Relief almost weakened her knees. He was only taunting her again, making her sweat.

That was when her fear changed abruptly to anger. What a fool she was to let him tie her in knots with nothing but words! He was playing with her like a cat played with a mouse, tightening the tension, viciously increasing the terror while he gloated with power. Damn him, she wasn't going to let him get away with it! He was the scum of society, lower than dirt. She'd be damned if she'd let a man like that turn her into a helpless female who jumped at her own shadow while he walked the streets like he owned them!

Straightening her shoulders, she dragged in a deep breath and waited for her pulse to steady. Only when she knew she could speak calmly did she reach for the phone and punch out Dugan's extension.

"Magee."

He didn't waste time bothering with a hello, but bluntly identified himself with a brusqueness that was all business. He couldn't have known how reassuring it was just to hear his voice on the other end of the line. Sarah knew that would bother her later more than she cared to admit, but for now, she could only thank God that he was there for her. "Dugan, it's Sarah."

She would have sworn her voice was perfectly level, but the words were hardly out of her mouth when he demanded, "What's wrong?"

Taken aback, she stuttered, "N-nothing," then could have bitten her tongue. She hadn't called him to cry on his shoulder. "I just wanted to let you know I've thought about what you said about tracing the line, and I've decided to do it."

She'd thought he'd be elated. Instead he repeated harshly, "What happened? And don't tell me nothing. We've only been in the building five minutes, Sarah. Less than twenty minutes ago, you were arguing with me about this in the car. What happened to make you change your mind so quickly?"

She'd known she couldn't keep the call from him, but she'd hoped he wouldn't press her about it while the memory was still fresh enough to chill her blood. She should have known better. "The rapist called again."

"I'll be right there."

"No, that's not necessary—"

But she might as well have saved her breath. For the second time in five minutes, a man had hung up on her.

He burst into her office five minutes later, his rugged face carved in grim lines, his eyes running quickly over her as if he'd half expected to find her hurt. "Are you sure you're all right?"

"Yes, of course. If you hadn't hung up so quickly, you would have heard me tell you it wasn't necessary to come charging over here. I'm fine."

She may have regained her composure, but her eyes still had that hunted look that made him want to snatch her into his arms. But that would only put her through more hell, and he didn't know if he could stand having her fight free of his touch a second time.

Moving to the chair in front of her desk, he sat down before he could be tempted to step around it and gather her close. "What did he say this time?"

"He saw everything." The nightmare image that brought to mind started a fine trembling deep inside her, but she ruthlessly ignored it and picked up her notes. In a flat voice totally devoid of the terror that was still lurking in the shadows of her mind, she began to read the transcript of the call.

By the time she was finished, her cheeks had lost their color and Dugan was seething. If he could have gotten his hands around the throat of the son of a bitch who was doing this to her, he would have made him regret he'd ever been born. Unable to sit still, he rose to his feet and paced restlessly to the window. "I'll check with the neighbors about the dog, but I don't think he'd taunt you with a lie," he said, glancing back at her over his shoulder. "He's one of those lowlifes who gets off by teasing us with everything he knows, and a lie isn't nearly as effective as the truth."

She'd already come to the same conclusion, but it was still daunting to have him agree with her. "Do you think he followed us to your house?"

"No, we'd have seen him if he had. There was very little traffic at that time of the morning, and there wasn't a soul behind us. There's no way he could possibly know where you're staying. You're safe."

For now.

The words weren't spoken aloud, but they both knew that the rapist was too clever to accept her evasion of him as anything less than a challenge. He was out there somewhere, patiently watching, waiting for her to make a mistake. Her fingers tightened on the notepad until they ached. "How long do you think it will take to set up the trace?"

"I'll have to get departmental approval, but that's not going to be a problem," he said. "We should be able to have it in place by this afternoon. The next time he calls, we'll be ready for him."

As he'd promised, Dugan had the trace approved by that afternoon. The telephone company was notified, and a button was installed on the side of Sarah's phone. All she had to do was press it, and the call would be traced immediately.

But the rapist, as if guessing the trap set for him, didn't call. Instead she was flooded with other calls—informants wanting to know if indictments had come through on whoever they'd turned in so they could collect their re-

ward money, detectives wanting to discuss possible reenactments with her, a writer wanting to know how the
program worked. By the time she met Dugan at the elevator for the ride home, her nerves were knotted with tension from a call that had never come.

But when she slid into Dugan's car a few moments later,
another kind of tension gripped her. Too late, she realized
that while she'd been worrying about the rapist, she hadn't
given a thought to her more immediate problem—Dugan.
The weekend stretched before them, and for the next two
days she would be cooped up in his house with him, with
nothing to distract her from an attraction that refused to
go away. How was she going to make it through the days,
let alone the nights, without going quietly out of her mind?

She lost track of the number of times she asked herself
that over the next forty-eight hours. By unspoken agreement they tried to stay out of each other's way, which
should have been easy, considering the size of the house.
For a while it actually worked. Sarah holed up in her room
with a book and Dugan escaped to the garage and the old
MG he was restoring. When his daughter called several
times, she left him to his privacy, then couldn't help noticing later how the calls always left him pensive and with-
drawn. More than once she opened her mouth to ask him
what was wrong, only to shut it with a snap. His worries
were none of her business.

Hunger, however, always tugged them each to the
kitchen, usually around the same time. The second their
eyes met, a kiss that should never have happened hung
between them, teasing their senses. The air stilled and
thickened as it did before an approaching storm.

Her heart racing at the sight of him, there were times
when Sarah was so tempted to stay and ride out the storm

that she could taste it. Instinct warned her he wouldn't hurt her. But her instincts had let her down before. If anyone had asked her what she'd thought of Trent Kingston before he'd forced himself on her that fateful night in May three years ago, she would have sworn she could have trusted him with her life. So much for instincts.

So she ran. From Dugan, from the feelings he stirred just by being in the same room with her, from the past that refused to stay buried. Because she had no choice. If she lingered in his presence for too long, it would only be a matter of time before she found herself back in his arms again. And that was something she couldn't allow to happen. She could somehow learn to live with the fact that there was a stranger out there determined to rape her, but she never again wanted to see the look that had been on Dugan's face when she'd fought free of his touch.

By Sunday night tempers were short, and they were both thankful the weekend was almost over. Exhausted, Sarah went to bed early, convinced she'd fall asleep the minute her head hit the pillow. But hours later she was still wound tighter than a broken watch and wide-awake. Every time she closed her eyes, she was hit with images of Dugan in bed, his dark hair tousled and his granite jaw rough with a night's growth of beard, his large hands unbelievably gentle as they found her in the darkness.

Her heart tripping over itself, she sprang up, her breathing ragged in the utter stillness of the night. This had to stop! she told herself fiercely. But her mind had a will of its own, and the fantasies continued, each succeeding one more detailed and titillating than the last. Restless and aching and on the verge of tears, she finally admitted defeat. She knew from experience that there was only one way she could get to sleep when she was this wired.

Throwing off the covers, she pulled on her robe and belted it at the waist before padding barefoot to her bedroom door. Opening it a crack, she held her breath, listening. But the house was as quiet as a tomb and just as dark. Relieved, she released a soundless sigh. Good, Dugan was asleep. The last thing she wanted to do in her present state was run into him in the dark.

Feeling her way carefully, she silently glided down the hall to the stairs. Once, when a board creaked, she froze, her eyes flying down to the darkened doorway at the back of the entrance hall that led to Dugan's bedroom. But nothing disturbed the quiet of the night. Her knees knocking loud enough to wake the dead, she hurried down the rest of the stairs and made her way to the kitchen.

The smell of baking bread dragged Dugan out of a hot, fevered sleep. Fighting the pull of the enticing aroma, he buried his face in his pillow and told himself he was dreaming. No one baked bread in the middle of the night. The wind had to be out of the north again, he decided groggily. It was just the bowling ball factory he smelled. All that fiberglass was making him light-headed.

Dismissing the mouth-watering, yeasty smell as nothing more than a mere figment of his imagination, he punched his pillow and wadded it up in his arms just the way he liked it. Then he heard what sounded like a pan drop in the kitchen. Sleep vanished in the blink of an eye. What the hell!

Between one heartbeat and the next, he was out of the bed and soundlessly jerking on his jeans. Not bothering to button them, he moved to his bedroom door and slipped out into the hall. The noises from the kitchen were louder here, the scent of the bread intoxicating. Frowning, he made his way to the kitchen door and silently pushed it open to find Sarah busily baking as if it were the middle of the afternoon. "What the devil are you doing?"

The loaf pan she held crashed to the floor. Her eyes wide, she stared at Dugan, standing in the open doorway bare chested and barefoot, his jeans zipped but unbuttoned. He looked nothing like the buttoned-down detective who drove her to work. Her throat suddenly parched, she had to swallow twice before she could answer him. "I c-couldn't sleep so I thought I-I'd b-bake some bread."

"At two in the morning?"

He didn't have to sound as if she was out of her mind, she thought indignantly. *He* was the main reason she couldn't sleep! Lifting her chin, she said stiffly, "It's good therapy. Kneading the dough helps take my mind off... things."

He didn't have to ask what types of things; the answer was there in her face for him to see. Shadows of the past, fear, worry, vulnerability. He felt the anger drain out of him and wanted to hold onto it so he wouldn't get any crazy ideas about holding onto her instead. But it was too late.

Go back to bed, Magee, while you still can.

It was good advice his conscience threw at him, and any man with brains in his head would have followed it. It was late, they were both tired and half dressed, and defenses that were anything but sure in the daytime were damn shaky in the middle of the night. But as his eyes swept down the length of her in a lazy journey, he knew there was no way in hell he could leave her to her lonely baking.

She was a woman who didn't like to be touched, but with her wild red hair sleep-tousled and tumbling halfway down her back, she looked like a sex kitten who'd just stepped out of one of his fantasies. She was covered from neck to ankle in a white cotton gown and robe whose only adornment was the lace at her throat. There shouldn't have been anything provocative about it, but the material was as soft as tissue paper, gently molding the curve of her breasts and hips and the long length of her legs, just giving him a hint of the womanly body hidden from view.

Dugan felt his blood rush at the tempting sight of her, and fought the need to step closer. If he made that mistake, he knew it wouldn't be the last one he made tonight. Forcing his eyes back to the paraphernalia she'd spread out on the counters, he frowned. "Where did all this stuff come from? I don't remember having any pans like that."

"You don't," she said quietly. "They're mine. I brought them with me."

Which revealed a lot about her, whether she knew it or not. Obviously there had been a lot of nights she couldn't sleep if she felt the need to take her bread-baking supplies with her wherever she went. Damn it, just how often did she find herself alone in her kitchen in the middle of the night?

"Sarah—"

"I'm sorry—"

Like two teenagers awkward with the silence that stretched between them, they both spoke at the same time. When he motioned for her to go first, she said quietly, "I'm sorry if I woke you. I just couldn't lay there any longer."

He knew what it was like to lie in the dark and think of someone who refused to leave you in peace. He wondered how shocked she'd be if he told her she was that someone. "It doesn't matter," he said tightly, waving off her apology. "I wasn't sleeping very well, anyway. How much longer before you finish up here?"

She shrugged. "A half hour or so. Why?"

Ignoring the question, he leaned down, picked up the loaf pan she'd dropped when he'd walked in on her, and held it out to her. She should have taken it and turned away to check the bread that was browning in the oven, but she couldn't make her fingers work. Soundlessly she stared at him, her eyes moving over him as if she were committing every square inch of him to memory.

He was so close she could see a faint scar that trailed just above his right nipple, so close that she only had to reach out to stroke the whiskers that shadowed his angled jaw. No man had a right to look so good half dressed and still warm from sleep, she thought shakily as her pulse began to pound. Wordlessly she reached for the pan and hugged it to her breast, as if it would protect her from the heat spilling through her veins.

"How about some coffee?"

"No!" The last thing she wanted was to have a coffee klatch with him in the middle of the night. She was already too aware of him, too conscious of the coziness of the small kitchen and the darkness outside pressing in on them, closing out the world. But she might as well have saved her breath. He was already brushing past her to the coffeemaker and starting a fresh pot.

"Dugan, you don't have to stay up with me," she said in exasperation. "There's no use both of us being dead in the morning just because I couldn't sleep. I don't need you to baby-sit me."

"Good," he retorted. "Because the last thing I think of you as is a baby."

He never took his eyes off what he was doing, but the husky words wrapped around her, warming her all the way to her toes. Suddenly the kitchen was twenty degrees hotter and the increased temperature had nothing to do with the oven. "Dugan—"

He'd have to be deaf to miss her warning tone. Shrugging, he let the matter slide. For now. "So, you bake your own bread," he said casually as he turned to face her. Leaning back against the counter, he crossed his arms over his naked chest and once again gave her the once-over. "I wouldn't have figured you for an old-fashioned woman. Who taught you to cook?"

Caught off guard, she blinked, heat stinging her cheeks. "My grandmother. And just because I know how to bake bread doesn't mean I'm old-fashioned. I happen to like to cook."

His mouth twitched at her defensiveness. "I didn't mean it as an insult. I'm just surprised, that's all. What else did your grandmother teach you?"

"How to skip rocks." She saw his eyes widen and couldn't help but grin. "My grandmother was born fifty years before her time. She could run as fast as a deer when she was sixty and hiked the Grand Canyon when she was seventy-two. She never let her sex—or age—get in the way of anything she wanted to do."

The coffee was ready then, and he poured them both a cup. Taking his to the bar that separated the cooking area from the dining alcove, he settled himself on a bar stool and said quietly, "Tell me about her."

She shouldn't have. It was late and talking about her grandmother didn't make the kitchen any less intimate, or Dugan any less threatening to her peace of mind. But the shadows of the night encouraged confidences and talking about her grandmother always brought back warm memories that never failed to cheer her. Before she could stop herself, she found herself telling him about her childhood and her adventures with another Sarah, her mother's mother.

Caught up in her memories, she didn't realize she was showing him a side of herself she allowed very few people to see. The reserve that usually dictated her movements was stripped away, revealing the carefree, fun-loving young woman she must have been before the rape. Fascinated, Dugan couldn't take his eyes from her. She moved gracefully about the kitchen, removing the last of the fresh-baked bread from the oven, then cleaning up the mess while she laughed over another one of her grandmother's antics. She was totally captivating and sexy as hell and hadn't a clue as to what she was doing to him.

Dugan knew he should have ended their little tête-à-tête right then and there. It had been a long time since a woman had made his blood swim with just a smile, especially when it wasn't even directed at him. He was too drawn to her and much too close to losing his head over her. And that was something he couldn't afford to do. Even if he'd been interested in jumping into another relationship—which he damn well wasn't—giving in to his need for Sarah would be nothing short of disaster. She might want him—her eyes, had she but known it, told him that much—but what her heart wanted and the memories her mind allowed were two different things. The last thing either of them needed was his coming on to her.

But he wasn't going to be able to go back to bed without kissing her.

Inevitability tugged at him like an undertow, infuriating him. It wasn't like him to let desire overrule his common sense, but from the moment he'd first laid eyes on Sarah, nothing was as it had been before. No woman had ever unbalanced him so quickly, so effectively, but there didn't seem to be a damn thing he could do about it. Except want her.

"My God, I didn't realize it was so late!" she suddenly said, horrified as she glanced at the clock and saw that she'd been reminiscing for nearly forty-five minutes. "In another couple of hours, it'll be time to get up again. You should have stopped me."

He shrugged. "I've survived on less sleep. Anyway, I was enjoying listening to you."

Something in his eyes seemed to steal the breath right out of her lungs, and too late, she realized that the walls she'd unconsciously let down while she talked of the past were not quite as easy to rebuild once she returned to the present. Jerkily, she turned to wipe the counter one last time. "I'm just about through here, so you don't have to stay up with me any longer. I'll turn out the lights before I go upstairs."

"That's all right. I'll wait for you."

His voice whispered over her nerve endings like sand-paper, making her heart skid. Panic, quick as lightning, shot through her bloodstream. With shaking fingers she spread out the dish cloth on the edge of the sink to dry, then turned, her smile forced, her eyes unwittingly wary. "See? All finished. If you're as tired as I am, you'll crash the minute your head hits the pillow."

Since he was already picturing her in bed, preferably his, it was a foregone conclusion that sleep would be a long time coming. He shrugged noncommittally and motioned for her to precede him. "Go ahead. I'll get the light."

Her palms damp and her throat dry, she escaped into the entrance hall and headed for the stairs, stopping only to turn on a light. Before she could do more than take the first step, she heard him behind her.

"If you have any more trouble sleeping," he said softly, "wake me."

Instinct told her to thank him for his concern and keep on walking, but she couldn't. Thanks to him, she'd managed to escape the worries nagging at her for at least a little while, and she couldn't run from him like a scared rabbit. "I don't think that'll be necessary," she replied, turning to face him. "But thanks for the offer. And thanks for letting me bore you to death about my childhood. It helped."

"I wasn't bored, but you're welcome."

He stood less than a foot away, his eyes level with hers since she still stood on the first step, her mouth just a heartbeat away. There was flour on her cheek, a fine dusting of white he wanted to taste with his tongue. He felt need, hot and pulsing, hit him in the gut and just barely resisted the urge to snatch her into his arms. Careful, he warned himself as his hands curled into fists to keep from reaching for her. She had been through so much. He wouldn't, couldn't add to her pain.

A kiss, he reasoned. Just a kiss. He could make it through the night with nothing more than that. Clinging to the half-truth, he started to lower his head, only to stop abruptly when he saw her eyes widen in distress. Her panic stabbed him right in the heart, surprising him. He hadn't expected her to be able to hurt him without saying a word.

"A kiss, Sarah," he whispered thickly. "I just want to kiss you good-night, nothing more than that."

He held her gaze unwaveringly, his hands at his sides, his eyes solemn with a promise that she instinctively knew he would break his right arm to keep. If she'd turned and fled, he wouldn't have made a single move to stop her. "Dugan—"

She breathed his name on a sigh and that was all the encouragement he needed. With infinite patience, he leaned toward her, giving her time to accept his nearness, to accept him. His eyes open, his body straining, he watched her brace herself even as her mouth lifted ever so slightly to his. Steeling himself not to rush her, his lips settled on hers.

It lasted the span of three heartbeats, no longer. A brush of lips, a tangling of breaths, the dark, secret glide of a tongue. As kisses went, it was brief, innocently sweet, nonthreatening. Yet it made Dugan burn as nothing else ever had and still managed to pull a tenderness from him that left him gasping.

Staggered, he jerked back abruptly, his stunned eyes searching hers. Given half a minute more, he could have lost himself in her, he thought dazedly. He could have wrapped her close and sank into her softness...and scared the hell out of her.

The thought sobered him as nothing else could. Putting a step between them, and then another, he muttered roughly, "Good night," and turned toward his room.

Feeling as if she'd been caught up in the breath-stealing winds of a whirlwind only to be dumped back to earth with a jolt, Sarah stared after his retreating back for a long moment and knew she was in trouble. Once, long ago, she'd never thought to question the wisdom of touching someone she was attracted to. Then Trent had hurt her and she hadn't been able to shake the feeling that somehow, some way, she must have misled him. She hadn't voluntarily touched a man since.

But tonight she'd been tempted, she admitted shakily. For one wild, heart-stopping moment, when Dugan had tilted the world beneath her feet with nothing more than the brush of his mouth against hers, she'd had to fight the instinct to move closer, to be the person she'd been in the past, to touch him as she longed for him to touch her. And that was something she just couldn't allow to happen. What, dear God, was she going to do now?

Chapter 6

By morning Sarah had convinced herself that tiredness and the lateness of the hour had blown her reaction to Dugan's kiss all out of proportion. She'd read tenderness and yearning into what had been nothing more than a simple good-night kiss. A kiss, she reminded herself, that hadn't seemed to affect him in the least. In fact, he'd ended it as quickly as possible, then walked away from her without a backward glance. And who could blame him? What man would want a woman who would turn into a scratching wildcat the minute he got too close? No, she didn't have to worry about him pressing for anything more than a kiss. Nothing had changed.

Yet the minute her eyes met his across the breakfast table, she felt as if nothing was as it had been the day before. Heat still sizzled between them, but suddenly it was something more than desire, something more than physical that reached out to draw her in. He never made a move to touch her but she could still feel its tug. And so could he.

She could see the knowledge in his eyes, the quiet thoughtfulness, as if he were trying to figure out where they went from here.

Emotions she wasn't ready to handle were closing in on her, and she knew she was losing control of her heart. But even when they got to work and she was finally able to put some distance between them, the feelings he stirred in her so effortlessly, refused to go away. She missed him. If she hadn't been so horrified by the idea, she would have been stunned. How could you miss someone you'd spent the weekend constantly snapping at? But she did, and she didn't realize how much until she looked up from the paperwork she was trying to lose herself in and he was there, standing on the threshold.

Her pulse jumped and her palms dampened at the sight of him. His dark hair was ruffled as if he'd been out in the wind or he'd been running restless fingers through it, the flowered tie that had been so neatly knotted hours earlier when they'd left for work now pulled slightly askew. The scowl that sat upon his face was the same one that had sat upon it for most of the weekend, but it was the hot intensity of his eyes that had her breath backing up in her throat. They'd held that same heat only moments before he'd kissed her.

Quickly, before she dropped it, she set down the pen she was holding. If she'd been able, she would have risen to her feet rather than sit there and let him tower over her, but she had a horrible suspicion her knees wouldn't support her. "What—" She winced at the revealing huskiness of her voice and tried again. "What's wrong?"

Wrong? he wanted to shout at her. What was wrong was that he couldn't stay the hell away from her! He'd been fighting the need all morning to stop by her office with one excuse or another just so he could see her. Every time he got up for a cup of coffee, every time he stepped into the hall, he found himself wanting to turn toward the administrative wing. In desperation, he'd insisted on doing some of the legwork on one of Buck's prostitution cases. When Buck had looked pointedly at the paperwork piled high on Dugan's own desk, then lifted a brow inquiringly, Dugan had muttered a curse and told him he just needed some air. But the air obviously hadn't helped. The minute he'd stepped back into the station, his feet had ignored the dictates of his brain and led him straight to Sarah's office. He was losing it, he thought furiously. Well and truly losing it.

"Nothing," he retorted. "I've been away from my desk and just thought I'd stop by and see if you'd gotten any interesting calls today."

Foolish disappointment flooded through her. So he hadn't dropped by just to see her. Why did that hurt so when she was determined not to get any more involved with him than she already was? "No calls," she said stiffly. "In fact, it's been pretty quiet. If that changes, I'll give you a call." She picked up her pen and dropped her eyes back to the script she'd been fine-tuning when he'd walked in.

It was a clear dismissal, the kind she'd become famous for whenever any man pressed a little too close. But damn it, he wasn't just any man! He was the man who'd wanted her so badly last night he could taste it, yet he'd still somehow managed to keep his hands at his side. She could trust him, and he wasn't letting her give him the brush-off like he was some nobody who'd just crawled out from under a rock!

Strolling over to her desk, he dropped down uninvited to the chair in front of it and stretched out his legs as if he intended to camp there all day. "So how are you feeling?"

Her fingers tightened on her pen, but she didn't look up. "Fine. Why do you ask?"

"You didn't get a lot of sleep last night."

He didn't move so much as a muscle, but with nothing more than his words he stole her breath and dragged her back to the moment on the stairs when he'd kissed her. Had he known she hadn't been able to sleep after that without dreaming of him? Had he, too, tossed and turned in the darkness and reached for someone who wasn't there?

Heat climbing her cheeks, her eyes lifted to his. "Dugan—"

The sharp ringing of the telephone cut off whatever she was going to say next, and with a sigh of relief, she reached for it. "Crime Watchers."

"Did you enjoy your weekend, Sarah?"

Dugan saw her stiffen, her face go as pale as the white blouse she wore under the jacket of her green suit. He didn't have to hear what the caller was saying to know that it was the rapist. Swearing, he jerked upright in his chair and almost reached for her. He wasn't going to sit there and watch the creep put her through hell! he thought, enraged. All he had to do was reach across her desk and push the button that notified the phone company to trace the line. Then they'd see how cocky her tormenter was!

He started to lean across the desk only to stop, his eyes locking with hers. She didn't make a move to stop him, didn't say a word in protest, but his hand froze, his fingers curling into a tight fist of frustration. The look in her eyes clearly warned him this was her move, her call. *She* had to make sure it was the right thing to do. Uttering a short, pithy oath, he moved back. She was right, damn it.

Sarah wanted to thank him for understanding, but all her concentration was focused on the familiar, sinister voice of the man purring in her ear like a sick lover. "So you're not going to talk," he chuckled. "Then let me tell you about my weekend, Sarah. I couldn't get to you—you were out of my reach. So I had to get someone who looked like you. Only she wasn't you. We both know she wasn't you, Sarah. But your time is coming. Just wait."

Horror rose in Sarah like bile. "No!" She didn't know if she was protesting his claim that he'd raped another woman, or that her unavailability made it all her fault, but she knew she couldn't continue to let this man flaunt his horrendous crimes in her face. Shaking with sudden fury, she jabbed at the button on the side of the phone.

"Good girl," Dugan breathed softly in a voice that wouldn't carry to the man on the phone. He wanted to sweep her up in his arms and give her a big hug, but even if she hadn't been on the phone, that wouldn't have been possible. Instead he had to be content with giving her free hand a squeeze before she picked up her pen and started taking notes again. "Keep him talking, sweetheart," he whispered encouragingly. "Remember what they say about sticks and stones. He can't hurt you."

When he smiled at her like that, she felt as if nothing could ever hurt her again, but she only nodded, warmed by the endearment that had fallen so easily from his tongue. When had his approval come to mean so much to her?

Shaken, she turned her attention back to the ugly words echoing in her ear. She knew that the trace had gone through instantly, but it would take the phone company a few minutes to track down where the rapist was calling from. Once they were able to get that information to the police, a patrol car would immediately be sent to the address. Meanwhile, Sarah had to keep him talking so he wouldn't have time to get away before an officer arrived on the scene.

"You're lying," she retorted angrily. "There hasn't been a report of any more rapes. I would have heard."

"Am I?" he taunted, his phony accent stronger than ever. "Watch the evening news. In fact, maybe I should call one of the TV stations myself. They might be real interested in knowing why I've developed an interest in redheads. Should I do that, Sarah? Hmm?" he goaded. "Should I let today's victim and the ones to come know they have you to thank for my sudden interest in them?"

"No! This isn't my fault! You can't blame me for something you did—"

Behind her the phone that wasn't used for hot line tips rang shrilly. Dugan quickly hurried around her desk and answered it in a low voice. "This is Detective Magee. What have you got?"

"The call's being made from a pay phone on the first floor of the courthouse."

"Son of a bitch!" Dugan swore under his breath. The caller was less than three blocks away! Damn his daring! Muttering his thanks, Dugan hung up and quickly buzzed the police dispatcher. "C'mon, c'mon," he grumbled impatiently. "Answer the damn phone!"

Sarah hardly heard Dugan give the dispatcher instructions to get all available units to the courthouse pronto. Caught up in a nightmare, all too familiar accusations slapped and tore at her. How many nights had she lain in the dark and replayed Trent's accusations after he had hurt her? she wondered, forcing back a sob. For months afterward, she hadn't been able to crawl into bed without his words ringing in her ears, mocking her, blaming her. She'd been the victim, yet he'd raged at her as if he was the wounded one, as if he was the one who'd been taken advantage of and defiled, until she'd begun to wonder if maybe he was right.

"You miserable excuse for a man," she said witheringly, her eyes blazing. "Does it make you feel more manly to blame your shortcomings on your victims? Well, I've got news for you, you're nothing but slime—"

"You'll pay for that, lady. Just wait."

"I don't think so," she tossed back, unwisely taunting him. "I don't think you've got the guts—"

She was so furious she would have said more, but he didn't give her the chance. A soft click broke the connection only seconds before she heard what sounded like a fleet of patrol cars, their sirens echoing eerily off the downtown buildings, shoot past the police department and up the street to the courthouse.

Only then did she realize what she'd done. Stricken, she looked up to find Dugan standing right next to her. "Oh, God, Dugan, I'm sorry! He made me so mad, I didn't even think about keeping him on the line. I shouldn't have taunted him that way!"

No, she shouldn't have, but Dugan couldn't help but grin. If he hadn't thought it would bring that haunted look back to her eyes, he'd have snatched her into his arms and kissed her. "I don't know what he said to you, honey, but you ate his lunch. I'm proud of you."

She would have laughed, but she was too close to tears to chance it. Giving in to a need she couldn't fight, she reached out and took his hand. She saw surprise widen his eyes, then pleasure darken them to slate. Ever so lightly, his fingers closed around hers, holding her, but not trapping her. Dragging in a shaky breath, she felt the contact steady her and didn't question why this man could make her feel safe when she'd thought she'd never again feel anything but panic in the company of a man who wasn't family.

"He claims he committed another rape," she said quietly. "Another redhead. Because he couldn't get to me. He threatened to call the TV stations."

Dugan uttered a short, terse curse that Sarah had never heard anyone say aloud. So that was the guilt trip the maggot was trying to lay on her. "You're damn right he couldn't get to you, and he's not going to. We may have him this time. Half the force is surrounding the courthouse. Instead of threatening to call the media, he'd better worry about calling his lawyer. He's going to need one."

He didn't try to convince her that there couldn't have been another rape; they both knew the rapist didn't make idle threats. Giving his hand a final squeeze, Sarah turned away to the window, which gave her a limited view of the courthouse in the distance. Black and white police cars were pulled up at odd angles, blocking traffic and turning the red rocked courthouse and Main Plaza, directly across the street from it, into what looked like a war zone. Hugging herself, she whispered, "I can't believe he'd be stupid enough to let himself get caught so easily."

He hadn't.

Leaving Sarah safely ensconced in her office, Dugan rushed to the courthouse to join Buck, who was directing the search, but it soon became apparent that the criminal had slipped through their fingers. The phone he'd used was deserted, the receiver he'd held still warm from his touch. There was no doubt that he'd been there—he'd boldly left a cassette tape with Sarah's name written on it on the shelf under the phone, then taken the time to wipe everything free of his fingerprints. In the hustle and bustle of people coming and going in the always crowded building, no one had noticed him.

Infuriated, Dugan and Buck had the building searched from top to bottom, every broom closet and out of the way niche checked out even so they knew it was probably a waste of time. Without a physical description to go on, they'd have had a better chance of finding a needle in a haystack then the rapist among the throngs of people in the building.

An hour later they were forced to admit defeat. The criminal could have walked right through the line of cops outside and they never would have known it. Frustrated and furious at the man's cunning, they headed back to the station with the tape the first officer on the scene had found at the phone.

The minute they stepped off the elevator onto the second floor, Dugan hesitated, his eyes going to the hallway that led to Sarah's office. She was probably wearing out the carpet by now, waiting for him to return. How could he face her and admit that once again the slimeball had gotten away? Damn it, they'd been so close! He could almost smell the guy. His jaw rigid, he stared down at the tape he held. He could just imagine the filth on it, the threats and vile promises that would drive the blood out of Sarah's cheeks and bring that desperate, panicked look to her eyes. Did she have any idea what it did to him when she looked that way? It tore him up inside and made him ache to hold her, to make her forget, and he could do neither. Instead he had to stand by and watch her pretend that she could handle her fear alone, even though she became jumpier with every passing day.

Damn it, she'd been through enough, he thought angrily. Her nerves were already stretched to the limit and Dugan didn't like to think what it would take to make them snap. It damn sure wasn't going to be the tape that had been left for her. What she didn't know couldn't hurt her. The decision made, he turned right, away from Sarah's office. When Buck shot him a questioning look, he said, "She doesn't need to hear this now. Not until we know what's on it.

Sarah, however, had no intention of letting him protect her from the ugliness of the case. When they stepped into the large, desk-filled room that served as home to the detective unit, she was seated at Dugan's desk, one long, slender leg crossed over the other, her foot tapping the air agitatedly as she waited. Dugan swore, his fingers unconsciously tightening on the tape. How the hell was he supposed to protect the woman if she wouldn't cooperate?

Coming to a stop at his cluttered desk, he scowled down at her. Her skin was parchment white, her brown eyes anxious. A muscle ticked in his jaw. "What are you doing here?"

Unable to sit still, she rose quickly to her feet. "I just couldn't stay in my office and wait. What happened?"

"Not a damn thing," he retorted, his mouth flattening into a thin line. "He got away."

"But how? The first patrol car was there only seconds after he hung up."

"It only takes seconds for a faceless man to step into a crowd and disappear." He watched her shoulders slump, her eyes blink rapidly, forcing back tears, and almost reached for her. "I'm sorry, honey."

Perched on the corner of his own desk, Buck lifted a brow in surprise, his gaze bouncing between his friend and the woman he'd been grumbling about working with only last week. His mouth twitched, amusement stealing into his eyes, but he kept his comments to himself. "He was probably gone before we even pulled up at the curb, Sarah.

He wouldn't have tried a stunt like this without having an escape route already worked out."

"I know that, but—" Suddenly spying the tape Dugan held, she asked, "What's that?"

Dugan could have kicked himself for not slipping it into his pocket the minute he saw her at his desk, but it was too late now. "It was found at the scene," he said with a shrug that wasn't quite as casual as he'd have liked.

If Sarah hadn't spent the past few days in his constant company, she might have thought he wasn't the least concerned about the tape. But something in his tone, in the stiffness of his shoulders, set alarm bells clanging in her head. "It's from him, isn't it?" she guessed shrewdly.

"Sarah—"

"Isn't it?" she pushed, ignoring his warning tone. "Damn it, Dugan, don't lie to me! Don't try to wrap me in cotton like some porcelain doll that'll crack at the least bit of pressure. I don't break easily."

No, she was strong, he admitted, studying her through narrowed eyes. Maybe too strong. She drew that cloak of reserve around her and took whatever was thrown at her, refusing to accept any help, any protection, unless she was forced to. Because, to accept help, she had to trust, and that was something she didn't do easily. It hurt—more than he'd expected. He wanted, *needed* her to trust him, and she was fighting him every step of the way.

"All right," he sighed in defeat. "Yes, it was apparently left by the rapist. It has your name on it."

She paled ever so slightly, but she didn't hesitate. "I want to listen to it."

"No."

"It's a message for me. I have a right to listen to it."

Scowling, he glanced over at Buck, who only shrugged. Muttering a curse under his breath about stubborn women, he jerked open the bottom drawer of his desk and pulled out a tape-player. "You want to let the man terrorize you, who am I to complain? Listen, then, but don't blame me if you're up in the middle of the night again baking bread!" And with that, he shoved in the tape and jabbed the play button.

"Sarah..." Oozing a false British charm that was nonetheless sick, the rapist greeted Sarah as if he were right there in the room with her. "Can you hear me, lady? I'm close. So close I can almost reach out and touch you. The cops think they can keep me from you, but they're wrong, Sarah. They've got you safely tucked away for now, but one of these days I'll slip right through their fingers and find you." He laughed mockingly. "Fools, Sarah, you're surrounded by fools. But even a fool can get lucky, so I'm not taking any more chances by calling you again. The next time we talk, it'll be in person. Just you and me, Sarah, with no cops to protect you. Watch for me."

The tape fizzled off into static, and with an abrupt movement, Dugan punched the stop button. Silence fell like a stone, but Sarah hardly noticed. It wasn't the threats that echoed in her ears, chilling her, but the man's confidence. He sounded so damn sure of himself. And why shouldn't he? she thought, fighting the hysterical sob that threatened to choke her. So far he'd kept every perverted promise, and no one had been able to lift a finger to stop him, least of all the police. Shivering, she rubbed her hands up and down her arms, trying to warm herself, but the cold seemed to touch her very soul. Time, she thought in rising panic. She was running out of time.

She didn't make a sound, but Dugan could see her struggle to hang onto her control, and something inside him tore free. Like it or not, she wasn't going through this alone! he thought determinedly. Damning the consequences, he reached down and pulled her to her feet, and then into his arms. He felt the surprise that rippled through her, the first faint traces of wariness that threatened to stiffen her muscles one by one. His grip instinctively tightened before he could bring himself to relax his hold a little.

"Dugan—"

Her startled whisper reminded him that they were at work, in full view of Buck and anyone else who cared to walk in, but he didn't give a damn. She was the one he was worried about, and whether she knew it or not, she needed to be held. And that was just what he was going to do! "Easy," he murmured, stroking his hand down her back, soothing her. It seemed like ages since he'd had her this close. "You're safe, honey. Relax. No one is going to hurt you again. You have my word on that."

She strained against him, and for a moment he thought she was going to push out of his arms like a startled virgin. But just when he braced himself for the rejection, she wilted suddenly and let her hands tentatively crawl around to his back, until she was unconsciously clinging to him. "I don't want to be afraid," she said in a whisper that was so low he had to bend his head closer to hers to catch it. "But he sounded so sure of himself. God, Dugan, what if he's right? What if he finds a way to get to me? I...I don't think I . . . I could go through it again."

The faint, stuttered admission slashed at him like a switchblade, cutting his heart to ribbons. He swore, a muscle working in his hard jaw, and tugged her closer. If he ever got his hands on the dirtbag who was doing this to her—and he promised himself he wouldn't rest until he did—he was going to make his life a living hell. "He'll have to go through me first to do it," he growled. "And that ain't gonna happen, baby. Trust me."

She tried to tell him that she wanted to, that it frightened her just how much she was coming to depend on him, but she couldn't get the words past the lump in her throat. Then the phone rang on his desk, and the moment was gone.

Seeing Dugan's reluctance to release Sarah, Buck shot him an amused glance that warned him he would be in for some ribbing later, then leaned over and snatched up the phone. "Detective Roberts," he said, identifying himself. The laughter fell from his face abruptly as he listened to whoever was on the other end of the line, and with a curse, he reached for pencil and paper. Scribbling furiously, he jotted down notes. "Yeah, I got it," he said grimly, tossing down the pencil. "We'll get right on it." When he hung up, his gaze moved regretfully to Sarah before returning to Dugan. "There's been another rape."

Within two hours the news was all over the station that the latest victim was the spitting image of the chief's goddaughter, except for the fact that her hair was more brown than red. But she had the same delicate features, the same tall, slender body, the same quiet dignity that nothing seemed to shake. Until now.

Staying close to her office, Sarah heard the hushed rumors, the speculative whispers, and wanted to clamp her hands over her ears and scream out a denial. The rapist couldn't be systematically, *deliberately* limiting his latest victims to women who looked like her. He couldn't be that cruel, that sadistic. Someone's imagination was playing overtime, and as soon as Dugan got back from the hospital, where he was questioning the woman, he would tell her that she no more looked like Sarah than the man on the moon. It was all just a tragic mistake.

But when Dugan walked in hours later, well after four o'clock, she took one look at his chiseled face and knew that the rumors that had been flying about the station all day were true. "Oh, God, it's true, isn't it? She looks like me."

He would have given anything to deny it, but he was still reeling from his meeting with the thirty-two-year-old salesrep who'd had the misfortune to have her car break down on a lonely stretch of road on the northwest part of town while she was making her cosmetic deliveries. The fact that it'd been broad daylight hadn't saved her. She'd looked so much like Sarah, it was frightening.

"Yes."

He didn't even try to candy-coat the truth. The minute he'd walked into the hospital emergency room and seen Rebecca Hawkins, he'd stiffened like someone had slammed a fist into his ribs. She'd been as white as the sheet that covered the gurney she'd sat on, her brown eyes wide and lost, her teeth gripping her bottom lip to keep it from trembling. She hadn't shed a single tear, hadn't murmured a single protest when he'd asked the probing, intimate questions he'd had to ask her. Her voice low and carefully devoid of emotion, she'd given him all the information he'd needed as if she were reading it from the classifieds. She hadn't once looked him in the eye.

Instinct told him Sarah must have looked much the same way the night she'd been date raped. She wouldn't have screamed and cried and demanded to know why a woman's worst nightmare had happened to her. No, she'd have drawn into herself like Rebecca Hawkins did. She'd have closed off her emotions—herself—from the rest of the world and refused to let anyone get close enough to see her hurt, let alone offer her comfort.

For the first time he really began to understand the horror Sarah had gone through, the violation, and he ached to hold her so badly he nearly shook with need. But if he touched her now, there was no way he'd be able to keep the embrace light. He wanted her close, so close he could all but pull her inside him, where no one could ever hurt her again. And she wasn't ready for that. She might never be ready for that.

Keeping his distance, he said tightly, "I'm getting you out of here, but first I've got to meet with the chief. He'll have my butt if I don't fill him in on the latest developments. After that, I'll take you home."

But that was the last place she wanted to go. Too much had happened for her to just go back to his place and pretend nothing had changed. She wasn't that good an actress. Dugan hadn't said anything, but he was obviously worried about the recent turn of events. The rapist was clearly getting impatient and taking more and more risks in his attempt to get to her. And they still didn't have a clue as to who he was. "I can't just sit around the house and wait," she said huskily. "I'll go stir crazy."

The desperation in her voice called to him, testing his resolve to keep his hands to himself. But just the thought of her pulling away from him now, when she was the only thing he'd been able to think of since he'd left the hospital, had him moving toward the door. "Then we won't go home," he said simply, and stepped into the hall.

Minutes later he was being shown into the chief's office, and it wasn't a meeting he was looking forward to. Russell Fletcher was a hard-nosed cop who had used guts, intelligence and uncanny instincts to work his way up in the ranks. He wasn't just an administrator, but a damn good cop who didn't like excuses. He hadn't been too happy when he'd learned about the package that had been left on

Sarah's doorstep, the same one that had driven her to accept Dugan's offer of shelter and protection at his house. In a private meeting with Dugan the following day, the old man had made it clear he would have felt better if Sarah had come to him for help, or better yet, returned to Houston, but he wasn't going to interfere with her decision as long as she was safe. Dugan didn't even want to speculate how he was going to react to today's developments.

"Magee," the older man greeted him the moment he stepped through the door. "Sit down and tell me what you've got on this latest rape. I've heard the victim is a dead ringer for Sarah."

Dugan bit back a curse. He should have known nothing got past Fletcher. "She could pass for her sister," he said flatly, taking the chair in front of the desk that dominated the far end of the spacious office. Quickly and succinctly, he gave him a detailed report on the circumstances of the rape, the fiasco at the courthouse, the tape that was being examined by the lab. Even to his own ears, it was obvious that there was pitiful little progress in the case.

The thinning of the older man's lips said as much. "What about snitches? And a profile on this bastard? He didn't just appear out of nowhere. You know as well as I do that a serial rapist rapes again and again until he's caught. He's done this before."

"We're checking it, getting the word out, hoping his M.O. and the profile strikes a chord with someone. But so far, we've got squat. As for the snitches, it's quiet as a church on the street. If our boy's talking, he's doing it to a few select friends who know how to keep their mouths shut."

The hard angle of Fletcher's jaw eased ever so slightly. He knew enough about Magee to know he would turn over every stone until he turned over the one this snake hid under, but that took time. Meanwhile, Sarah was in danger. That was unacceptable. "Then I don't have to ask if there was any response to the reward being offered by Crime Watchers. Damn it to hell, Magee, I want this scum caught!"

An image flashed in Dugan's head of Sarah baking bread in his kitchen in the middle of the night because she couldn't stand to stay in bed. His gray eyes turned cold and deadly. "No more than I do, sir. I'll get him even if I have to break every rule in the book."

That was an admission the chief chose to ignore. Leaning back, he drummed his fingers on the arms of his leather chair and studied Dugan through eyes that missed little. "How is Sarah?" he asked finally. "Whenever I see her, she claims she's up to her ears in work, and she hardly has any time to talk. How is she handling all this?"

Dugan hesitated, the image of her in his kitchen at three in the morning once again taunting him. "She's... coping," he hedged.

The other man nodded. "Sarah's good at ... coping," he said, using Dugan's own words and timing to let him know he'd noticed his evasiveness. His gaze speculative, he suddenly made a snap decision and straightened in his chair. "I'm not in the habit of betraying confidences, Magee, but there's something you should know about Sarah, something that isn't to go beyond the walls of this office. I presume I have your word on that?"

Dugan stiffened, guessing what was coming. "Sir—"

"Your word, Magee."

"You have it," he snapped, "but it's not necessary. I already know."

Russell Fletcher eyed him suspiciously. "Know what?"

"That Sarah was date raped three years ago in Houston," he replied. "She told me all about it."

Whatever Russell had been expecting, it wasn't that. As far as he knew, Sarah had never told anyone but her immediate family and a few very close friends about the rape. Understandably, it wasn't something she liked to talk about with just anyone.

"Well," he said, expelling his breath in a rush. "I'm surprised. But pleased," he quickly added. "Sarah's cut herself off from the world for too many years now. I was really starting to worry about her. It's nice to know she's finally letting another man in her life. You'll be good for her."

This time it was Dugan's turn to be surprised. Stunned, he opened his mouth to tell the chief that he was mistaken—he wasn't involved with Sarah now, nor would he be in the future—but the words just wouldn't come. Because he was involved with her. Somehow she had made him care, whether he wanted to or not.

Chapter 7

Just as Dugan had promised, they didn't go home. Instead the minute Sarah was safely buckled in beside him in his car, he headed for the one spot in the city where he knew it would be easy for her to forget the hellish day—the River Walk. Located below street level along the banks of the San Antonio River in the heart of the city, the meandering walkways of the Paseo del Rio were a mecca for tourists and local people alike. Here, among the shops and sidewalk cafés and restaurants that lined the river, the mood was always festive, and life moved at a less hurried pace. With water taxis chugging up the slow-moving river and the sound of music and laughter floating on the air, even uptight, antacid-popping businessmen found it easy to relax.

In no rush to eat, Dugan and Sarah strolled up and down both sides of the river, trying to decide between Mexican, Chinese and French food, as well as seafood and steaks. It was the live band at the Mexican restaurant that finally decided the issue. Settling down by the river at a table with a bright yellow umbrella, they ordered margaritas to go with their tostadas and hot sauce, then sat back to people-watch.

Late afternoon softened into twilight, the colored lights decorating the different restaurants sprang on, and an evening breeze carrying the promise of summer rippled across the water, gently stirring Sarah's hair. As Dugan had hoped, she wasn't immune to the carefree atmosphere. Unaware of his shuttered eyes on her, she watched couples stroll by hand in hand, children dart over the arched bridges that crossed the river and pigeons waddle among the tables, searching for crumbs. Gradually the tension knotting her shoulders and tightening the set of her jaw eased. Unconsciously, her foot tapped to the beat of the conjunto music the band was belting out, and a smile flirted with the corners of her mouth. Although she wasn't looking at him, Dugan felt the powerful punch of that smile slam into his gut.

"Would you like to dance?"

Feasting on the sight of her, Dugan didn't realize the question had popped out until she glanced at him in surprise, the light in her eyes fading with apprehension. God, he hated it when she looked at him like that! Had nothing he'd done over the past week convinced her that she could trust him? Swallowing his disappointment, he jerked up the menu the waiter had left for them when he'd taken their drink orders. "Never mind," he said abruptly before she could say no. "Forget I asked. We probably should think about ordering anyway."

Stricken, Sarah watched him retreat behind the menu, his dark brows knitted in a scowl, his eyes hard, and found herself wanting to call back the easy, relaxed man who had sat across from her only seconds before. Giving in to impulse, she leaned forward to lay her fingers over his. "Dugan..." she began softly, helplessly, wishing she could make him understand, "It isn't that I don't want to dance..."

"You don't have to give me an explanation. I understand."

He didn't look at her, but under her fingers she felt the tension running through him like steel threads. He had so much unleashed power, she should have been pulling her hand back in fright, but all she could think of was soothing him. "Then you should know that it has nothing to do with you," she replied. "I haven't danced with anyone in three years. I haven't even wanted to. But I think I would like to with you."

Over the top of the menu, his eyes met hers. She'd guarded her heart for so long, refusing to allow herself emotions that most people took for granted, that Dugan knew the admission hadn't been an easy one for her. "Why do I sense a *but* coming?"

One corner of her mouth turned up in a wistful smile. "It's just...difficult. I'm afraid..."

She couldn't voice her fears, only that they existed, but it was the sad regret in her eyes that had his hand turning in hers and capturing her fingers. He warned himself that he couldn't fight her dragons for her, to try would only drag him deeper into her problems. But, from the moment he'd admitted to himself in the chief's office that he was involved, he'd known that his chance to walk away from her had long since passed.

"Nothing's going to happen on the dance floor, babe," he assured her, giving her a crooked grin. "You couldn't be safer in church."

She had to laugh, a blush climbing her cheeks, the sudden sting of tears burning her eyes. Did he have any idea how she hated being a victim? Especially with him? He was so strong, so sure of himself. With nothing more than a grin and a teasing quip, he made her want to throw off the chains of fear that had held her in bondage for years and finally live again. It was so easy. All she had to do was take the first step into his arms. If only he knew how she wanted to!

Still holding her hand, he rose to his feet and tugged gently. Startled, her heart thumped madly. What she read in the steady gray depths of his eyes only confirmed what she'd always secretly known in her heart—he was a man of his word, a man she could trust with her deepest secrets. Without a word, she let him pull her to her feet.

The minute they stepped onto the small dance floor, the music changed from the lively beat of conjunto to the slow, liquid purr of a Mexican love song. Her eyes wide, Sarah stiffened, her heart tripping at the sound of the blatantly sensuous beat. Dismayed, she looked wildly around for an escape, but more couples had crowded the floor, and she cringed at the thought of pushing through them. "Maybe it would be better to sit this one out."

"You'll do fine."

"But—"

He ended her protests simply by taking her into his arms. Sarah gasped, her hands automatically flying up to brace against the hard wall of his chest, holding him at bay, while her stomach plunged to her feet. Slamming her eyes shut, she knew what would happen next. He would drag her closer, until their hips and thighs brushed with every movement of the dance, and then the panic would start to rise in her, choking her. Sick with dread and stiff as a broomstick, she waited.

But the sinewy arms that encircled her made no move to eliminate the distance between them. The music rose and dipped and swirled around them until most of the other couples on the dance floor melted into each other, content to simply sway to the seductive melody. But Dugan appeared not to notice. Hardly touching her except where his hands linked at the small of her back, he kept a good six inches between them, silently telling her that he asked nothing more from her than that she share the music with him. Still, even though her heart told her she was perfectly safe, it was a long time before her head sent out the message to her rigid limbs that it was okay to relax.

Later Dugan never knew how he kept from pulling her snugly against him, where he ached for her. The music shifted again, and then once more, becoming slow, languid, dangerous. Dugan could feel the rhythm in his blood, drumming in his head, until the need to feel her soft curves pressed to the hard angles and planes of his body became compulsive. Fighting the pull, he sent up a silent prayer of thanks that she was still straight as a board in his arms. Then, just when he thought he was going to make it through the rest of the evening hanging onto his sanity by a thread, she sighed and her muscles turned fluid under his hands. Suddenly he understood the type of torture that could break a man who thought he was unbreakable. He'd never wanted to draw a woman against him so badly in his life.

It was late when they finally left the restaurant and headed back to Dugan's house in a silence that neither seemed willing or able to break. Tension throbbed, heating the air between them and tightening nerves. Sarah couldn't sigh without him being aware of it; Dugan couldn't so much as shift in his seat without her eyes flying to his. Staring straight ahead, the set of his jaw unyielding, Dugan flicked on the radio, hoping the music would be a distraction. Mellow jazz seeped into the car. It didn't help. With a muttered curse, he switched the radio off again.

Clutching her purse to her as if it were a shield, Sarah was sure he could hear the hammering of her heart in the sudden silence. Her gaze drifting to his shadowed face in the darkness, she tried to tell herself that the emotion scraping along her nerve endings was just leftover tension from a day she wouldn't soon forget. But leftover tension didn't make her breathless. Leftover tension didn't foam in her veins like champagne bubbles and make her light-headed. Leftover tension didn't explain her longing to be back in his arms.

She wanted him.

Her thoughts frantically tumbled over themselves in search of another explanation, but she knew in her heart she was only postponing the truth. She wanted him. Why had it taken her so long to accept the inevitable? From the moment she'd met him, the glint in his eyes had warned her he would be a force to be reckoned with, and he hadn't disappointed her. Where other men had backed off when she'd thrown up a wall of ice between them, he'd only taken it as a challenge. He'd forced her to feel when she didn't want to feel, to ache in the night even when she refused to admit it, to need in a way that she hadn't thought possible. And now that she was no longer fighting the truth, her hunger for his touch was only going to get worse before it got better.

Because she was still afraid to let him get too close.

Caught up in the turmoil of her thoughts, she didn't realize they'd arrived at their destination until he pulled into his driveway and cut the engine. Stillness fell, the echo of silence ringing in the night. The windows of Dugan's house were dark, not a single light burning. Sarah glanced up at

the shadowy house and just that quickly, another moonless night stirred in her memory. She shuddered, fighting
the pull of the past and another date that had ended in a
driveway before an unlit house, but the images were too
powerful, too stark, to be ignored. Hands, rough and
ruthless, only hinting at the hurt to come. The click of the
power locks. God, would she ever hear that sound again
without her blood running cold and bile backing up in her
throat?

Releasing his seat belt, Dugan half turned to her in the
dark. He made no move to touch her, but Sarah suddenly
knew she couldn't sit there another second without falling
apart. Biting her lower lip to hold back a sob, she fum-
bled for the release to her own seat belt, then reached for
her door handle, her movements clumsy in the dark. She
felt rather than saw Dugan's start of surprise, but she was
already pushing from the car on shaky legs, her only
thought to get away from the memories that wouldn't leave
her alone. Whimpering, she stumbled up the sidewalk to
the porch.

"Sarah, wait! Damn it, what's the matter?" Confused,
Dugan pushed open his own door and started after her.
He'd just spent most of the evening trying to give her all
the room she needed and now she was running from him
like she was scared to death he was going to jump her
bones! Damn it, what the hell was going on? What had he
done? Unthinkingly, he reached for her. "What—"

The second he touched her, she whirled, shrinking back
against the doorjamb, her eyes wide in her pale face.
"Please...don't."

Dugan froze. In the nearly opaque darkness he could see
the traces of fear in her eyes, the nightmare that for some
reason pressed close tonight. Had something he'd said—
done—pushed her to this? The thought sickened him,

squeezing his heart. Careful not to scare her any more than he already had, he slowly lowered his hands to his sides, the need to take that look from her eyes almost more than he could bear.

"Let's go inside, honey. We need to talk and the front porch isn't the place to do it," he told her evenly. Turning, he shoved his house key into the dead bolt on the front door and turned it sharply, unlocking it. Silently he pushed open the door, flicked the wall switch to flood the entrance hall and living room with soft, inviting light, then stepped back for her to precede him. The minute they were both inside, he shut the door and leaned against it, his gaze fixed unwaveringly on her face. "Did you enjoy the dancing?"

Whatever she'd been expecting, it wasn't this. Her eyes softened. "Oh, yes! It was wonderful. I hadn't realized how much I had missed . . ."

Her words dwindled off, her smile faded, as if she were afraid to admit what she had missed because it would only make the loss more tragic when it was spoken aloud. Struggling with the need to take her into his arms, Dugan forced himself to keep his distance. "Then I didn't do anything to frighten you?" he persisted, his eyes searching.

How could he even think such a thing? "No, of course not. I wouldn't have danced dance after dance with you if I'd been scared of you."

"Then why did you run from me the minute we got home?"

She winced. She'd been so caught up in escaping the flashback, she'd never thought of him, what he must be thinking. "Oh, no," she said, stepping toward him, her words tripping over themselves in her haste to make him understand. "It wasn't you. I loved dancing with you . . .

being held by you. For a while there, I—I could almost pretend the night would end the way it does for most couples when they spend a romantic evening together. W-with a kiss. And I wanted to kiss you," she said fiercely, uncaring that she was admitting more than she should. "But then when we got home—"

She trembled, suddenly cold again. "It was too... similar," she whispered, her eyes trained on a nightmare he couldn't see. "Sitting in the driveway in front of the dark house...the sudden silence closing in on me, trapping me. I c-couldn't stop the memories."

Dugan knew she needed to talk, to get it out of her system, but he couldn't just stand there and watch her relive the horror. "Honey—"

She blinked, bringing him back into focus. "It's called post-traumatic stress disorder," she said stiffly. "Some women still suffer from it fifteen years after they were raped. There are times when I want to believe I'm finally recovering from it, but then something happens—like tonight—and I know I'm only kidding myself. I may never be able to handle intimacy again."

The warning wasn't lost on Dugan. She'd stripped herself bare and laid the truth flat out before him so there would be no misunderstandings. She wanted him, but she feared anything that bordered on intimacy more. A smart man would cut his losses and run.

A rational voice buried deep in his brain advised him to listen to her. He didn't know where their relationship was headed, whether the attraction they felt for each other was anything more than the result of being thrown together at a time when she was at her most vulnerable. It might be wise to cool down and do whatever it took to set their relationship back on a strictly professional footing. Otherwise, she was going to twist him into knots that might never be unraveled.

It was sound advice, but there was only one thing wrong with it—he couldn't take it. Her honesty only made him want her more. If she had a problem with being trapped, with being held, then he wouldn't hold her. Even if it killed him, he promised himself. He would let her set the pace and not press for more than she was ready to give. He didn't fool himself into thinking it would be easy. Letting someone else take control had always been damn difficult for him, but he'd find a way to be satisfied with nothing more than the most innocent of touches if that would help her to finally get past her fears.

Crossing to her, he stopped two steps away from her and shoved his hands into his pockets to keep from reaching for her. Challenge lighted his gray eyes as they locked with the dark, turbulent depths of hers: "It seems to me, sweetheart, that you're giving that Kingston bastard more power over you than he deserves. He hurt you and got away with it, but you can still get revenge by getting on with your life. If you want a good-night kiss, take one."

Stunned by the offer, her gaze flew to the sensuous lines of his mouth and lingered there in fascination. Temptation beckoned. Unconsciously her tongue flicked out to skim her suddenly dry lips, dragging a muffled groan from him. Startled, her eyes lifted to his, the heat she saw there scorching her. "I don't think—"

"That's right," he growled huskily. "Don't think. Go with your gut instinct, honey. Take a kiss. Make it as hot and deep and wet as you're comfortable with. We'll go as far as you want, stop when you want, do nothing more than touch if you want. It's all up to you."

Her eyes wide, she could do nothing but stare at him. She didn't know another man who would have made her that offer. "Why?" she whispered, searching his face for some sign as to what he was feeling. "Why are you doing this?"

"Because I don't want you to be afraid of me anymore," he said simply. "If letting you take control will reassure you that nothing's going to happen that you don't want to happen, then that's what I'll do. So take what you want, sweetheart," he urged, his grin rakish and his hands spread as if to say *here I am*. "I'm yours for the taking."

A week ago she would have turned him down flat. But a week ago she hadn't really known him and had no reason to trust him any more than she would trust any other man. But a lot had changed in the past week. He was the only man she had dared to let herself trust in three long years, let alone want. How could she resist him?

She didn't remember taking the two steps that would eliminate the distance between them, but suddenly she was only inches away from him, so close her breasts almost brushed against the hard plane of his chest. Suddenly temptation took on a whole new meaning. Heat staining her cheeks, she glanced up, intending to look him right in the eye and make him promise this was no trick, but her gaze didn't make it past his mouth. Firm, sensuous and slightly parted lips patiently waited for hers. She only had to lift her chin mere inches to bring her mouth into contact with his.

No sooner did the thought enter her head, and the deed was done. Balancing herself with a steadying hand against his chest, she shyly, hesitantly, brushed her lips against his in a fleeting kiss that lasted no longer than a heartbeat. Soft as the fall of the morning dew and just as sweet, the caress wasn't meant to arouse, but rather to thank him for not pressuring her for more than she was prepared to give. But the minute she drew back and saw the smoldering depths of his eyes, she realized that Dugan wasn't the type of man a woman gave a light kiss of thanks to. He wanted her and made no attempt to hide it. But still he didn't reach for her.

Something in her eased, a guardedness, a wariness she hadn't even been aware of, releasing yearnings she'd submerged in the darkest corners of her mind. For the first time she realized the implications of his offer. Freedom. He held it out to her without restrictions, urging her to touch and taste him, to explore the boundaries of her own sensuality without having to worry that he would expect more from her than she was ready to give. It was a heady feeling.

Murmuring his name, she crowded closer and lifted her mouth to his again. Her eyes drifted shut, the fingers that pressed against his chest curling into his tie as hot, enervating pleasure drifted through her. It had been so long, she thought dreamily as she allowed herself a second kiss, and then a third, learning the shape of his mouth, the heat of his response, the hunger that both thrilled and alarmed her. So long since she'd felt like this.

By the time she drew back, her cheeks were flushed, her eyes dazed, her breathing ragged. "I . . . I should go up now," she said huskily. "It's g-getting late—"

His hands clenched into fists and the muscles along his jaw bunched, Dugan dragged in a hissing breath and just barely fought the need to jerk her into his arms and give her the kind of long, hot, mind-destroying kiss she'd so innocently been begging for. But he'd promised, damn it, and if she needed to keep things light and teasing between them right now, then, by God, he'd find the strength to let her!

"You don't need to give me an explanation," he said with an easy smile that cost him dearly. "You wanted to give me a good-night kiss and you did. It's okay, honey. Go on to bed and I'll see you in the morning."

Swallowing the lump in her throat, she nodded and turned toward the stairs—while she still could. "Good night, then," she said, glancing back over her shoulder at him as she took the first step. "Thank you again for tonight. I really had a good time."

Not trusting himself to speak, he nodded curtly and watched her disappear up the stairs while his body burned in protest. If tonight was just a sample of how they would end their evenings from here on out, he thought with a groan, what kind of sweet torture had he set himself up for?

Sarah lost track of the number of times she relived those kisses. As she lay in bed that night, in her dreams, at work, every time her eyes would innocently stray to wherever Dugan was. He didn't betray by so much as a flicker of an eyelash that he'd attached the slightest bit of importance to those few precious moments when she'd given in to her needs—or the fact that she hadn't made any indication that she wanted to repeat the experience—but she knew he hadn't forgotten. Every time they came within twenty feet of each other, the air almost sizzled between them. And the strain was beginning to tell.

She wanted him. Now, more than ever, and the strength of that need was frightening. Frowning at the report she was preparing for the monthly board of directors' meeting, she warned herself she was becoming too dependent on him. He was a strong man, a gallant man who would have winced at the label. She couldn't let herself get dragged into the illusion that their time together meant anything personal. It would end the moment the rapist was caught, so she would be wise to protect her heart. If it wasn't already too late.

The phone on her desk rang sharply, and Sarah welcomed the interruption thankfully. The trace button was still on the phone if she needed it, but Dugan had insisted she leave it there only as a matter of precaution. The rapist had said on the tape there would be no more calls, and so far, he'd been as good as his word, though it had only been a day. But with every passing hour, she found it easier to answer the hotline without her heart plummeting to her feet.

Her eyes still on her report, she picked up the receiver and balanced it between her shoulder and ear as she made a notation on the paper in front of her. "Crime Watchers."

The voice on the end of the line was male, obviously young, and shakily lacking in confidence. "Uh...m-my name's Joseph P-Peters. I'm a student...at Incarnate Word College. I...uh, I need to talk to someone about being in a Crime Watchers' reenactment."

Sarah had to grin as he rushed out the entire second half of the sentence, as if he didn't spit it out all at once, he would lose his nerve. "You already are," she chuckled. "My name is Sarah. I'm the Crime Watchers coordinator. I take it you're an actor."

"Oh, yes! I mean, I plan to be," he quickly added, flustered. "In Hollywood, after I finish school in May. But the only experience I have so far is in drama productions at school. I thought it would really help me when I went out there to have some work on film to show an agent. You know what I mean?"

Oh, yes, she knew what he meant. She got at least two or three calls a week from young, starry-eyed would-be actors who thought they would make it as easily in Hollywood as they did in their school plays. They had no idea what kind of odds they were up against, and probably wouldn't have cared if they had known. She had to give them credit. She'd never dared to dream that big when she was their age.

"I'm always in need of actors, Joseph," she said easily, "but we don't use film, only videotape. The work is strictly volunteer and you won't get any screen credit. That's for your own protection, but if you're looking for some local fame and fortune, I'm afraid I can't help you."

"Oh, no, I'm just looking for exposure," he quickly assured her. "And tape's fine. Really! So do I need to come down and audition, or what?"

Sarah grinned and reached for the small notebook where she kept a list of potential actors. If he had half as much talent as he had enthusiasm, Joseph Peters would go far. "Just give me your phone number and physical description, and I'll give you a call when I can use you." Scribbling quickly, she started to take down the information he rattled off, then laughed. "I don't know how to tell you this, Joseph, but your timing's perfect. We're taping a reenactment of a convenience store holdup tomorrow night, and none of the actors on my list are available to play the male lead. You sound like you're just the man I'm looking for to play the robber. What do you say? Are you interested?"

"Hell—I mean, yes! Of course!"

"Good. Then the cameraman and I will meet you at the Quick Stop at the corner of San Pedro and Oblate at eight o'clock tomorrow night. You'll need to wear jeans, a blue T-shirt and a red bandanna."

"*All right!* I'll be there."

His thanks ringing in her ears, Sarah hung up with a sigh of relief. She hadn't expected to find someone to play the thief so easily. Now all she had to do was find a plump blonde to play the cashier. Groaning, she picked up her talent notebook and started flipping through it.

The night of the shoot was cool and moonless, and as usual whenever the reenactment was taped at a commercial place of business, there were several last-minute details that had to be taken care of before they could begin. Dugan, who had insisted on coming with her in case there was any kind of trouble, checked out the premises to make sure they were safe, while Sarah consulted with the manager, who had already agreed to clear the store out once they were ready to start taping. Freddy worked around existing displays, setting up lights and a microphone, and within minutes, the stage was set. Janey, the actress Sarah had finally found to play the cashier, then announced that she was ready. All they were waiting on was Joseph Peters.

"I hope I didn't make a mistake in not getting a backup in case that boy doesn't show," Sarah grumbled to Dugan. "But he was so excited, I just felt sure that I could depend on him."

The words were hardly out of her mouth when a battered white Camaro raced into the parking lot and screeched to a stop. The engine was cut at the same time the driver's door was thrown open, and a tall gangly youth wearing jeans and a blue T-shirt exploded from the car, half his face concealed by the red bandanna he was already tying into place. Above the mask, recognition flared in his eyes the minute he saw Sarah standing just outside the entrance to the store, obviously waiting for him.

"God, Sarah, I'm sorry!" he said, hurrying toward her. "I had a flat, and then the spare was flat and I couldn't find a phone anywhere. I never should have cut the time so close, but the car belongs to a friend, and how was I to know he was driving around on nothing but thin air? I know that's not much of an excuse—it's my responsibility to be here on time—but it won't happen again, I can promise you that." Suddenly running out of steam, he looked past her into the shop, his eyes widening when he saw everything was set and waiting. Visibly bracing himself for a chewing out, he asked reluctantly, "Have I held you up long?"

"Not enough to worry about," she replied, amusement gleaming in her eyes. "Five minutes more or less isn't going to make any difference, so calm down. It's okay."

He dragged in a deep breath and expelled it in a rush, his hazel eyes alight with a rueful grin. "I guess I do sound a little frantic. It's just that I don't want to blow this."

"You'll do fine," she assured him. "Let me introduce you to everyone and we'll get started."

She performed the introductions and then gave both him and Janey a quick rundown of their lines. The directions they were to follow were simple enough. Joseph was to walk into the store while Janey's back was turned to him as she refilled the cigarette racks behind the counter. When she turned at the sound of the bell on the door, she would find herself staring down the barrel of a Saturday Night Special. At a curt order from Joseph to open the cash register, she would move too slowly and he would push her up against the racks behind her and hold the gun against her temple while squeezing her throat.

When both the actors assured her that they had their parts down pat, Sarah gave a nod to the manager to empty the store of patrons, and they began. But it soon became apparent that Joseph wasn't at all clear about the character he was supposed to be playing. He was too timid, too hesitant, and obviously afraid he would hurt Janey by the way he gingerly pushed her back from the counter. Struggling to hold onto her patience, Sarah quietly explained again and again that it took body language as well as a gun to carry off this kind of robbery. He had to convince the viewers that he really meant business. But Joseph still couldn't seem to get it right.

"Cut," she said in exasperation when the third take was only slightly better than the first. "We're just wasting tape here and getting nowhere. Janey, take a break. Joseph and I are going to rehearse."

"I'm sorry, Sarah," he apologized for what seemed like the hundredth time. "I guess I'm just nervous."

"Don't be," she retorted with a quick grin that was meant to reassure. "Nobody expects an Oscar-winning performance from you, Joseph, so quit taking everything so seriously. Relax and enjoy this, and stop worrying about hurting Janey or me. We're not made of spun glass, so put some grit into it."

He nodded. "I'll try."

"No, Joseph, just trying leaves room for failure. *Do it!*"

"Y-yes. I will. I'll do it."

Sarah just barely resisted the urge to roll her eyes at Dugan, who was watching from the sidelines, and turned back to the cigarette racks. "Okay. Try it again."

The bell behind her rang and Sarah whirled to see Joseph standing on the other side of the counter, the bandanna covering all but his eyes, the prop gun he pointed at her steady for the first time that evening. She almost sighed in relief. Finally! Glaring at her, he gruffly ordered her to open the cash register. But before she could do as the script called for and move too slowly, he was rushing around the counter and shoving her up against the cigarette racks, hands at her throat, body pressing forcefully against hers.

Sarah froze. Somewhere on the edge of her consciousness, she heard Dugan swear and start toward her, and she knew she was perfectly safe. Joseph hadn't meant to hurt her, she told herself. He was just a little too enthusiastic. But her heart slammed against her chest and her blood ran cold as a terror she'd thought she was finally putting behind her clawed at her throat.

"Don't!" She didn't remember crying out or pushing him away, but suddenly she was free. Shuddering, she gasped for breath.

"Oh, God, I hurt you!" Stricken, Joseph reached out to touch her as if in apology, then snatched back his hands, looking down at them at horror. "I'm sorry! I don't know what happened. I guess I just got carried away—"

"You sure as hell did," Dugan snapped, stepping past him to get to Sarah. At the sight of her wide eyes and ashen face, he wanted to turn and knock the kid up the wall to see how he liked it, but the last thing Sarah needed was more violence. "Are you all right?" he asked quietly.

She nodded, struggling for control. But the concern in his eyes as he stood in front of her, blocking her from the interested eyes of the others in the store, was almost her undoing. Choking back the lump in her throat, she said thickly, "I just need a minute."

He ached to hold her then, to take her into his arms until she was no longer shaking; but since the night she'd driven him half out of his mind with her hesitant kisses, she'd shied away from any physical contact. He couldn't touch her now without her asking him to, but her silence spoke louder than words, and that obviously wasn't going to happen. Stifling his frustration, he said, "Take your time. I'll be right here if you need me."

Silently she took his hand and felt his fingers tighten around hers. The contact grounded her as nothing else could. Straightening her shoulders, she was finally able to take a few steadying breaths. Only then was she able to step around him and give the others a smile that wasn't wobbly. "Okay, guys, now that I've made a fool of myself, let's get back to work. I'm fine, Joseph," she said quickly before he could apologize again. "Keep that same intensity, just tone it down a bit, and you'll do fine."

Within thirty seconds she had everyone in their places and the camera rolling. She was the picture of calm, cool professionalism, but inside she felt like she was falling apart piece by piece, shattering in slow motion as old fears crowded her. By the time she'd thanked everyone for their help and she and Dugan headed for his car, she'd started to shake with delayed reaction.

When Dugan opened her door and she slipped into the seat, all she could think about was having his arms around her. With the memory of his gruff voice echoing in her ears, telling her that from now on she would set the pace, she lifted stricken eyes to his. "Hold m-me," she whispered brokenly as he got into the car. "Please."

Before the words were out of her mouth, she was pressed close to his chest, the reassuring cadence of his heart drumming in her ears. "God, honey, I thought you'd never ask!"

"I . . . I couldn't before. I would have cried and Joseph really w-would have thought he h-hurt me."

"I know, sweetheart, I know," he murmured, carefully tightening his arms around her as her voice broke on a sob. "Go ahead and cry if you want to. Whatever makes you feel better."

She buried her face against his throat and sighed, letting the spicy, masculine scent of him drive away the tainted memories that tried to linger. "Just hold me," she whispered. "That's all I need."

Uncaring that they were still parked in the convenience store parking lot, Dugan could have held her for hours without a word of complaint. But a few minutes later he got a call on his police radio, and there was no way he could ignore it. Still cradling her close with one hand, he snatched up the mike. "Magee. What is it, Dodsen?"

"A call just came into the station from your ex-wife," the disembodied voice of the dispatcher replied. "She tried getting you at home but got no answer. I hate to break it to you this way, Dugan, but she said your daughter's missing. She thinks she's run away."

Chapter 8

"Oh, no!"

Dugan hardly heard Sarah's softly whispered cry as he dropped his arm from around her. Sitting as if turned to stone, he told himself that he must have misunderstood the dispatcher. Tory wouldn't run away. Not his daughter. She was too obedient to be rebellious, too cautious, too aware—as a cop's daughter—of the hidden dangers out there on the streets. She would never worry him or her mother by doing something so dangerous.

But the dread that dropped into his stomach like a chunk of ice told him there had been no mistake. Tory not only would, she had. His fingers tightened on the mike he held to his mouth until his knuckles ached.

"Dugan? Hey, Magee, you still there?"

The dispatcher's voice pulled at him, snapping him back to attention. "Yes," he retorted curtly.

"Your ex-wife wants you to call her. She left her number—"

"I already know it," he broke in grimly. "Thanks, Dodsen."

Tense silence filled the car after Dodsen signed off, leaving a too still quiet. Her heart breaking for him, Sarah could almost hear the worried thoughts that carved such deep lines in Dugan's face, aging him. Tentatively she reached out to touch the harsh set of his jaw. "Don't look like that," she pleaded softly. "It may not be as bad as it sounds. You know how kids are. They blow up about something and storm off to one of their friends' houses until they cool off. She could be on her way home any minute."

Dugan wished like hell she was right, but he knew better. "You don't know Laura, sweetheart. She wouldn't have called me unless she was desperate. By now, she's already turned L.A. upside down." Regretfully returning her hand to her lap, he pushed open his door. "You stay here. I'm going to call her and find out how the hell this happened."

Striding over to the bank of phones against the outside wall of the convenience store, he punched in a string of numbers that would charge the call to his home phone, and waited impatiently for the call to go through. The phone on the other end of the line only rang once when it was snatched up, and Laura cried anxiously in his ear, "Hello?"

"It's me, Laura."

"Dugan . . . Oh, God," she choked in a thick whisper. "I—I was hoping you were Tory."

"Then you haven't heard from her." It wasn't a question but a flat statement of fact. When her only response was a shaky no, a muscle jumped in his jaw. He told himself he was going to remain calm, that throwing accusations was only going to make the situation worse. But the image of his daughter out on a dark, sinister L.A. street somewhere, without any money or anyone to help her, was not a pretty one. Impotent rage built in him, making his voice as sharp as a barber's razor. "Damn it, Laura, what the hell happened? And don't try to tell me nothing because I'm not buying it. Tory isn't the kind of kid who would run away without a damn good reason."

She caught back a sob. "It was j-just a stupid argument."

"Between you and Tory?"

"N-no. Between me and Joe."

Dugan bit off a vicious curse. He should have known! "Wonderful," he ground out coldly. "You're so wrapped up in your fights with your husband, you don't even realize what you're doing to your daughter. Either that, or you just don't care."

"That's not true," she cried. "We don't argue in front of her anymore. We were in our bedroom, but she must have heard us anyway. She left a note on the kitchen table saying..." Her voice broke, and it was several moments before she could continue. "She s-said she couldn't l-live like that anymore. Dugan, she took all the baby-sitting and birthday money she was saving in her piggy bank to buy a car when she turned sixteen. She must have had over five hundred dollars! If anyone finds out she's carrying that kind of money—"

She could be in serious trouble, Dugan silently finished for her, fear balling in his throat. Before he could stop himself, he found himself echoing the suggestions Sarah had made only minutes before. "Call her friends. She could be at one of their houses right now, working up the nerve to come home."

"I already did. I've been on the phone for the past three hours calling everyone she knows. No one's seen or heard from her. I . . . I even called the police here. I didn't know what else to do."

That, more than anything, told Dugan just how worried she was. She was a woman who prided herself on appearances. Her private life could be pure hell, but she'd die before she'd let the rest of the world know it. She'd have to be desperate to call the cops and admit to a perfect stranger that her marital problems could have driven her daughter away.

"And?"

"And nothing. They sent out an officer, but Tory hasn't even been gone long enough to file a missing persons report."

"She's going to be all right, Laura," he said firmly, praying it was true. "She's got a good head on her shoulders. As soon as she calms down, she'll call home and let you know she's okay. Stay off the phone and give her a chance to call."

"This is all my fault," she said with a sob. "I just didn't realize . . ." She made an audible effort to regain control, then admitted shakily, "I'm scared, Dugan. Really scared."

So was he, but he couldn't increase her worry by telling her that. "I'm at a pay phone right now, but I'm going home as soon as I hang up. If you hear *anything,* you call me immediately."

He hung up with her promise ringing in his ear, but all he could think of was that he'd waited too late to get any promises from her. He should have made her give him her word months ago that she and her husband would get some therapy or marriage counseling, or whatever the hell it took for them to straighten out their home life. Maybe then he'd know where Tory was tonight.

Sarah watched him return to the car as if the weight of the world was on his shoulders and more than he could bear. She'd never seen him look so grim. Her heart twisting in her breast, she had to bite her tongue to keep from asking what his ex-wife had said. It wasn't any of her business, and there was nothing in their relationship that gave her the right to ask about his private life, she reminded herself. He would tell her if he wanted her to know. But still, this was the first time since she'd moved into his life that he was in need of comfort. She ached for him.

He started the car without a word and turned left out of the convenience store parking lot, heading for home. With every passing mile, the silence grew louder, until it echoed in Sarah's mind like a scream in the night. Leaning against the passenger door, she waited, for what, she wasn't sure. An explosion of rage, a cry of helplessness, a curse against the fates that had placed his only child in danger while he was more than a thousand miles away. His face was set in implacable lines, but Sarah didn't doubt for a minute that the fury was building in him. Even if she hadn't felt it emanating from him in waves, she knew all about a frustration and hurt that made you want to blindly strike out at the world and deny what was happening.

"Laura and her husband had another fight and Tory overheard them."

His words were low and angry and filled with disgust. Watching his face in the light from the passing street lamps, Sarah saw his mouth flatten into a thin line and had to fight the need to scoot across the seat to him. He seemed so alone. "Another fight?" she repeated, frowning. "Just how often do they argue?"

"Apparently all the time," he retorted. Suddenly, unable to hold in the fury any longer, he hit the steering wheel with the palm of his hand. "Damn it, I should have seen this coming! I knew how unhappy Tory was, how she hated the constant bickering. Every time we talk lately, she begs me to let her come live with me, and I put her off. I promised her that if she'd just hold on until summer, I'd pressure Laura into giving me custody." He laughed, a low, tortured sound of pain that came straight from his soul. "No wonder she ran. She knew as well as I did that it would be a cold day in hell before Laura would let her live with me, so why stick around for her old man to help her?"

"Dugan, don't . . . please." Unable to just sit there and listen to him tear himself apart, she abruptly released her seat belt and slid across the seat until her hip and thigh were pressed to his. But she still wasn't as close as she needed to be. Her heart breaking for him, she slipped her arm around his shoulders and, careful of his steering, just held him. "Don't do this to yourself. You weren't the one causing Tory's unhappiness. Her mother was. How can you possibly take the blame for Laura's marital problems?"

"Because I called her and talked to her about it," he admitted. "I knew just how bad things were between her and Joe. I should have threatened to take her to court right then if she didn't get immediate help."

"And if she'd still said no?" she tossed back. "What would that have accomplished except to antagonize her? You'd be up to your ears now in a custody battle, which would only make Tory's home life more miserable than ever."

She spoke nothing less than the truth, but that didn't make it any easier to accept. He'd never felt so helpless in his life, and it ate at him like a cancer. "If anything happens to her . . ."

At the sound of the agony thickening his voice, her arm tightened around him. "Don't even think about it. She'll be fine. She has to be."

He wanted to believe her more than he'd ever wanted to believe anything in his life. "I want you to meet her," he said as he turned onto his street and pulled into his driveway. "You two would like each other—"

He broke off suddenly as the headlights swept across the darkened windows of the house and came to rest on the porch, ruthlessly stripping away the shadows concealed there to reveal a forlorn figure sitting on the steps. Her slender shoulders were slumped, her head down, a curtain of long dark hair concealing her face, but Dugan would have known her anywhere. "Tory!"

Her head snapped up, her hair falling back to reveal a face that was a soft, feminine version of her father's. Lifting a hand to her brow to shield her eyes from the bright glare of the headlights, she called shakily, "Daddy? Is that you?"

Dugan was out of the car like a shot. "Honey, thank God! I've been worried sick about you!" His long strides eating up the distance between them, he caught her as she launched herself at him, his arms banding her to him. "How did you get here? When? Why didn't you call me?"

Her answers came as fast as his questions while she huddled against him. "I was afraid you'd tell me not to come, and I had to! I just couldn't stay there anymore and listen to all that fighting. So I took my savings and called a cab to take me to the airport. I just wanted to get to you. Please don't send me back!"

Dugan wanted to assure her that he would never let her out of his sight again, but he glanced up to see Sarah getting out of his car, the glint of tears in her eyes, and he was suddenly reminded of all the reasons Tory couldn't have come at a worse time. His arms tightened around her before he reluctantly drew back and slipped an arm around her shoulders. "Let's go inside," he said quietly. "There are a few things you should know, honey."

"Mom called, didn't she?" she asked in alarm. "She wants you to put me on the first plane to L.A., doesn't she?"

He tugged her closer at the note of panic in her voice. "Of course she called, but not because she thought you were coming here. She didn't know where you were and she was worried sick. But this has nothing to do with your mother."

"Then what—" Tory suddenly spied Sarah standing just a few feet away and stiffened in surprise. "Oh, I didn't realize . . . *Oh!*"

Dugan read that second *oh* as clearly as if his daughter had spoken her thoughts aloud. Since the divorce, she'd never seen him with a woman, and she obviously thought her unannounced arrival had interrupted an intimate evening for two. "It's not what you're thinking," he growled, irritated by the heat that warmed his cheeks. Quickly introducing them, he said, "Sarah is—" *Living with me.* Suddenly realizing what he was about to say, he snapped his teeth shut on an oath. Hell. "Sarah is . . . staying here for a while," he finally bit out.

"Oh."

Sarah had never felt so awkward in her life, but she had to laugh. She'd never seen anyone who could say so much with only one word. "It's not what you think, Tory. Let's go inside and we'll tell you all about it."

"Good idea," Dugan grumbled, and strode over to the car to cut off the engine and retrieve his keys from the ignition.

The minute he opened the door and the three of them stepped inside, he moved to the phone. "I'm going to call your mother—"

"Daddy!"

He ignored Tory's wail of protest and punched out the familiar number. "I'm just going to let her know you're okay," he assured her. "For now. Later, after we've had a chance to talk, you're going to call her back and we're going to get a few things hashed out. Understand?"

She knew that tone, and there was no arguing with it. "Oh, okay," she sighed heavily. "But I thought you'd be happy to see me."

"I am, but I'd also like to ring your neck, young lady," he retorted bluntly. "You scared your mother and me to death." His call went through then, and he held up his hand, stopping any further discussion with Tory so he could turn his attention to his ex-wife. "It's me, Laura. Tory's here. I found her on the porch when I got home."

"Oh, thank God! Is she all right? Let me talk to her. I need to—"

"She's fine, but she'll have to call you back in about fifteen minutes," he said firmly. "We just walked in the door and I wanted to let you know she's okay. She'll answer all your questions when she calls you." Laura wasn't too happy about that, but he didn't give her a chance to complain. Hanging up, he turned back to his daughter and Sarah, who had each settled onto opposite ends of the couch.

Running his hand through his hair impatiently, he struggled to find the words that would explain the situation to Tory without making her think that he didn't want her. Dear God, he'd wanted her from the first moment he'd known she was conceived. Surely she knew that by now? "Honey, your timing really stinks," he finally sighed. "You know I want you here with me, but you can't stay. Not now."

She grew pale, tears welling in her eyes. "You're going to send me back?" she cried accusingly. "But how can you after I told you how awful it is living with Mom? How can you do that to me?"

"Honey, I don't want to—"

"Then don't!"

Sarah had promised herself she was going to let Dugan handle the explanations, but she couldn't sit by and let his daughter think she'd misjudged his love of her. "Tory, your father wants to send you back because of me," she said quietly.

"Why? Because you're having an affair?"

"Tory!"

She winced at her father's thunderous roar but met his gaze head-on. "You don't have to sound so outraged, Daddy," she chided innocently. "I wouldn't mind if you had an affair with a nice lady. And Sarah seems nice. And if you're already living together..." She shrugged, as if to say, "What's wrong with that?"

Dugan felt his face become uncomfortably hot. Was he actually getting permission from his fourteen-year-old daughter to take Sarah to bed? Scowling at her, he snapped, "Remind me to talk to your mother about this. For your information, Sarah is staying here because someone is trying to hurt her. I'm protecting her."

He gave her a slightly edited version of recent events, telling her only enough to emphasize the danger Sarah was in. "The man who's chasing Sarah is extremely clever. He hasn't been able to track her down here yet, but I'm sure it's not from lack of trying. He's not going to give up without a damn good fight, so Sarah is in constant danger until he's caught. So you see, it just wouldn't be safe for you to stay here, honey. With that maniac still on the loose, it's too risky."

"But I'll be careful," she promised, her gray eyes, so like Dugan's, pleading. "I won't answer the door to strangers or even answer the phone when you're not here. Please, Daddy? You've got to let me stay!"

His jaw set, he shook his head, cursing the fates. From the moment Laura had announced her intention of getting a divorce all those years ago, he'd fought tooth and nail for Tory, wanting nothing more than to have her with him. But not like this. "I'm sorry, sweetheart, I can't. It's too dangerous."

Desperate, she jumped to her feet, her face filled with resolve, her chin lifted defiantly. "Then I'll run away again!" she said wildly. "I mean it, Daddy! I can't live with Mom and Joe again. I can't! I hate it. You don't know what it's like... the fights, then the cold silences." A shiver skated down her spine. Choking back a sob, she wrapped her arms around herself, and suddenly she wasn't a rebellious teenager but a lost little girl with hurt, wounded eyes. "God, I hate the silence," she whispered.

Stunned by her threat, Dugan told himself she didn't mean it. She had always been an obedient child, eager to please and easily disciplined, though she'd never had any reservations about expressing her opinion when she wasn't happy about something. She would back down real quick if he called her bluff.

But something in her eyes warned him she wouldn't this time—a pain that no child should have to deal with, a hurt that pushed her into adulthood before she was ready for it, a glint of determination that he'd seen in his own eyes when his back was to the wall. Dear God, how could Laura and Joe have made her home life so miserably unhappy that she'd rather take her chances on the street than go back there?

Swearing, he glanced helplessly at Sarah. What the hell was he supposed to do now?

He looked at her as a man looked at his wife when faced with a problem that left him floundering. *Help me with this.* The words rang in her ears as clearly as if he'd spoken them, and if she let herself, she could almost believe Tory wasn't just his problem, but *theirs.*

Common sense warned her to back off. This was something he needed to discuss with Laura first before making a decision. Instead she heard herself say huskily, "I've never felt safer with anyone than I do with you. If you can protect me, you can protect your daughter."

"Oh, listen to her, Daddy," Tory begged. "Please?"

He was. His eyes locked with Sarah's. She trusted him. She had to or she wouldn't feel safe with him. The knowledge stunned him, rocking him to the core. He wanted to hold her, to kiss her, to give in to the needs that he'd been fighting longer than he cared to remember. But he couldn't. Not yet. She might trust him, but she still had a long way to go before she would welcome anything more intimate than a kiss from him.

Dragging his eyes from hers, he turned back to Tory. "If I agree to let you stay...and that's still an *if,*" he reminded her sternly, "there are going to be some ground rules laid down that you will not break." Struggling to hang onto a fierce frown when she let out a whoop and threw herself at him, his arms closed around her as if he would never let her go. God, it felt good to have her home! "Is that understood, young lady?"

"Oh, yes! I'll do anything you say. I'll be good as gold, I promise!"

Dugan only snorted at that and ruffled her hair. "Yeah, right. Tell that to someone who doesn't know you." Drawing her away, his smile faded as he thought of the phone call he still had to make. "You do realize, don't you, that your mother's going to give us some flack on this? She wants you with her."

"She's had me for six years," Tory said simply. "She's just going to have to understand it's your turn."

Dugan doubted it would be quite that easy, but he'd do whatever it took to gain Laura's cooperation. Tory was right. It was his turn. "Then I'd better go call her and get this over with. You're going to have to talk to her when I'm finished, so just get prepared. She's probably going to be pretty upset."

He went into his bedroom to make the call, leaving Sarah and Tory alone in the living room. Plopping back down onto the couch, Tory studied Sarah with unabashed curiosity. "You know, I was really surprised when Daddy said you were living here with him. He never brings women home."

Sarah knew she shouldn't be discussing Dugan with his daughter, but before she could stop herself, she lifted a brow in surprise and asked, "Never?"

She shook her head. "He says he doesn't want the hassle. That's why I was hoping you and he...you know," she said with a shrug, grinning.

Sarah felt the heat in her cheeks but met the inquisitive girl's eyes unflinchingly. "We're not lovers, Tory," she said bluntly. "When this is all over with, I'll go back to my life and Dugan will stay in his. This house and the time I spent here will just feel like a dream." Unwilling to think about the loneliness she would be going back to, she jumped to her feet and headed for the kitchen. "Are you hungry? I think there's some ham in the fridge. I could make you a sandwich.''

But Tory had no intention of being distracted so easily. She followed her into the kitchen, puzzlement narrowing her eyes. "No sandwich, but a soda sounds good.'' She retrieved a glass from the cabinet and moved to the refrigerator to fix the drink herself. Dropping ice cubes into her glass, she glanced up suddenly and asked, "What's the matter? Don't you like my dad?''

"Of course, I do.'' The response popped out automatically, but it wasn't something Sarah just said to appease Tory. She did like Dugan. More than she should. She liked his strength, his honesty, his integrity, even his dogged persistence that could, at times, infuriate her. He was a man of his word, a man to have at your side in a dark alley, a man who unashamedly showed his concern and love for his daughter. Oh, yes, she liked him. That was the problem. When a woman found herself both liking and desiring a man, he was next to impossible to resist. And that could only lead to heartache.

She turned away, unable to bear the younger girl's scrutiny, and needlessly wiped the counter with a dish cloth. "It isn't a question of liking,'' she said unevenly.

Unaware of the shadows clouding Sarah's eyes, Tory took her answer at face value and sighed in relief. "Good. Daddy really needs someone, you know,'' she confided. Dropping her gaze to her soda, she stared at it as if she were gazing into the past. A look that was too sad for someone of her years passed over her face, maturing her. "He's been alone a long time now, ever since Mom married Joe and we moved to California. I tried to talk her into letting me stay—she had Joe, but Daddy had no one—but she wouldn't listen. She said Daddy would get by just fine, but he hasn't. He works hours and hours of overtime just so he won't have to come home alone to this empty house." She glanced up then, her expression somber. "Sometimes I really worry about him."

The images her words stirred up tugged at Sarah's heart. She didn't want to think of Dugan alone and lonely, coming home only when he was too exhausted to think and didn't have anywhere else to go.

In his bedroom, Dugan sat on the side of his bed with the phone pressed to his ear, his frown fierce. "It's not going to do you any good to cry or threaten, Laura," he said wearily. "I'm not sending her back. Your marriage is a mess, you're unhappy, and you and Joe are making Tory miserable. I told you to get help, but you wouldn't listen."

"I did, too. I was going to call someone this week—"

"Oh, give it up," he snapped. "If you'd really intended to get some counseling, you wouldn't have put it off. You were just going to let things slide and hope whatever was wrong would fix itself. I'm not sending Tory back into that kind of atmosphere. Even if I would," he added, "she'd just run away again. She doesn't want to come back home, Laura."

Silence buzzed on the line, threatening to stretch into infinity. Dugan was beginning to think they'd been disconnected when she choked softly, "She told you that?"

Dugan heard the hurt in her voice, the pain, and felt the tension drain out of him. "I'm not saying these things to hurt you," he told her quietly. "But there have to be some changes made, Laura. For all our sakes. Surely you can see that."

She sniffed tearfully. "I don't want to lose her, Dugan. But I don't want to lose Joe, either. And things have been tough the last couple of months with him out of work, but he's got a job interview tomorrow. I think he's got a good chance of getting it.''

"I hope he does." He meant that sincerely. He'd let go of his animosity concerning Laura and her husband a long time ago and wished them no ill will. But he also wanted his daughter. "A little help and some time alone may be all you need to work things out. As for Tory, she'll always be your daughter, Laura. Living with me won't change that. You might even find that you're closer with some distance between you.''

"She always did want to live with you rather than me," she replied with just a trace of resentfulness. "Maybe this is the time to try it. Just until the end of the school year," she added warningly. "We'll see how it goes and talk about it again then.''

Dugan almost let out a shout of triumph, but there was still one more hurdle he had to jump. "Fine," he agreed. "Now that we've got that settled, there's something else you should know.''

Quickly and succinctly, he told her about Sarah and the rapist stalking her. "Tory won't be in any danger, Laura. If the rapist knew where Sarah was, he damn sure would have taunted her with it by now. But I'm going to have a security system installed anyway. Tory will be alone in the house after school until we get home from work, and I'm not taking any chances.''

Laura hesitated. "I don't know, Dugan. I don't like the sound of this at all. What if the rapist discovers where you live?''

"He won't," he assured her. "The only way that could happen would be if he followed us home one day after work, and I've done everything I can to make sure that hasn't happened. So you don't have to worry about her being in any kind of real danger. As much as I want Tory with me, I wouldn't let her stay if I didn't think I could protect her. I don't want anything to happen to her anymore than you do."

"I know that. And I know you'll do everything you can to keep her safe. I just . . . worry," she admitted huskily. "But if I insisted that she come home and she ran away again, I'd worry even more. So I guess you're the lesser of two evils."

"Gee, thanks," he drawled.

"You know what I mean," she laughed. "Let me speak to Tory now. I'd like to tell her myself about what we've decided."

"Okay, I'll go get her." He started to set the phone down on the nightstand, then hesitated. "Laura? I want to thank you for going along on this," he said gruffly. "I know I strong-armed you, but if you'd have stood your ground, we both know there's nothing I could have done about it. It means a lot to me to have her with me." Before she could form any kind of reply, he said abruptly, "Hang on. I'll get Tory."

He found the two women in his life in the kitchen chatting like old friends. Stopping unnoticed in the doorway, he just watched them for a moment, enjoying the sight of them together. They sat at the kitchen table with a huge bowl of popcorn between them and glasses of soda within reach, laughing as Tory joked about her efforts to buy her airline ticket with the change and small bills she'd take from her piggy bank. Grinning, Dugan found it all too easy to picture them this way over the years as Tory grew up, sharing laughter and confidences, becoming a family. *His family.*

Longing twisted his heart, bringing his fanciful thoughts abruptly back to reality. What the hell was he doing? Tory was with him for now, but if Laura decided to throw a wrench into the works, that wouldn't last beyond the school year. And as for Sarah, the future was an intangible blur in the distance. She was here now, too, but only because she had to be. He knew what he felt for her was much more than lust, and there wasn't a doubt in his mind that she was attracted to him. But how deep did her feelings run? Had she turned to him tonight after the taping of the reenactment only because she knew she could trust him and he was the first man she'd let herself get close to since the rape? Or because she felt what he felt, something neither of them was willing to put a name to yet?

Suddenly spying him in the doorway, Tory turned, apprehension dampening the laughter that lighted her round face. "Well? What did she say?"

"She wants to talk to you," Dugan said simply, stepping further into the room.

"She said no, didn't she?"

Dugan had to laugh—she sounded so tragic. "She wants to tell you herself, sweetheart. But I will tell you you can unpack your suitcase."

"I can? Really, Daddy?"

Chuckling, he pulled her out of her chair for a hug. "Really. Now go talk to your mom. She's waiting."

"All right!" Grinning broadly, she ran out of the kitchen.

Sarah watched her dash off, then turned twinkling eyes to Dugan. "She's a good kid. I like her."

"Even after she embarrassed you to death?" he teased, leaning across her to grab a handful of popcorn. "She can be exceedingly blunt. Laura says she gets it from me."

Resisting the urge to squirm, Sarah felt her cheeks warm and could do nothing but chuckle. "Well, she certainly made no secret of the fact that she'd like to see you involved with someone—"

"I am involved."

At his quiet statement, Sarah almost choked on her popcorn. Coughing, her eyes watering, she reached for her soda, but before she could take a swallow, Dugan was pounding on her back. "Easy, sweetheart. It's nothing to get all choked up about. You've known for a long time that I want you."

"Yes, but—" Swallowing the lump in her throat, she wiped the tears from her eyes and shot a quick glance at the door where Tory had disappeared only moments before. "Dugan, y-you can't just go a-round saying things like that. Tory—"

"Isn't blind," he finished for her, his pounding of her back slowing changing into a circular, rubbing caress that threatened to drive them both to distraction. "She's not a child. She's old enough to pick up on the sparks between us."

The blush firing her cheeks deepened. Was the attraction between them that obvious? "I know, but this is her home, not mine. I don't want her to be uncomfortable just because I'm here."

Dugan grinned. "Did she look uncomfortable to you? I got the distinct impression that she was disappointed that we *aren't* having an affair."

"Well, yes, but that's just because she doesn't like the idea of you being alone," she argued. "She probably would have felt the same way about any woman you had here."

"I don't think so," he growled, the movement of his hand sweetly arousing as it slid up her spine to the back of her neck. "Anyway, that's beside the point. You're here, and I want—"

"Mom wasn't exactly thrilled—" Tory's words died on her tongue as she burst into the kitchen and saw how close

Dugan was standing to Sarah. She grinned cheekily. "Oops. Should I get lost? I can always go up to bed."

She started to turn, but Sarah was already rising to her feet. "No, wait, Tory. I've been sleeping in your room. I'll need to get my things out before you go to bed."

The younger girl stopped, obviously realizing for the first time that Sarah had been telling her the truth about her and her father not being lovers. "Oh. But where will you sleep?"

"The couch will be fine—"

"*I'll* take the couch," Dugan interrupted. "You can have my bed."

An image of herself in his bed flashed before Sarah, heating her blood. "Oh, no. I couldn't let you do that."

"Then we'll both take my bed," he retorted, shooting her a wicked grin, "because you're not taking the couch when there's a perfectly good bed available. So what's it going to be? Me on the couch, or in bed with you?"

Aware of the dancing eyes of his daughter watching the interplay, she just barely resisted the urge to kick him. "Well, if you want to put it that way, then you're on the couch."

He groaned good-naturedly. "I had a feeling you'd say that."

Chapter 9

Sarah told herself she was so tired she didn't care where she slept, even a bathtub would do. It was late, it had been an emotionally draining day and evening, and she'd crash the second she was horizontal. Clinging to that thought, she took a quick shower in Dugan's bathroom and slipped into her nightgown, studiously ignoring the warm, intimate feelings that settled low in her stomach at the sight of his things surrounding her. Tempted to explore the brand of his after-shave and toothpaste, the feel of his robe hanging on the back of the door, she hurriedly snapped out the bathroom light and found her way in the dark to his bed. The minute she crawled between the sheets, the silence of the night closed in on her. Her heart started to pound. Closing her eyes, she tried to relax, but from the inkiness of the night, Dugan's scent reached out to her. Suddenly wide awake, her senses sharp and throbbing and her imagination working overtime, it was all too easy to picture Dugan coming to her, loving her until they were both boneless and sated.

There was no way she was going to be able to sleep in his bed without wanting him.

The thought echoed through her like the ringing of a bell, setting her body humming. She should have gotten up right then and found another place to sleep, even if that meant settling for the floor. But she couldn't. As much as she wanted him, she knew she'd never be able to let him make love to her except in her dreams. Unshed tears stinging her eyes, she clung to his pillow and the only type of loving her past would allow her to have.

She never knew when she slid into a restless sleep. Hours slipped by unnoticed, and the deep darkness of the night eased, giving way to the shifting shadows of dawn. Wrapped in her dreams and the quiet stillness of early morning, Sarah didn't hear the door open soundlessly. She didn't see Dugan step into the bedroom clad in nothing but jeans and quietly head for his closet, his eyes straying to her sleeping figure every few seconds as if he couldn't deny himself the sight of her in his bed. He didn't make a sound, but suddenly she knew he was there.

Lying on her side facing him, she sleepily opened her eyes and found him reaching for a shirt in his closet. Her heart caught in her throat at the sight of him. He hadn't shaved yet, and his jaw was darkened with stubble, his dark hair uncombed and tumbling over his forehead, giving him a boyish look. But when he glanced over at her suddenly, as if he felt her watching him, there was nothing boyish about the hot look in his sleepy gray eyes. With nothing more than a glance, he made her ache for the feel of his arms around her.

"Good morning."

If she'd been cool and sophisticated, she'd have greeted him easily, and casually reached for her robe, as if she wasn't the least affected by the fact that they were alone in his bedroom, both half dressed and all too aware of each other. But her whispered greeting was revealingly husky, and she knew by the way his eyes darkened in the early morning light that he'd noticed. Warmth singed her cheeks.

"Mornin'," he muttered in a voice that was as rough as gravel. "Did you sleep well?"

She considered lying and saying she'd slept like a rock. But instead she pushed herself up to a sitting position and clutched the sheet to her breast and admitted softly, "I dreamed about you."

Dugan sucked in a sharp breath. That was the last thing he needed to hear after tossing and turning on the couch all night, tortured by the image of her in his bed, her head on his pillow, her hair spread around her in sweet abandonment. Biting back a groan, he thought, Two steps. That's all it would take for him to join her.

Fighting temptation, he turned back to his closet. "Sweetheart, that's something you shouldn't admit when you're sitting half naked in my bed," he growled. "Not after the night I just spent on the couch. Now go back to sleep. I just came in to get some clothes. You still have another hour before you have to get up."

Sarah should have let it go at that. She should have laid back down, turned her back on him, and ignored her ever-growing desire for him. But she was so tired of hiding her feelings, so tired of pretending to herself that she could control the yearning he stirred in her. She had no more control over her need for him than she did over the panic that threatened to strangle her whenever she let him get too close. Ignoring either emotion wouldn't make them go away, so somehow they would have to learn to deal with them. Together.

Gathering her courage, she slipped from the bed and crossed the room until she was standing directly behind him. "I don't want to go back to bed," she said quietly. "Not alone."

She made no move to touch him, but Dugan stiffened as if she'd reached out and trailed her fingers all the way down his spine to the low-riding waistband of his jeans. "Sarah—"

"You said you were letting me take control," she reminded him, ignoring his warning tone. "Not to think, to take what I wanted, right? To go with my instincts. Isn't that what you said?"

"Yes, but—"

"I want you to hold me. To kiss me. To—"

"But when I said that, I didn't expect you to take me up on it at the crack of dawn in my bedroom," he retorted, whirling to face her.

At the sight of her standing just inches away, her auburn hair sleep-tousled and wild, her blue gown giving him teasing glimpses of the feminine curves it covered so delectably, his breath caught in his throat. God, she was gorgeous in the morning! Soft and mussed and innocently sexy, so close he only had to lift his hand to her pinkened cheeks to touch her. She faced him bravely, daring him to deny them what they both wanted, but peeking out from the depths of her brown eyes was an apprehension she wasn't even aware of.

With infinite care, he traced the rosy color spilling into her cheeks. "Honey, this isn't a good idea," he cautioned huskily.

She swayed toward him, nearly undone by his gentleness. "Why not?"

He could have given her a dozen reasons. His daughter was upstairs and was a notoriously early riser. In a little while they would both have to get ready for work. His defenses were down and he was afraid if he touched her now he might never be able to let her go. But the real reason began and ended with his desire for her. "Because I want you too much," he admitted thickly, nudging up her chin until her eyes locked with his. "I want you so damn much I'm afraid I'll scare the hell out of you."

His eyes were dark with longing, the fingers at her chin not quite steady, his tone filled with self-disgust at his inability to repress emotions she had no control over yet he thought he should have a handle on. Tenderness squeezed her heart. Crazy man! Didn't he know yet that she didn't expect him to be Superman? Smiling, she took the single step that eliminated the distance between them and hugged him. Hard. She felt the struggle in him, the battle to resist her before his arms moved to lightly encircle her. Her eyes closed on a sigh as peace stole through her. Home. When had being this close to him started to feel like the only place in the world where she belonged? "I'm not scared of you," she murmured, rubbing her cheek against his bare chest. "Do you think I would be here in your arms if I was?"

"No, but—"

"Kiss me, Dugan. Please."

It was her husky please that did him in. When her voice turned low and sexy like that, she could have asked for the Taj Mahal and he'd have started looking for a realtor. Groaning her name, he swooped down and covered her mouth with his.

He promised himself he would take nothing more than a kiss. A slow and easy, light and breezy kiss that didn't threaten, didn't demand, didn't press for more than she was ready to give. He might be burning for a hell of a lot more, but she would never know it because he'd break his arm before he'd do anything to scare her ever again. It was that simple.

He had it all worked out in his head, but he'd forgotten that nothing was ever simple where Sarah was concerned. His mouth touched hers, and it wasn't caution he was thinking of, but sweetness. Sarah's sweetness. The sweetness of her lips parting, her tongue shyly greeting his, her arms tightening around his waist just seconds before her hands climbed up his back, clinging to him as if she would never let him go. After nothing more than a kiss, he wanted to drown in the honeyed heat of her response, to love her slowly and leisurely until her every thought began and ended with him.

She was trembling, but he knew it wasn't with fear. Her mouth was too eager, her tongue too welcoming, the delicate body melting against his yielding with a softness that could drive a man right over the edge. No, she wanted him, and the knowledge went to his head like a double Scotch on an empty stomach. With a groan of need, he pulled her closer.

A kiss. It was all she'd asked of him, all she'd expected. Instead she got a dozen. Short and sweet, long and hungry, teasingly innocent and sizzling with passion. Before she could even gasp, he was stealing her breath with another, then another, until she was light-headed and dizzy and her arms were wrapped around him as if he were the only rock in her suddenly reeling world. Intoxicated, exhilarated, she hung on for dear life.

In the very back of her dazed mind, a voice reminded her that the fear should have touched her by now. He was so close she could feel the hammering of his heart against her breast, the heat of his growing arousal against her stomach. Hungrily answering kiss for kiss, she waited for the familiar panic to strike, for terror to chill her blood, for the icy fingers of revulsion to claw at her throat until she couldn't breathe. This time she would handle it, she promised herself, shuddering with need as his hands swept over her. But it was heat that engulfed her, not ice, hot tongues of flame that licked at her senses and threatened to melt her bones one by one. Whimpering, her mouth moved hungrily under his.

The early morning sunlight slipped in through the open windows, coating them in a golden glow, but the last thing Dugan cared about when he had her in his arms was the passage of time. Wrenching his mouth from hers, he pressed hot, desperate kisses to the curve of her cheek, her rounded chin, the pulse pounding at the base of her throat. She smelled of the dawn—fresh and sleepy and all soft woman. Closing his eyes, he drew in the tempting scent of her and teased his senses until he groaned. A man could look forward to sunrise if he knew he had her to wake up to every morning.

Unconsciously his hands tightened even as a voice in his head warned him to take it easy. But it was too late. He'd dreamed of having her in his arms like this, ached for the feel of her, the taste of her, too long. Unable to stop himself, he let his fingers roam over the curves hidden under her gown until he found her breasts. His breathing turned ragged, his loins tight. She was small but full, perfectly fitting his palm. And so damn responsive. His thumb sought and flicked her sensitive nipple and her back arched like a bow, her startled gasp of pleasure sweet music to his ears.

That's when he should have let her go. He should have reined in his self-control and put her from him. But his blood was hot and thick in his veins, his body heavy, his need for her unlike anything he'd ever known before. He couldn't let her go. Not then. Maybe not ever. Whispering her name, he swept her up into his arms and carried her to the bed.

With every fiber of her being focused on the urgency of his mouth on hers, Sarah never felt him lower her to the mattress. Pleasure seeped through her like hot honey, then he was coming down on her, gathering her close, pressing her into the sheets.

Cold. It came out of nowhere like a bitter north wind, rushing over her, stealing her breath and dropping her body temperature twenty degrees between one heartbeat and the next.

She stiffened. No! This was Dugan who held her, Dugan who covered her with his hard, lean body, Dugan who was making love to her with such rough tenderness. There was no force, no taking, no rape. He would never, ever hurt her. She knew that, would stake her life on it. But the panic was already racing through her like wildfire, destroying reason and setting her heart slamming against her ribs. Her teeth gritted on a sob as her hands curled into fists.

Dugan felt the change in her immediately. One moment she was a hot, giving woman in his arms, and the next she was as still as an ice statue. Alarmed, he rasped, "It's okay, sweetheart. There's no reason to stiffen up. You're just as safe now as you were a moment ago. Relax."

But when he pulled back slightly to sweep her hair back from her face, he knew nothing he could say now was going to reach her. Her eyes were tightly squeezed shut, her jaw locked on a cry of protest, her usually creamy skin ashen. He'd pushed her too far. Swearing savagely at his own thoughtless stupidity, he rolled off her and onto his back, his curses turning the air blue as he flung his arm across his eyes. Every nerve in his body tightened in revolt. Idiot! What had he been thinking of? He was no better than the slimeball who had raped her in Houston!

Shaking, her breath shuddering through her lungs, Sarah winced at every vile curse. Aching and empty, cold all the way through to her soul, she fought back tears, but the battle was lost before it had begun. Her eyes filled and overflowed. He lay only inches away, but there might as well have been a chasm between them. Careful not to touch her, he wouldn't even look at her. He didn't throw a single accusation at her, but he didn't have to. She'd heard all the ugly names before, all the insulting labels men had for women who aroused them to the brink of mindlessness, then backed out at the last minute and left them hanging. Oh, God, he didn't—couldn't—think she'd deliberately done that to him, did he?

Unable to bear the thought of him thinking such a thing of her, she whispered brokenly, "No, don't...please." Bursting into tears, she threw herself against him. "I'm not a tease!" she cried, burying her face against the hard muscled wall of his naked chest. "I'm not!"

Caught up in his own self-castigation, Dugan's arms automatically came up to surround her, but it was a long moment before the meaning of her words penetrated. When they did, his eyes snapped down to her bent head, his frown fierce. "Would you like to tell me where the hell that came from?" he asked in a voice that was dangerously soft. "Who called you a tease?"

She hadn't meant to tell him, but the words just came tumbling out. "Trent. He said I t-teased him, then cried rape," her voice broke, "when he took wh-what I was offering." She swallowed the lump in her throat, her eyes stark with pain as they lifted to his. "It wasn't like that," she choked in a whisper he barely caught. "I never encouraged him to think I wanted...that—"

"Sweetheart, I never thought you did." His jaw tightened, the glint in his eyes deadly. One day, he silently promised himself, if he lived long enough, he'd track Kingston down and make him pay for the hell he'd put Sarah through for the last three years. Five minutes was all it would take for him to make the bastard regret he'd ever been born.

His fingers trembling with gentleness, he lifted his hand to her face and tenderly cupped her cheek. "But even if you'd taken him to the very edge and then pulled back, that doesn't justify rape, honey. Nothing does. You always have the right to call a halt."

"But you're angry."

"Not at you. Never at you," he stressed. "I'm the one who needs his butt kicked. I lost my head when you were trusting me to keep it."

The guilt and disgust that flattened his voice tore at her. What had she ever done to deserve this man in her life? she wondered, warmth flooding her and filling the empty chambers of her heart. Yes, he'd lost his head, but not without a great deal of encouragement from her. They both knew he had every reason to be furious with her, yet he insisted on taking the blame. Only a special man could be so generous, so giving, so protective of a woman's feelings.

Her eyes searching the rugged lines of his face, she felt the barriers that guarded her heart start to crumble, convictions she'd carved in stone three years ago start to blur. She'd been so sure she'd never again let anyone get close enough to touch her, let alone hurt her. But Dugan had not only touched her, he'd made her feel . . . everything. And she was falling in love with him.

She would have given anything to deny it. There could be no future for them, nothing but heartache. He deserved a woman who was as special as he was, someone who would love him with no holds barred, the way he needed to be loved. Not someone who couldn't go to bed without shaking with fear.

"Honey? Are you all right?"

She blinked and found his watchful eyes waiting for hers, his frown gentle but worried. She wanted to hug him, to kiss him, to forget, just for a moment, that all they would probably ever have was here and now. But pretending only made reality that much harder to face.

She forced a smile and had no idea just how sad it was. "It's getting late. We'd better get ready for work."

It was a clever ploy, distracting him with the passage of time. But she still hadn't answered his question, and in spite of her smile, he knew something was wrong. He could see it in the shadows in her eyes, in the way she avoided his direct gaze and began to withdraw. If he'd had his way, he would have kept her there until he got the answers he wanted, but she was right. It was late, and they had a busy day ahead of them. He had to drop her off at work, then see about enrolling Tory in school. Reluctantly releasing her, he watched her scramble off the bed. "We'll talk tonight," he promised her.

The station was filled with its usual morning crazies as shifts changed, newly arrested perpetrator's made bail and the drunks were released from the drunk tank. Sarah hardly noticed. Dugan had let her out at the curb, then waited for her to go inside before he'd driven off with Tory to take care of the paperwork at school. For the first time in days she'd walked into the station without him by her side, and she was already starting to miss him.

She was falling in love with him.

She'd thought of nothing else since she'd left his bed and escaped to the bathroom almost two hours ago to get ready for work, but the knowledge still shook her. How could it have happened? How could she have *let* it happen? And what was she going to do now?

That, more than anything else, plagued her the most. She hadn't planned on loving him, didn't know how to handle it. She needed time. Time to think, time to get her free-falling emotions back into some semblance of order, time to regain her balance. But when? Until the rapist was caught, they would continue to live in each other's pocket. She was even sleeping in his bed, for goodness' sakes! How could she expect to think clearly under such conditions when he only had to walk into the same room she was in to scramble her pulse?

Lost in her thoughts, she wound her way through the madness around the front desk and slipped into the hallway that led to the administrative offices. Message boxes lined one wall, and she automatically stopped to retrieve the mail and memos crammed into her In box. Her arm was halfway stretched out to the box when she saw the black cassette tape lying in it.

Apprehension skittered along her nerves even as she tried to convince herself there was no reason to be alarmed. It was just a harmless tape that could have been left there by any one of a half dozen people. Her godfather's secretary had been promising to give her a copy of a creative visualization tape that was supposed to be great for stress reduction. And her godfather knew she liked jazz and was always leaving her little surprises in her box. He could have left it for her. It could even be the tape left for her at the courthouse, the one the lab had been going over with a fine tooth comb.

But it wasn't. Without touching, she knew it wasn't from her godfather or his secretary or the lab. It was another tape. A new one. From him. Whirling, she hurried out to the front desk.

The desk sergeant was Jorge Luis Rivera. He'd been on duty less than an hour, and his graying hair was already mussed, his tie loosened, his expression harried. Impatiently waiting for him to get off the phone, she stepped to his side as soon as he hung up. "Jorge, there's a tape in my In box . . ."

He growled at the angry businessman who had just been brought in for five hundred dollars' worth of unpaid parking tickets to shut his trap, then said distractedly, "Yeah, what about it? It's yours, ain't it? It's got your name on it."

"Yes, but who left it? I wasn't expecting—"

He didn't have time to let her finish. Scowling at the businessman, who didn't have the good sense to shut up when it was in his best interest, he snapped, "Peter Pan could have left it for all I know. The place has been a zoo ever since I came on duty. Keep pushing, mister," he warned the parking ticket king when he belligerently demanded to be released immediately. "You ain't in no condition to be demanding anything!" His black eyes as hard as onyx, he turned back to Sarah. "Like I said, I didn't see nothing. One minute it wasn't there, and the next it was. Sorry, but that's all I can tell you."

Disappointed, she thanked him for his help and returned to her In box. Telling herself not to look for trouble because it would find her soon enough, she gingerly picked up the tape with the rest of her mail and headed for her office. Her curiosity demanded she immediately pull out her cassette player once she'd unlocked her door, but she studiously ignored the temptation. Rigidly following her regular morning routine, she first turned on the computer, then punched in the numbers on the phone to have the hotline calls transferred back to her office from Public Services, who handled all calls that came in from five in the afternoon until she arrived in the mornings. The filing cabinet was then unlocked, the blinds opened, the few plants she kept to add some color to the somber office were watered. Only then did she allow herself to sit down at her desk and reach for the tape.

"I'm sorry I was late last night, Sarah—"

The minute she pushed the play button, the rapist's raspy voice jumped out at her like a mugger, a sinister threat vibrating just under the surface of his words. Cold, ugly, horrifyingly confident. The blood drained from her cheeks.

"I didn't mean to be so rough with you in front of all those people at the convenience store. But you pushed me, Sarah. You know you did. If you have bruises this morning, you have no one to blame but yourself."

Horror curled into her belly like a snake. "No!" Staring at the cassette player, she shook her head, refusing to accept what she'd just heard. She must have misunderstood. Jerkily hitting the rewind button, she started the tape at the beginning. But the message was the same.

Suddenly, without warning, the rapist dropped the phony English accent he hid behind every time he called her and spoke in the unsteady treble of Joseph Peters as he'd struggled to get his lines right in the reenactment last night. "One word and I'll blow you away, lady," he said, repeating word for word the lines Sarah had given the young actor last night. "Open the cash register. Now!" He chuckled evilly. "Isn't that what you told me to say, Sarah? I admit I'm not much of an actor, but I thought I did pretty good."

Strangling on a gasp, she jumped up from her chair so quickly, she sent it crashing into the wall behind her desk. The truth, refusing to be denied, echoed obscenely in her ears. His voice was the same as Joseph Peters, the inflection the same, the words identical. He couldn't have seen the reenactment already and just imitated Joseph Peters—the segment hadn't even been edited yet, let alone aired. So the only way he could have known about last night was if he'd been there, spoken to her, touched her.

"Oh, God!"

As if he heard her horrified whisper, he laughed triumphantly. "Next time will be better, Sarah," he promised in the grotesquely innocent voice of Joseph Peters. "Next time we won't have an audience. Next time I can get as rough as I want. Next time will be sooner than you think."

The tape ended abruptly, but over the wild hammering of her own heart, Sarah could still hear the threats echoing in her head, taunting her. The memory of his hands on her rose up before her, sending goose bumps skating over her cold skin. Revulsion clogged her throat. He'd touched her last night, held her, been in the police station this morning. She started to shake and couldn't stop. Terrified, she snatched up the cassette player and ran.

Buck was searching through the mountain of paperwork that had once been his desk when Sarah rushed into the detective unit as if the devil himself was hot on her heels. He took one look at her face and jumped to his feet, the report he'd been looking for forgotten. "What is it? What's wrong?"

"Dugan . . . where—"

"He called in. He's registering his daughter in school. Didn't you know? I thought you were staying with him."

Oh, God, how could she have forgotten? Her head swam dizzily. "Yes, I just forgot—"

She swayed, and Buck was at her side in a flash. "Hey, are you all right? Here, sugar, sit down before you fall flat on your face." Jerking out the chair behind Dugan's desk, he didn't give her time to protest, pushing her down into it. Taking the cassette player she was clutching, he tossed it on the desk, then forced her head down to her knees. "Just take a couple of deep breaths and relax. That's it." Crouching down beside her, he grabbed her hands and gave them a brisk rub. "God, you're cold! You want some coffee? The stuff in the pot's lethal, but at least it's hot. You just stay there and let me get you a cup."

She started to object, but he ignored her and quickly crossed the room to the coffeepot that was in operation twenty-four hours a day. When he returned seconds later, he held a large mug out to her, the scowl on his face daring her to refuse it. "I added cream and sugar, otherwise you'd never get it down."

Afraid she'd drop it if she didn't wrap both hands around it, Sarah took the mug, but only because he clearly had no intention of giving her a choice. She took one sip and almost choked. "That's awful!"

Buck chuckled. "Yeah, but it's got enough caffeine in it to wake the dead. Drink up."

Reluctantly she gulped down another swallow and pushed the mug back into his hands. "That's enough," she gasped. "Really. I feel much better."

Buck only snorted at that and set the barely tasted coffee on Dugan's desk. If she was better, then he was Howdy Doody. She was as pale as waxed paper, her fingers still shaky, more rattled than he'd ever seen her. He'd only have to yell boo at her to have her jump out of her skin.

Sitting on the edge of his own desk, he frowned down at her. "All right, what happened?" he asked, glancing at the cassette player. "Did you get another message from the rapist?"

She nodded stiffly. "It was in my box this morning. He...he must have delivered it right to the station himself." Her fingers twisted together, the fear stronger than it had been in a long time. "He was at the reenactment we taped last night...one of the actors. He touched me." Her eyes filled with abhorrence. "He sounded so smug! Like he isn't afraid of anything." Her laugh was brief, short, and too close to hysteria for comfort. "Of course he's not afraid! He just walked into the station, as bold as you please, without anyone noticing. What's to stop him from walking up the stairs like he owns the place and tracking me down? He's already proven he thrives on daring. He could slip into my office and lock the door and no one would even know I was in trouble until it was too late."

"The hell he could!" Buck swore, surging to his feet. "He'd have to be totally wacko—"

"What the hell's going on here?" Dugan demanded, striding into the detective unit suddenly, his dark brows snapping together when he saw Sarah sitting, visibly shaken, at his desk. His eyes narrowed on the fear she made no attempt to hide. "What's happened?"

From the second she'd realized just how close the rapist had managed to get to her, she'd known she wouldn't feel safe again until Dugan's arms were around her. But now she couldn't move, couldn't manage to do anything but whisper his name.

Seeing her dilemma, Buck said flatly, "She got another tape from the rapist. Apparently he left it at the front desk."

The curse Dugan spit out was succinct, furious and unprintable. Reaching for Sarah, he pulled her into his arms and wrapped her close, uncaring of who might be watching. "Are you okay?"

She nodded, the strength of his hold loosening the words lodged in her throat, and everything just came spilling out. The horror, the revulsion, the panic that had sent her blindly searching for him. "It was him," she said hoarsely. "Last night. Joseph Peters. It had to be him... he knew things he couldn't possibly have known if he hadn't been there. And his voice... it was the same. I know it was the same!"

"I believe you, honey. I believe you," he assured her, hugging her fiercely. Anger whipped at him, along with an exhilaration that dragged an unexpected laugh from him. They had him. Damn it to hell, they had him!

He didn't realize he'd spoken aloud until Sarah pulled back in surprise and looked up at him in bewilderment. "Dugan, he walked into the station and no one even knew it. How can you possibly say we have him?"

"Because we've got him on tape, sweetheart. Twice! Last night and this morning. No one steps foot in the building without the cameras at the front desk picking it up, and you can bet this week's paycheck he didn't walk in with a mask on. We've got the bastard! Come on, let's go see what he looks like."

The three of them hurried downstairs, but Sarah was afraid to let herself hope. The rapist had been too clever, too conniving, too slippery, to have made such a big mistake. Last night he'd made sure to keep his face covered, slipping back into the darkness before he'd dared to remove his mask. Regardless of his smugness, she just couldn't see him walking into the police station bold as brass and letting himself be captured on film.

Ten minutes later the three of them stared at the video image of the rapist as he casually walked into the police station earlier that morning. He had a slouch hat pulled down low over his eyes and kept his head down as he wove his way through the crowd that surrounded the security desk just inside the front door. The desk sergeant had his hands full and didn't see the small man wearing a wrinkled suit and hat carefully make his way to the side of the desk.

"His head's down," Sarah said in disappointment. "This doesn't help at all."

Buck swore, but Dugan's eyes were glued to the screen. "Wait! Look!" He punched a button, freezing the scene on the screen. The rapist, his hand frozen as he slipped the cassette onto the desk, stood with his chin up, his profile clearly visible as he sent a furtive glance around to see if anyone was watching.

"All right!" Dugan breathed in satisfaction. "Now we're cooking! It's not a front shot, but it's enough to nail the dirtbag." He turned to Sarah quickly. "Honey, did he give you an address, a phone number, anything when he called you about being in the reenactment?"

"Yes, I have it in the files upstairs."

"Good. Then let's get it. You're going with us to check it out."

Chapter 10

For most of the day, it looked as if they were going to run into nothing but brick walls. The address Joseph Peters had given Sarah a couple of days ago turned out to be that of an apartment he had abandoned the same day he'd called her. Disappearing into the night like a dark shadow, he'd just walked away, leaving behind an apartment that was mockingly empty. Swearing, Dugan and Buck had searched it from top to bottom and came up with absolutely nothing. Questioning the neighbors had been equally unproductive. Peters had taken the apartment only a few weeks ago, under the name of John Peterson, and since then he'd been careful to keep a low profile. No one in the cheap rent complex had even seen him, let alone had a chance to talk to him.

Except the landlady.

As Dugan pulled into his driveway hours later with Sarah at his side, he almost laughed aloud at the thought of Lillian Ferguson. White-headed and on the downhill side of eighty, she'd only seen Peters once—the night he'd rented the apartment. But when Dugan had made the mistake of questioning her ability to give an accurate description of the man after meeting him only once weeks ago, she'd almost taken his head off. She'd indignantly assured him that she knew all her tenants, then reeled off a detailed description of the rapist that would have done a seasoned cop proud. Unknowingly, she'd described a man that matched the video profile shot they had of Peters to a tee. Dugan could have kissed her.

Close. They were so close to nailing him, Dugan could taste it. Finally, they were getting somewhere! Joseph Peters was clever, he had to give him that. Both of the names he had used had turned out to be aliases and there was no public record of him anywhere. He'd led the authorities on a merry chase by abandoning the battered white Camaro he'd driven last night on the south side, mockingly sending every cop in the city down another blind alley when the car turned out to be stolen and wiped clean of fingerprints. Success—and his obvious greed for Sarah—however, had made him sloppy. He'd started to believe his own press and overplayed his hand.

Fury gleamed in Dugan's eyes as he thought of the other man arrogantly strolling into the station and leaving that tape for Sarah. Oh, yes, Joseph Peters had made some serious mistakes, and for that he was going to pay. Soon. With Lillian Ferguson's input and the video pictures they already had, the police artist had been able to come up with a composite sketch of Joseph Peters, a.k.a. John Peterson, or whatever the hell his name was, that would be shown on all local newscasts come evening. Tomorrow that same sketch would be on the front page of every newspaper within a three hundred mile radius of San Antonio. By noon tomorrow Peters wouldn't be able to lift his head out of the hole he'd crawled into without somebody recognizing him.

As if she'd read his thoughts, Sarah watched him cut the engine and said quietly into the silence, "It's almost over. I can't believe it."

"Believe it, honey," he said, squeezing her hand. "In a matter of hours, Joseph Peters will be a hunted man looking for a way out of town. And when a man's in a panic, he makes stupid mistakes. The minute he makes the wrong move, somebody out there is going to see him and pick up the phone. All we've got to do is wait."

For weeks she'd been running from a faceless, nameless man who had the power to terrorize her without even touching her. During that time she'd told herself she'd be able to handle her fear much better if she only had a name to go with it, a physical description, anything that would identify her tormentor in a crowd. But now that she had that and it was only a matter of time before he was arrested, it didn't really help. A few hours, she thought. She only had a few more hours and then it would all be over. It sounded like an eternity.

"I hope you're prepared to eat a lot of homemade bread," she said ruefully as she reached for her door handle. "Until I know for sure Peters is in custody, I've got a feeling I'm going to be spending most of my time in the kitchen."

Dugan almost told her that he had no intention of letting her while away the hours baking bread—if she needed a distraction, he would be more than happy to provide it. But after what had happened in his bed that morning, he wasn't sure he should push the issue. They were making progress—she hadn't fought her way out of his arms, thank God. But the rigid set of her jaw as she'd silently struggled to get past her fear had cut him to the quick.

Lord, it was getting harder and harder to let her go! What was he going to do when this mess was all over and he no longer had a reason to keep her close?

"Then I guess I'll be right there with you," he said easily as he joined her on the sidewalk. "And Tory, too. One of her biggest complaints about her mother's cooking is that it comes out of the freezer or a fast-food place. You probably won't be able to turn around without her asking you questions about what you're doing."

But the minute Dugan opened the front door and followed Sarah inside, it was blatantly obvious that Tory had already made plans for them that didn't include her. Dugan took one look at the living room and nearly dropped his teeth. "What the—"

If ever a room had been better set for a seduction, he had yet to see it. A just lit fire crackled merrily in the fireplace, even though the temperature had been in the eighties that afternoon and it was still warm outside. A Frank Sinatra album—good Lord, where had she dug that up?—played on the stereo, and in front of the fire sat a card table, its slightly warped surface covered with an old flowered sheet in lieu of a tablecloth. From the fat red candle dripping wax in the middle of the table, he could see his grocery store china arranged in an intimate setting for two.

"I'm going to wring her neck," Dugan growled under his breath, shooting Sarah a quick glance to see how she was taking the obvious matchmaking. For a moment he saw her mouth twitch as if she wanted to laugh, but he couldn't be sure. "Tory! Damn it, where is that girl?"

"Oh, hi!" She strolled in from the kitchen, her gray eyes dancing, her grin cheeky. "I see you've seen my surprise. I knew you'd like it."

How she could conclude that, when Dugan was glaring at her as if he couldn't decide whether to chew her out or strangle her first, Sarah hadn't the foggiest. Stifling a giggle, Sarah struggled to hold back a grin and failed miserably. "Tory, you didn't have to do this."

"I know," she said with a shrug, "but I wanted to. I mean, you don't have to worry about me being a third wheel just because I turned up unexpectedly on the doorstep. I'm cool. I know even people Dad's age need some time and privacy for a sex life. I know when to make myself scarce."

Dugan nearly choked on a curse when she started up the stairs, only just then noticing she had a peanut butter and jelly sandwich in one hand and a glass of milk in the other. "Where the devil do you think you're going?"

She gave him a chiding look. "C'mon, Dad, my counselor warned you this morning I'd probably have a lot of homework until my teachers figure out if I'm ahead or behind the classes here. I've got a lot of work to do." Winking at him, she turned to Sarah and said conspiratorially, "If you're worried about me barging in on you at an inopportune moment, don't be. As soon as I finish my homework, I'm going straight to bed." She started up the stairs again. "G'night," she called breezily over her shoulder. "Dinner's on the stove when you're ready for it. See you in the morning."

A tense silence reigned for all of five seconds before Dugan broke it with a muttered, "When I get a chance, I'm going to have a long talk with that girl about poking her nose into things that are none of her business. I'm sorry, Sarah."

She laughed, she couldn't help it. "For what? You're just as much a victim of this as I am."

"Yeah, but she's my daughter, so that makes me responsible for her actions. She's too old to be pulling this kind of stunt." He walked into the living room and stared helplessly at the romantic setting. "Look at this! The only thing she left out was champagne chilling on ice and that's probably because we don't have any in the house."

Sarah spied an ice bucket sitting on an end table by the couch and started to laugh. "You're right. There's no champagne. Instead we've got—" she pulled two cans of soda out of the ice and grinned "—Dr. Pepper."

Dugan groaned, but his eyes had started to dance. "The drink of choice for the sophisticated palate. Shall we check the kitchen and see what she's left us on the stove?"

"Well, it would be a crime to let everything go to waste after she's gone to so much trouble," she said, chuckling. "We wouldn't want to hurt her feelings."

Dugan snorted at that and took her hand to pull her with him into the kitchen. It was an instinctive move, an unthinkingly romantic gesture that set the air sizzling hotly between them the minute his fingers closed around hers. Their eyes locked, smiles faded, while Sinatra crooned a love song in their ears. Suddenly the evening that had been planned for them looked too tempting to resist.

"C'mon," Dugan said softly. "Let's eat."

Expecting to find Tory's only culinary accomplishment—tuna casserole—waiting for them, Dugan stared in surprise at the egg drop soup, pork fried rice and almond chicken warming in pans on the stove. "I'll be damned! How—"

The empty take-out containers from a popular Chinese restaurant sat on the counter. Impressed with Tory's ingenuity, Sarah said, "Dugan, this was so sweet of her. She must have started setting everything up the minute she got home from school."

"I know." And tomorrow, he would give her a big hug and kiss for it. Not for her matchmaking, but for having unwittingly found a way to distract Sarah from the long hours they had ahead of them while they waited for Joseph Peters to be captured. "She's got all the subtlety of a blow torch, but she's a good kid."

"Do you think you could talk her into joining us? Surely she'd rather have Chinese than eat a sandwich in her room."

"Usually, yes. But she's made it pretty clear this is our night," he replied quietly. "She wouldn't thank us for spoiling all her plans."

Their night. Sarah stared up into his darkening eyes and knew he was right. It was their night, a moment carved out of time, stretching out before them like infinity, free of worry and fear and stress. The ugliness of the last two weeks couldn't touch them tonight. The pain of the past was forgotten, the uncertainty of the future unimportant. There was only the here and now and a world that consisted of nothing but the one they saw in each other's eyes. For as long as they could cling to the illusion, nothing else mattered.

Glancing down at her black slacks and yellow silk blouse, then at his blue cambric shirt and plaid tie, she smiled. "Think we should change? We're hardly dressed for a romantic dinner."

"You look fine," he said, his eyes glowing as they followed the same path over her figure hers had. "Just fine."

Somehow Sarah felt as if he'd just told her she was beautiful.

They ate, but Sarah couldn't have said if it was good, bad, or indifferent. Trapped in the gray heat of Dugan's eyes, she couldn't taste anything but anticipation on her tongue. All her senses were finely tuned to Dugan's every move. He smiled and her heart thundered in her ears; his eyes gazed into hers as if he could see into her very soul and she forgot her own name. He talked and laughed and gently teased her, and for one incredibly sweet, timeless moment, he gave her something more precious than gold. He gave her back herself. If he hadn't already had her heart, she would have fallen in love with him right then and there. Without realizing what he was doing, he gave her the room to be the woman she had once been, open and giving and affectionate. The freedom of it went to her head like fine wine, making her dizzy with wanting. Completely dropping her guard, she touched him and laughed with him, her feelings there in her eyes for him to see if he only cared to look.

And he did look. He looked until they were both breathless and aching, the music that swirled around them drowned out by the frantic drumming of their hearts. Fingers brushed fingers, heat simmered, their eyes met, and he told her he was just as caught up in the fantasy as she was. All without saying a word.

But as with all fantasies, it had to end. The fire burned down until it was nothing but glowing embers, the melted candle sputtered, the music drifted into silence. From upstairs they could hear the water running in the bathroom as Tory prepared for bed. In the blink of an eye reality returned, bringing with it all its problems.

Unconsciously Sarah's gaze moved to the darkened windows of the living room, Joseph Peters' sinister threats echoing in her ears. She tried to tell herself that by now, he knew his days were numbered. The police would be hunting him down like a rabid dog, and the only thought in his head would be getting as far from San Antonio as quickly as possible. She was safer than she had been in weeks.

But in the gathering quiet, she could almost hear the deadly promise in his voice when he had vowed that the next time he held her, there would be no witnesses. She shivered as though someone had stepped on her grave.

"Don't."

She looked up from her unsettling thoughts to find Dugan's eyes on her. "Don't let him ruin the evening," he growled softly. "Don't give him that kind of power over you. He's a two-bit dirtbag who isn't worth the energy it would take to spit on him. Forget him. He hasn't got time to hurt you now. He's too busy running for his life."

She wanted desperately to believe him, but they both knew that she was in danger as long as Joseph Peters was free. Rising to her feet, she reached for their empty plates. "That's what he should be doing, what a man with any sense at all would be doing. But Dugan, we're talking about a man who's taunted the police for weeks," she reminded him. "He's called the station to mock you. He's walked right in the front door and dared you to catch him. If he has a lick of self-preservation, he hasn't shown it so far. There's no telling what he'll do when he realizes the noose is tightening around his neck."

"He can rant and rave and carry on like a madman for all I care, but the one thing he won't do is come after you. He still doesn't know where you are, sweetheart, so relax. You're safe."

"I keep telling myself that, and for long moments at a time, I actually believe it. Like tonight." Her face softened, her smile turning wistful as her eyes fell on the candle that had melted into a heap in the saucer Tory had stuck it in. "But then I start to think again, it all comes rushing back, and I just can't sit still."

She headed for the kitchen and began to clean up, loading the dishwasher with the dirty dishes, then looking around to find something else to keep her busy. Dugan stepped into the doorway and immediately recognized the desperate look in her eye. "You are *not* going to spend the night baking bread, Sarah. I mean it. I won't let you do that to yourself. Take a bubble bath instead. That'll relax you and help you get to sleep. By the time you wake up in the morning, this may all be over with."

If only it was that easy! But she knew herself too well. The minute she crawled into bed and turned out the lights, Joseph Peters would be there in the dark with her, the remembered feel of his hands at her throat, his body pressing intimidatingly up against hers, choking her. She wouldn't be able to stand it.

"I can't," she whispered. "I can't lie in the dark alone. Too much has happened. I wouldn't be able to think of anything but him." Needing his arms around her, she lifted pleading eyes to his. "Would you stay with me tonight?"

A stronger man than he would have had a hard time resisting such an invitation, and he'd never pretended to be a saint. He'd spent the past few hours losing himself in the dark depths of her eyes and all he wanted to do was hold her. He almost reached for her, but images of the two of them in his bed that morning flashed before his eyes, the memory of her sudden paleness, her frozen stiffness when he'd unthinkingly come down on top of her, haunting him. He couldn't put her through that again.

A muscle clenching in his jaw, he kept the width of the kitchen between them. "Have you forgotten what happened this morning? You were terrified—"

"But not of you," she said, crossing to him since he wouldn't come to her. Stopping directly in front of him, she reached up to lay her palm against his cheek. "It wasn't you I was fighting then," she said quietly. "It was the dragons inside me, and they're always worse at night. I know you can't fight them for me, but just having you close will help me feel stronger. Will you stay with me?"

How could he deny her after that? Covering her hand with his, he dragged her fingers to his mouth and pressed a lingering kiss to her soft skin. "Yes," he murmured, his gray eyes burning possessively into hers. "I'll stay for as long as you need me."

She wanted to tell him that would, in all likelihood, mean forever, but she knew he was thinking of hours, not years. Struggling to appear nonchalant, she forced an easy smile. "I've just got a few more things to finish up here. You don't have to wait up if you don't want to."

But he did. While she put away the last of the pots in the kitchen, he checked to make sure the fire was completely out in the fireplace, then folded up the card table and returned it to its place in the hall closet. By the time he was finished, Sarah was, too.

Awkwardness sprang between them the minute they headed for his bedroom. Surprised, Dugan tried to tell himself there was no reason to feel like a new groom facing a virgin bride on his wedding night. They weren't going to make love, just share his bed for what was left of the night. All Sarah asked of him was that he stay beside her in the dark, and after the fiasco earlier that morning, he was going to make damn sure nothing happened.

Since he had it all worked out in his head, preparing for bed should have been easy. But the minute he followed her into the bedroom and shut the door, nothing was quite as cut and dried as he'd have liked. Suddenly he felt like an untried teenager sharing a hotel room with a woman for the first time. Did he let her have the bathroom first or last? Did he ask what side of the bed she wanted or just take one? And why did he feel like he should shave? He wasn't going to touch her, damn it!

It wasn't like him to be so unsure of himself, and he didn't like it. To make matters worse, Sarah seemed to be as ill at ease as he was. Skittish, her cheeks flushed with color, she looked everywhere but at him as she pulled back the covers on the bed and nervously plumped the pillows before collecting her gown and robe. At any other time he probably would have been amused at their nervousness with each other when they wanted each other so badly they ached, but tonight he was not laughing.

"Why don't you take the bathroom first," he growled into the tense silence. "I'm going to make one last check of the house to make sure everything's locked up."

He was gone before she could utter a word, slipping out the door and firmly shutting it behind him. Clutching her nightclothes to her, Sarah sank down to the edge of the bed and struggled to control an unexpected giggle. Thinking about Joseph Peters every time she closed her eyes tonight was not going to be a problem. Staying out of Dugan's arms was.

Fifteen minutes later Sarah was in bed, lying on her side with her back to the rest of the room, when Dugan returned. The covers pulled up to her throat, she stiffened as he stopped in the doorway. She didn't have to look over her shoulder to know that his eyes warmed at the sight of her in his bed. She could feel the heat from their stroking touch clear across the room. Time slowed to a crawl.

Unconsciously holding her breath, she was beginning to wonder if he was going to stand there all night watching her when he quietly closed the door and crossed the carpet to the bathroom. Again a door shut, softly, wordlessly telling her that it was better for both of them if they pretended she was asleep.

It was a pretense, however, that neither of them could keep up for long. Within moments he'd doused the lights and was slipping under the covers with her, carefully keeping to his side of the king-size bed. The air stilled and grew so hushed Sarah was sure he could hear the wild thumping of her heart. He made no move to touch her, to breach the invisible wall that lay between them in the dark, but she could feel his need with every uneven breath she took. An answering ache lodged deep inside her, a burning ember that seemed to burn hotter with every slow tick of the clock on the bedside table. Fighting the urge to turn to him, to seek the warmth of his arms in the night, she lay as unmoving as stone, afraid that if she allowed so much as a single muscle to relax, she would be lost.

Her eyes tightly closed, her fingers clutching the sheet as if it were the only thing that could protect her from the temptation teasing her senses, she never knew how long she lay there when he spoke. "Are you asleep?"

The rough timbre of his words was so soft, it hardly caused more than a ripple in the dark. Her answer was equally soft, equally telling in its huskiness. "No."

Dugan groaned and rolled to his back, his eyes trained on the ceiling to keep from looking at her. If she'd just ignored his question, he would have found a way to go on with the pretense of sleeping. But now it was too late. The sensuous thickness of her voice had told him more than he wanted to know. She wanted him as badly as he wanted her, and he couldn't continue to share a bed with her without touching her.

He sighed heavily. "Honey, this isn't going to work. It'd be better for both of us if I just went back to the couch."

He started to throw the cover back, but in the blink of an eye, she was at his side, her fingers covering his in the darkness. "No... please! Stay."

Did she think he didn't want to? "If I do, I'm not going to be able to keep my hands off you," he warned bluntly. "I know I promised I'd let you set the pace, but damn it,

I don't have as much willpower as I thought I did where you're concerned. I'm sorry, sweetheart, but I can't share a bed with you and not make love with you.''

His eyes narrowed and gleaming in the shadows that engulfed them, he made no attempt to tie up his intentions in pretty words. She would either let him escape to the living room or they would consummate the attraction that had sprung up between them the moment they met. The call was hers.

Sarah knew if she let go of his hand and turned her back on him, he wouldn't utter one word of reproach. He'd just walk out, and when he did, she would lose something infinitely precious—the chance to take her courage in her hands and show him how much he had come to mean to her. She couldn't let that happen.

The fingers that had tightened on his, relaxed and turned caressing. ''Stay,'' she murmured. ''I want you to stay.''

His glance sharpened. ''And make love with you?''

''Yes.''

With a single word, she almost shattered his control. Only the memory of her in this very bed this morning, her jaw clenched to stifle an outcry of panic as he'd swept her under him, kept him from losing his head. His fingers covered hers, gently stilling them. ''Are you sure?''

She'd never been more sure of anything in her life. ''I want to be like other women,'' she said softly, earnestly, trying to make him understand. ''I want to be held by a man, loved by a man . . . by *you*,'' she stressed, ''without having my past rise up to haunt me. For three long years I've been a victim, denying myself any kind of real life because I was afraid of being helpless again . . . of feeling . . . of hurting. But every time I have to fight my way out of your arms, the pain only gets worse.''

Uncaring of the hot tears that spilled over her lashes and tracked down her face, she brought his hand to her cheek. "I'm tired of hurting. You're the best thing that's ever happened to me, and I want to love you."

Dugan groaned low in his throat. Did she have any idea how she touched his heart? How she made it impossible for him *not* to love her? His fingers tightened on hers. "Good. Because I wanted you five minutes after I met you, and that hasn't changed. Come here, sweetheart."

He gently tugged and pulled and maneuvered them both until he had her right where he wanted her—sprawled across his chest as he lay back against the pillow, the tantalizing soft mounds of her breasts resting intimately against him, her mouth just inches from his. He made no attempt to hold her, but lifted his hands to the dark wild curtain of her hair as it fell forward over her shoulders to brush teasingly against him. With a will of their own, the silky strands seemed to wrap around his wrist, capturing him, enchanting him.

His eyes lifted to hers. "We're not going to have a repeat of this morning," he assured her huskily. "There's no one here but you and me, and that's the way it's going to stay. Just take it slow and easy and everything will be fine. We've got all night."

As she ducked her head to tenderly take his mouth with hers, she knew he was telling her that she would set the pace in their lovemaking, but it wasn't until she tasted his slow, languid response that she really understood what he'd been trying to tell her. This time, their first time together, was totally and completely for her.

Sweetness flooded her, drizzling through her like warm honey. He was hers, to do with as she liked, to tease, to seduce, to love as she'd dreamed of loving him. And she had all night. Sinking more fully against him, she whisked her tongue across his bottom lip and tasted the fire in him. He moaned softly, the sound echoing through her in slow breaking waves. Suddenly the hours that stretched between now and dawn seemed pitifully inadequate. How could she be satisfied with mere hours when she'd been waiting for him for an eternity?

She wanted to hurry then, like a child set free in a candy store for too short a time, anxious to sample everything but unable to linger too long over anything, but she got sidetracked by the decidedly male, sandpapery texture of Dugan's whisker-roughened jaw. Lightly she skimmed her fingers back and forth from his chin to the chiseled plane of his cheek, loving the rugged feel of him under the sensitive pads of her fingers. Impulsively she leaned down to rub her cheek against his and laughed softly at the contrast in texture. "You feel so good."

He made a strangled sound, his hands moving to the back of her waist to hold her oh so lightly. "I thought if I didn't shave, that'd just give me one more reason to stick to my side of the bed. Honey, your skin—"

"Is fine," she assured him, pressing a whisper-soft kiss to the corner of his mouth. "And in case you hadn't noticed, Mr. Magee, you have stuck to your side of the bed."

Oh, he'd noticed . . . that and a hell of a lot more. Such as the fact that she hadn't stiffened up once since he'd pulled her on top of him. And that for the first time since he'd known her, she was freely giving in to the sensuality that she always tried so hard to keep under wraps. She didn't just touch his face, she teased and brushed and caressed like a woman who had denied herself the simple pleasure of human contact too long. No doubt about it, the lady was a toucher, and right now she seemed bent on driving him right out of his mind. He loved it.

And with every passing moment, her confidence grew. Kisses that had been shy, hesitant, delightfully innocent, slowed and deepened. Hot. Her tongue dueled with his, her teeth playfully nipped, and her sweet, knowing hands slipped over his shoulders and down his naked chest, charting him inch by slow, maddening inch, and his body suddenly burned like a furnace.

His breath tearing through his lungs, his limbs unbelievably heavy with the pleasure she steeped him in, he kicked at the covers tangling around them. "Sweetheart, you're burning me alive!" She only laughed huskily, the little witch, and leaned down to swirl her tongue around his nipple, turning up the heat. He cursed and pulled her closer.

Lost to everything but her desire to please him until he was so weak with pleasure he couldn't move, she'd intended to keep their loving light and playful, but suddenly there was nothing playful about the needs screaming through her. Caressing him, kissing him, wasn't enough. She ached for the feel of his hands on her. Everywhere.

Murmuring his name, she moved restlessly against him, her mouth blindly seeking his for a desperate, urgent kiss. "Touch me," she whispered, groping for his hands in the dark. "I need you to touch me."

He groaned, the quiet request going through him like liquid mercury. With unsteady fingers, he reached for the hem of her pale blue nightgown. "Here, sweetheart, let's get you out of this gown. You don't need it anymore."

He lifted her up until she was straddling him and whisked the flimsy garment over her head, tossing it onto the floor without even looking to see where it landed, his only concern was Sarah. He didn't want to move too quickly, to do anything that would scare her and bring back the past, but he also didn't want to give her any time to think, either.

But the minute his fingers closed over her breasts, cupping her, stroking her, tugging her nipples to tight, pouting peaks, he was the one who couldn't think. She was beautiful! In the darkness her body was a pale gleam of soft, tempting curves. His hands swept over her as she sank boneless to his chest and dropped hot, scattered kisses everywhere she could touch, the sweet, hungry sounds that came from the back of her throat nearly driving him wild.

Hanging onto the last of his reason by nothing more than a thread, he tried to be gentle, warning himself that anything else was unacceptable with Sarah. She needed, deserved, ached for a tender loving. But they were both suddenly breathing hard, their hands eager, demanding. His briefs met the same fate as her gown, and he couldn't for the life of him say whose fingers stripped them from him—his or hers. She didn't give him time to ask. Pushing him back down to the bed, she covered him like an electric blanket, her body hot and steaming, and kissed him hungrily.

He tried to slow her down, but then her fingers closed around him and the thought flew right out of his head. Flames licked from her to him and back again. He reached for her, dragging her close, his hands sweeping over her back, her hips, the melting liquid heat between her thighs. She bucked against him, his name a plea on her lips that completely destroyed him.

His hands, rough with emotion and a need unlike anything he'd ever known before, clamped around her slender hips, guiding her. If he'd seen the least hesitation in her eyes, he told himself he would have somehow found the strength to stop. But in the heated shadows that surrounded them, she was looking at him as if she'd die if he didn't take her, as if she'd found everything she'd ever wanted right there in his arms.

Slowly, carefully, he filled her, watching her face transform with wonder, a small smile of satisfaction curving her mouth. She was hot, tight, incredible. His jaw clamped against the need to set a hard, driving rhythm that would push them both over the edge, his fingers tightening on her hips. "Okay?"

"Oh, yes!"

"Then take us where we want to go, sweetheart."

Her eyes glowed as if he'd just given her the moon. She shifted her hips uncertainly, watched his eyes dilate, and felt the last of her inhibitions slip away. Her eyes drifting shut on a sigh that was his name, she moved against him until she found a steady, building pace that set the blood thundering in both their ears. Flames that had roared like a forest fire only seconds before blazed into an inferno.

Dugan thought he knew what to expect. He'd been married, for heaven's sake! And before that, he certainly hadn't been a monk. He knew all about sex. But when the first shudder took Sarah and she gasped in surprise, her startled gaze flying to his, he realized he knew squat about making love. Then she pulled him into the fire after her, and as the heat consumed him, he couldn't think of anything but Sarah. How was he ever going to live without her?

Chapter 11

A horn sounded out front, and Tory finished the last of her juice in one gulp. "That's my bus...gotta run." Grabbing her books off the counter, she pressed a quick kiss to her father's smoothly shaven cheek, grinned at Sarah and hurried out of the kitchen like a small whirlwind. Seconds later the front door slammed behind her, her hastily called "See you guys later" echoing in her wake.

Sarah stared after her, the smile that tugged at her mouth spilling into her eyes. It would take no effort at all on her part to fall into the fantasy of playing house with Dugan and his daughter. They made it easy to play.

The morning could have been—*should* have been—awkward. She had no experience with morning afters, and when she'd awakened to find Dugan already gone, the intimacies they'd shared last night had risen up before her, bringing with them a host of doubts. Did he have regrets this morning? Was that why he'd left without waking her?

Not knowing what to expect, she'd quickly dressed and gone looking for him, only to find him and Tory in the kitchen, laughing and teasing each other about the correct way to flip pancakes. The second they'd spied her lingering in the doorway, they'd pulled her into the good-natured fray. She hadn't had time to feel uncertain.

And any doubts she might have had were quickly put to rest by Dugan. With his daughter there, he didn't say a word that even hinted at what they had shared during the night, but his eyes held an unguarded heat that warmed her inside and out. He found a dozen innocent ways to touch her that were all the more potent for their casualness, silently telling her that he had no regrets. His hip nudged hers as he squeezed past her to get to the refrigerator; his fingers grazed hers when they both reached for the butter at the same time; his hand brushed her cheek to push a strand of hair back behind her ear when she leaned over the stove. And when they sat down to the table to eat, he slipped his foot out of his shoe and boldly played footsy with her.

Alone for the first time that morning, his eyes met hers across the table. "You okay this morning?"

Color blooming in her cheeks, she nodded. "How 'bout you?"

He grinned and leaned across the table to kiss her, his mouth tenderly brushing hers. "I could use a few more hours in bed with you," he admitted roughly, and gave into the hunger that demanded a longer, deeper kiss.

Breathless, her heart pounding out of control, Sarah finally pulled back, desire a sweet ache in her stomach. "If we don't leave for work soon, we're going to be late," she said softly.

He groaned in defeat, knowing she was right. His gray eyes dark with wanting, he rubbed the pad of his thumb across the damp softness of her lower lip. "We'll finish this later," he promised in a low growl, and then forced himself to release her while he still could.

By unspoken agreement, they agreed that was the only promise he could give her about the future. Working side by side, they cleaned up the kitchen just as they did every morning, then went outside to climb into his car to go to work. But when Dugan turned the key in the ignition, the motor sputtered and coughed and while it finally kicked to life, it shuddered in protest.

Dugan swore under his breath. "It looks like that tune-up I've been trying to put off just became a necessity. Sorry, honey, but I'm afraid we're going to be late for work after all. I'm going to have to get this thing to a garage."

Jolted by the rough, rocking motion of the motor, she looked at him skeptically. "Will it make it? It sounds like it's dying."

"Oh, yeah, it'll make it, but you'd better follow me just in case. We can take your car in the rest of the way to work."

Forty-five minutes later they walked into the station thirty minutes late to find the whole station buzzing with barely suppressed excitement. The composite sketch of Joseph Peters had hit the front page of the morning paper, and the phones were ringing off the wall with calls from people claiming to have seen him. Dugan and Buck already had a dozen leads to track down and the day had just begun.

Leaving Sarah in her office under the protection of a uniformed officer, Dugan and Buck divided up the city and hit the streets in separate patrol cars, backup just a call away. His adrenaline pumping, Dugan refused to be discouraged when he continually turned up in a spot that Pe-

ters had just left. He was so close he could smell the dark
sickness of the man, and Dugan took great satisfaction in
knowing he had the bastard running scared. It was only a
matter of time before the dragnet he and Buck and
thousands of watchful citizens were wrapping around the
city tightened like a noose around Peters' scrawny neck. He
couldn't wait to see him squirm.

Eight hours later nothing had changed. The calls were
still coming in and Peters was as elusive as a shadow, but
Dugan returned to the station feeling better than he had in
a long time. After weeks of having nothing to go on, the
case had finally broken wide open, and before he was
through, he'd have enough evidence to make sure Peters
never saw daylight again. And then there was Sarah.

She was waiting for him, a smile spreading across her
face and lighting her eyes the minute he stepped into her
office. She rose and started toward him, only then remembering the uniformed officer standing just outside the
open door in the hall. She stopped, suddenly unexpectedly shy, drawing a grin from Dugan. Stepping back into
the hallway, he told her protector, "I'm going to take Ms.
Haywood home now, Tom. Thanks for watching over
her."

"No sweat," the other man laughed. "This is the easi-
est duty I've drawn in weeks. Nobody stuck a foot in this
hall that wasn't supposed to."

"Good. If we need you again tomorrow, I'll let you
know."

Nodding, the young rookie wished them both a good
night and walked off down the hall, whistling. Dugan
quietly shut the door and turned to Sarah, his eyes gleaming as they swept over the white and black double-breasted
suit she wore. There was nothing provocative about it; it
effectively covered her from her neck to just below her

knee and was all business. It shouldn't have inspired a single lascivious thought, but all he could think about was taking it off her. Leaning back against the door, he teased his senses with the sight of her. God, she looked good!

"Ready to go?"

It wasn't what she wanted to ask. She didn't need to ask if he'd tracked down Joseph Peters yet—the news would have been all over the station by now and he'd have told her the minute he walked in the door. No, she wanted to know if he'd thought of last night as much as she had; if he'd spent the day replaying every touch, every kiss in his head the way she had; if he was looking forward to being together again tonight as much as she was. But she was still too unsure of herself where he was concerned, and she couldn't quite manage the words. What if he said no?

He never moved from the door. "In a minute," he promised softly. "Come here first."

His low, sexy murmur tugged at her, drawing her to him as surely as if he'd reached across the space between them and taken her hand. Needing his nearness more than she did air at that moment, she stepped toward him, a small smile flirting with one corner of her mouth as she stopped a foot away from him. "You wanted something?"

"Yeah. You." He promised himself he wasn't going to expect anything more from her than she was ready to give just because they'd spent one night together—even if it had been the most fantastic night of his life. If she decided she needed to step back and get a perspective on things, he'd find a way to deal with it. Later. Right now he had to kiss that teasing little smile off her face.

Pushing himself away from the door, he reached for her in one smooth move, pulling her into his arms before she could do anything but blink. A heartbeat after that, his mouth was on hers, stealing her breath, claiming her.

Lightning sparked; sudden heat set nerve ends sizzling. Just that quickly, the intimacy they'd shared last night was back, stronger and sweeter than ever. Sarah moaned and melted against him, boneless.

His tongue sweeping the dark, moist secrets of her mouth, Dugan found himself swamped by the need to drag her down to the carpet and take her then and there. Madness. How could she push him to madness so effortlessly? He was trembling, for goodness' sakes!

Jerking back abruptly, he pressed her face against his chest, his fingers buried in her hair so he wouldn't be able to wrap his arms around her and squeeze her closer than she might be able to stand. "This wasn't smart," he admitted ruefully, his breathing strained. "We've got to get out of here and go pick up my car before we can go home, and now I'm in no shape to go anywhere."

"Oh!"

He chuckled at her start of surprise and only had to dip his head to see the hot blush firing her cheeks. "Hey, where do you think you're going?" he demanded when she tried to step away from him. "Stay right where you are, woman. Talk to me."

"But—"

"I'll cool down in a minute. Tell me about your day."

Weeks ago, his blunt reference to his arousal would have sent her scurrying for cover. Now she couldn't imagine stepping away from him. "I spent most of the day calling the used car lots looking for a blue '68 Corvair. Can you believe that? Somebody actually used a Corvair as the getaway car in a bank robbery. Where am I going to find any Corvair, let alone a blue one?"

His laughter rippled through them both. "You got me there, sweetheart. What'll you do if you can't find one?"

"Check the junkyards and see if I can locate a wrecked one that isn't too badly damaged. I might be able to have it towed to the bank and shoot it from its good side. I guess your day wasn't much better."

It took nothing more than the mention of Joseph Peters to kill the last lingering traces of desire. "We're still running him to ground, but I'm not discouraged. We've finally got him right where we want him. We'll get him." Setting her away from him, he gave her hand a quick squeeze and released her completely. "Get your purse. We've got to get to the garage before it closes."

They made it with thirty minutes to spare, but so did six other people. When Dugan saw the line of car owners at the cashier window waiting to pick up their vehicles, he swore and went back outside to Sarah, who was waiting in her car. "It's going to be at least fifteen minutes," he said after explaining the situation to her. "Why don't you go on home? Tory'll be there, and there's no need for you to sit out here when I'll be along in a few minutes anyway."

"Are you sure? I don't mind waiting."

"No, go on. It'll be okay," he assured her. He never would have let her drive home from work alone, but there wasn't a chance in hell Joseph Peters could follow her from the garage since he had no way of knowing she was there. "I'll be right behind you."

She was still reluctant to leave him, but he was right. There was no sense in both of them waiting. "I'll start supper," she promised. "Unless Tory has another surprise for us."

Grinning, he watched her drive off, then went back inside the garage office. As he'd predicted, it was a good fifteen minutes before he was able to present his credit card to pay the bill. The cashier handed him back his card, had him sign the receipt, then handed him his copy. "The mechanic who worked on your car is bringing it up right now," she told him. "Just show him the receipt."

Dugan thanked her and stepped outside just as his car came to a stop almost right in front of him. The mechanic didn't give the receipt more than a passing glance. "She's all set and raring to go, Mr. Magee," he said as he wiped his hands on a red rag he pulled out of his back pocket. "She needed a tune-up, but that wasn't the main problem."

Dugan, walking around the front end to the driver's side, lifted a brow in surprise. "Oh? What else was wrong?"

"She was missing two spark plug wires." Scratching his head, the younger man frowned down at the car as if it was to blame. "A wire can become disconnected, but you don't usually lose one, let alone two. It's damned odd if you ask me."

"Yes, it is," Dugan said, frowning. "Damned odd. Thanks for telling me."

He slipped into the driver's seat and quickly headed for home. There was nothing to worry about, he told himself. It was just a freak incident. There were probably any number of ways he could have lost those wires. The neighbor's cat was always crawling up under the hood. And despite what the mechanic thought, normal wear and tear could have caused the problem. All right, so maybe it was a coincidence that he'd lost two wires overnight. But it could happen, he reasoned.

But the ice cold uneasiness knotting his gut reminded him he wasn't a man who believed in coincidence. His jaw rigid, he pressed down harder on the accelerator.

Sarah unlocked the front door with the key Dugan had given her and stepped inside, automatically setting her purse on the small table just inside the entrance hall. From upstairs, Tory's stereo blared, the hard, grinding beat of her favorite band vibrating the walls. Shaking her head, Sarah grinned ruefully. How could Tory study when she had the music so loud she couldn't possibly think?

Heading for Dugan's bedroom to change into jeans, she'd taken only three steps when she just barely heard the doorbell over the blasting music. Surprised, she turned back toward the door. Dugan had given her his key; surely he couldn't be home so soon—he'd said it would be at least fifteen minutes.

She started to open the door, then stopped abruptly, remembering Dugan's instructions to Tory not to open the door to anyone. Squinting through the peephole, she laughed in relief when the familiar logo of a local pizza restaurant filled her vision. It looked like Tory had planned supper again.

Grinning, she started to yell up the stairs for her, then realized she wouldn't hear her. Considering all Tory had done for them last night, Sarah decided the least she could do was pick up the tab for the pizza. Turning back to the table for her purse, she opened the door, her eyes dropping to her wallet and the bills she pulled from it. "I hope I've got enough. How much—"

"It isn't cash that I want."

She froze, her frightened eyes flying up to the man standing before her. He wore a baseball cap low over his brow and dark sunglasses hid his eyes, but she'd have known that accented voice in hell. "No!" she screamed and turned to run.

But he was on her in a flash, pushing her up against the wall, the knife he'd concealed beneath the pizza box jammed under her chin. "Oh, no, lady," he purred, his breath an obscene caress against her cheek as he leaned into her. "You're not getting away from me so easily. I've been waiting a long time to get my hands on you."

No! The scream echoed in her head, terror dark and cold and deadly nearly gagging her as the nightmare that stalked her in the night blurred with reality, terrifying her. Images flashed in her head...Trent Kingston, his eyes dark with purpose and his hands fierce, forcing his will on her, hurting her. She'd thought he'd taught her the true meaning of fear, but she had a horrible feeling the lessons she'd learned from him were nothing compared to the cruel degradation Joseph Peters would impose on her.

She could feel herself starting to shake and couldn't seem to do anything about it as panic tore at her. Gasping, she swallowed sickly and felt the cold, deadly edge of the knife slide against her throat. "Please . . ."

"You're the one who's going to do the pleasing," he growled. "But not here. Magee will be here any moment." He saw her eyes widen and grinned smugly. "Oh, yes, I know you dropped him at the garage to pick up his car. I figured that's what you'd do when I did a little mechanical work on his car last night."

"But how d-did y-you—" Hating the betraying quiver in her voice, Sarah tried to ignore the knife and steady her voice, but the fear was rising in her, threatening to snap what little control she had left. "How did y-you know where I-I was?"

"Have you forgotten the reenactment?" he taunted. "Magee got a call on his radio and you two took off like a bat out of hell for his house. All I had to do was lay back some and follow you."

Tory! Suddenly remembering her, Sarah's horrified eyes flew up the stairs, a sob almost escaping her throat when she spied the younger girl's ashen face peeking around the corner of the stairwell. *Don't!* she wanted to cry. *Don't be a hero!*

Joseph Peters, pleased with her distress, never noticed the direction of her gaze. "I've got a nice deserted apartment set up for us," he told her silkily. "So you're going to walk out to my car with me and get in without a word of protest. Understand?"

Eager to get him well away from Tory, she nodded. "Yes. Whatever you say."

Suspicious, he frowned at her acquiescence. "Don't think you can try anything on me," he warned. "I won't stand for it! I'll be right next to you with my knife in your ribs. You so much as look wrong, and I swear I'll stab you in the heart. You hear me? You'd better, 'cause I got nothing to lose at this point, lady. *Don't push me!*"

"N-no, I won't. I promise."

The quiver in her voice must have convinced him. Jerking her away from the wall, he pushed her toward the door, his breath hot on her neck, the knife pricking the skin over her ribs. Staring straight ahead, Sarah didn't dare look upstairs at Tory again. Her heart pounding painfully, she walked outside with Joseph Peters and climbed into his faded red pickup without a word. As they drove away, she never saw Tory at an upstairs window, her eyes narrowed on the truck's license plate before she ran for the phone.

He was being paranoid. His hands tight on the wheel, Dugan raced toward his house and hoped like hell he and Sarah would be laughing themselves silly over this later in the evening. But he had a horrible, gut-wrenching feeling that there would be no laughter for them tonight. God, no! If anything happened to her... Shying away from the thought, he slowed down for a red light, checked to make sure there was no cross traffic, and shot right through it. Seconds later he turned onto Cactus Way, the only major thoroughfare that led to his subdivision two miles away. Let her be safe at home, he prayed fiercely.

Praying as he had never prayed before, he didn't see the cat dart out from the side of the road until he was almost upon it. Swearing, he swerved to miss it and almost plowed into the faded red pickup abandoned at the side of the road instead. "Damn cat!" he growled, and quickly jerked the wheel back to the center of the road. His car fishtailed before he finally brought it back under control. He never checked his speed.

Four blocks later he stiffened as his police radio suddenly crackled with an all points bulletin. "Be on the lookout for a 1978 faded red Chevy pickup. license Baker-7-8-4-2," the dispatcher droned in an unemotional voice. "Driver is believed to be Joseph Peters and is wanted for four rapes and the kidnapping of Sarah Haywood, the chief's goddaughter. He was last seen leaving 407 Prickly Pear Drive at 0600 with Haywood and is considered armed and dangerous. All units in the area respond."

"No!" His hoarse cry ringing in his ears, Dugan's fingers bit into the wheel. The bastard had Sarah! He flattened the accelerator, but in the next instant the image of the faded red pickup he'd almost hit moments ago flashed before his eyes. Damn it, he was sure it was a Chevy, but he hadn't even gotten a glimpse of the license plate. Should he go back and check it out? Urgency tore at him. If Peters had gotten Sarah at his house, then this road was his only way out. Sometime within the last few minutes he'd come through here looking for a place to hide. Because he had to know Dugan was coming after him. And when he got his hands on him...

Rage burning like a fire in his stomach, he didn't finish the thought. Sarah! He had to get to her before that dirtbag touched her, hurt her. And what about Tory? She had to have been at the house when Peters got Sarah. What happened to her? Dear God, if she'd been hurt—

Grabbing the mike on the radio, he identified himself to the dispatcher. "My daughter," he demanded harshly, "is she all right? She was at the house, too. Is she hurt?"

"She's fine, Magee," came the response. "She called in the report. There are two officers with her now. They'll stay with her until you can get there."

He didn't wait to hear more. "I'm on Cactus Way heading north. There's an abandoned pickup matching the description of Peters' vehicle a half mile south. I'm going back to check the plates." After a quick check of his rearview mirror, he executed a sharp U-turn and gunned the motor.

Soon he braked to a gravel-throwing halt behind the pickup, his gaze locked on the license plates. B-7842. The relief that flared in him went out like a snuffed-out match when he tore his eyes from the abandoned truck to glance wildly around for any signs of Sarah and Peters. His throat went dry at the sight before him.

Peters had abandoned the truck in front of a deserted apartment complex that had been closed for renovations not yet started. What looked like nearly a hundred multifamily units were surrounded by an eight foot high chainlink fence topped with barbed wire. A long gash cut in the wire mesh of the fence told Dugan that this was where Peters had holed up. And somewhere in that maze of empty buildings was Sarah. How was he ever going to find her in time? Snatching up the radio transmitter, he barked out his location and requested backup.

* * *

Her lungs burning and her heart slamming against her ribs in fright, Sarah whimpered as Peters moved the knife to her throat and twisted his hand in her hair, practically dragging her down the dusty street running through the middle of the complex. She knew he was enjoying her pain, feeding on it like a shark on a helpless flounder, but she would have got down on her knees and begged for mercy if she'd thought for a minute it would slow him down long enough for Dugan to find her. And he would find her; she didn't doubt it for a minute. But would it be in time?

Terror a growing ball of ice in her stomach, she grabbed at the hand gripping her hair, crying out as he deliberately tightened his hold. "You're h-hurting me! I c-can't k-keep up with you if you keep pulling my hair."

"You'll keep up," he threatened, letting her feel the sharpness of the blade, "or you'll never see that lover boy detective of yours again. You understand? I got nothing to lose by killing you." Releasing her hair abruptly, he shoved her in front of him. "Now walk!"

She stumbled, then caught herself, a sob of relief ripping from her throat now that she was finally free of his revolting touch. On stiff legs, she started forward, her eyes searching, constantly searching for a way out. But the only shelter in sight were the vacant, barren buildings that cast lengthening shadows as the sun slipped lower on the horizon. There was nowhere to run, no escape in sight. Hysteria pushed closer, the acrid taste of fear bitter on her tongue. Now what? she thought frantically. What was she supposed to do now?

"Hold it," her captor ordered suddenly. "We're going in here."

He motioned to a building on their left that looked like it had been bombed. Windows were broken out, doors hung ajar and glass and debris littered the yard and walkways. Sarah took one look at it and felt bile rise in her throat. "No," she whispered. She couldn't go in there. He couldn't expect her to meekly walk into the place where he was going to brutally rape her!

But he not only expected it, he insisted, viciously pushing and prodding her, laughing as she stumbled through the broken down door of a two-bedroom apartment. He was crazy, she thought wildly, choking on a whimper as she shied away from him. She could hear it in his uncontrollable giggle, see it in the deranged depths of his eyes. He wasn't going to rape her. He was going to kill her!

Terrified, she could feel the walls closing in on her, trapping her. With a cry of panic, she broke away suddenly and darted into another room, her pulse frenetic. Only then did she realize where her fear had led her. The small room had high windows and only one door. And Joseph Peters was standing in it. Laughing.

"Oh, God," she whispered.

"That's right," he chuckled, tossing his sunglasses and hat aside as if he were getting ready to enjoy himself. "You're trapped, but you can scream if you like. I don't mind."

He wasn't just giving her permission to scream, he wanted her to. The knowledge pulled Sarah up sharp, dulling the terror that clouded her mind, steadying her. He wanted her not only to scream, but to panic, to fall apart, to turn into a sobbing, hysterical, *helpless* woman who would be too devastated by her own fear to fight him off. He wanted her to be a victim.

Rage hit her, hot and biting and bracing, a fury that had been building for three long, lonely years. "No." She didn't realize she'd spoken aloud until she saw his eyes narrow with anger. Her spine snapped straight, her chin lifting to a fighting angle. "No," she said again, her voice stronger. "I'm not going to scream for you. I wouldn't give you the satisfaction. I was a victim once, and I hated it. I won't let you or anyone else do that to me again, not without a fight."

"It won't do you any good," he said, his eyes furious as he crouched and spread his hands, the knife he held glinting wickedly as he urged her on. "I'm going to win, but come on. Give it your best shot."

He was so cocky she wanted to strangle him. She didn't kid herself into thinking she had even half a chance of besting him. He wasn't that much bigger than she was, but he was a man and there was no way she could match his strength. And the knife gave him the decided edge. But if, by some miracle, she made it through this alive, she'd be able to live with herself knowing that she hadn't wimped out.

Without a word of warning, she snatched up a splintered board off the floor and threw it at him, catching him off guard. Snarling, he jumped out of the way. A second later a broken bottle sailed by his ear, missing him by an inch. The war was on.

Breathing hard, his heart hammering in his ears, Dugan raced into one deserted apartment after another, his eyes stark with growing panic. Time. He was running out of time! He could feel it spilling through his fingers, slipping away, and there didn't seem to be a damn thing he could do about it. She was here . . . somewhere. He could almost hear her voice in his ear, calling to him, her need for him tearing him apart, but she was just out of reach. If he had to check every unit, every single apartment, he'd never get to her in time.

Frustration building in him like lava gathering in the belly of a volcano, he bolted out of the last unit at the eastern end of the complex and stopped, ready to yell the place down if he had to find her. But before he had time to open his mouth, he heard her scream. For one horrifying moment every muscle in his body turned to stone, the reverberations of her cry rippling through him over and over again, an echo without end that almost sent him to his knees. Then, in the next instant, he was running like a man possessed, his gray eyes murderous with rage.

His ears straining, he sprinted toward the very heart of the complex, stopping at every cross street he came to, holding his breath to listen. But all he heard was the soft whisper of the wind as it found its way through shattered windows and broken doors. Swearing, he ran on, praying he wasn't making a mistake. All his instincts warned him she was in the middle of the complex. If she wasn't, if even now he was running right by the building where she was being held, he'd live with the agony of his wrong decision for the rest of his life.

Hurry. Urgency pushed at him. Lungs straining, he stumbled onto the street that dissected the complex right down the middle. It was a short street, long enough for only four units. And Sarah had to be in one of them. But which one, damn it? Which one?

When she screamed this time, the hackles rose on the back of his neck. She'd just run out of time. Snatching his service revolver form his shoulder harness, he lunged toward the nearest unit.

Crouched for another assault, Sarah watched the devil tormenting her edge to her left, as if he planned to slip around behind her and grab her by the throat. He was so intent on her, he didn't realize that he'd left the doorway, unwittingly giving her her only chance of escape. Before her heart could pound out another frantic beat, she was running.

In the next instant he caught her in a flying tackle, slamming her into the dirty floor. A board gouged painfully into her hip; glass cut her hands as she instinctively threw them out in front of her to break her fall. She groaned, shuddering, and frantically pulled at the hands tearing at her clothes even as she felt her strength deserting her. Then he was forcing her onto her back and locking her hands over her head, and suddenly the nightmare swallowed her whole.

She screamed then because she couldn't help herself. Because there was no escape from the dark shadows closing in on her, weighing her down, stealing her breath, her soul. Because she was sinking deeper and deeper into the black inkiness of her worst fears and there was nothing else she could do to save herself. Because the man she unknowingly screamed for was the only one who could pull her out of the darkness and back into the light.

Lost in her own private hell, she never heard Dugan's hoarse cry, never felt Joseph Peters being ripped off her, never heard the scream of sirens right outside as Dugan slammed the other man up against the wall, knocked the knife out of his hands and clapped a pair of handcuffs on his wrists. Her hands suddenly free, she curled in on herself, hugging herself, tears silently streaming out from underneath her tightly shut eyelids.

A hand closed around Dugan's heart at the sight of her. Her hair was wild and tangled, her suit filthy, a button torn from the jacket, which had parted to reveal one breast still covered in a lacy bra. But he was in time, and that was the only thing that stopped him from burying his fist in the stomach of the bound man. His jaw tight, he pushed Peters at the army of officers suddenly swarming into the apartment in answer to the backup call he'd sent out what seemed like a lifetime ago. "Read him his rights," he snarled.

But when he turned back to Sarah and knelt down at her side in the glass, his tone was as soft as a summer breeze. "Sarah? Honey, it's all right now. You're safe." He ached to touch her, to pull her close, needing to hold her like he had never needed a woman in his life, but he was afraid. Afraid she would cringe from him, afraid that a touch from any man right now, even him, would push her right over the edge. So he talked to her instead, murmuring reassurances to her, his voice low and soothing and filled with love. Why did he have to come so close to losing her to realize how much he loved her?

Trapped in the darkness, Sarah stirred, the whisper of Dugan's words flowing over her like a healing balm, coaxing her, calming her fears, making her promises she'd only heard in her dreams. Gradually she realized that she was no longer being held, that she wasn't just hearing Dugan's voice in her head. He really was there beside her. Cautiously opening her eyes, she looked up to find him hovering protectively over her like a dark avenger, his eyes alight with a tenderness that flooded her with warmth.

"Dugan?"

Slowly, giving her time to pull back, he gently pushed her hair back from her face. "I'm here now, sweetheart. You're safe. No one's going to hurt you."

She glanced over to the doorway, in time to see Joseph Peters being led away in handcuffs, but it was the relief she heard in Dugan's voice and felt in his unsteady fingers that told her the nightmare was finally over. "Oh, Dugan!" Bursting into tears, she threw herself into his arms.

Chapter 12

The house was dark and quiet, the clock on the nightstand showing 1:15. Lying on his side, Sarah snug against him and finally asleep, Dugan tightened his arm around her slender waist, reassuring himself again that she was really there where she belonged—in his bed and so close he could feel her every breath. Even after Peters had been taken away and Sarah had thrown herself into his arms, he'd worried that he'd lost her. After that one brief burst of tears against his chest, she'd made a visible effort to tighten her grip on her emotions by withdrawing into herself, distancing herself from the nightmare, from him. She didn't shy away from his touch, but he knew he wasn't reaching her, and it had scared the hell out of him.

Battered, bruised and cut from Peters' knife and the shattered glass on the floor, she hadn't offered a word of protest when he'd insisted she let him take her to the hospital. But in the emergency room, she'd been pale and shaken, her dark eyes haunted with the past, and Dugan hadn't wasted any time in getting her out of there as quickly as possible. There was no reason she couldn't have gone to her own home then—Peters was in jail without a bond, his fingerprints identifying him as Peter Jackson, a suspect wanted for a series of rapes in Oregon. But Dugan hadn't even asked her where she wanted to go. He'd bundled her into his car and taken her home with him...where she belonged. And the only emotion she'd shown was when Tory had burst into tears at the sight of her and run into her arms.

That was hours ago. He'd hovered over her and pampered her and done everything he could to assure her that the nightmare was finally over and they could get on with the rest of their lives. But she'd been in no shape to discuss the future. Violet shadows lining her eyes and so exhausted she could hardly see straight, she'd avoided his bed—and sleep—like the plague, afraid of the demons that would come out of their hiding places in her mind the minute she let her guard drop. Aching to wrap her close, he'd offered her a brandy she hadn't wanted, but she hadn't had the strength to refuse. The liquor had spilled through her, slowly easing the tension that was the only thing holding her together. Only then was he able to convince her to lie down.

There'd never been any question that he would spend what was left of the night right there by her side. He hadn't planned to touch her, to do anything but be there for her if her dreams turned frightening, but she'd turned to him, snuggling against him until she was so close that nothing, not even air, could come between them. Her sigh a whisper of contentment in the night, she'd closed her eyes and slept.

Burying his face in the soft cloud of her hair, he dragged in the sweet scent of her, instinctively knowing he wouldn't sleep that night. He'd come too close to losing her. Five minutes more at the garage, a cat that decided not to dart across the road, a daughter who might not have had the presence of mind to run to the window and get a description of the truck and the license number, and he never would have made it in time. Chance. He'd never believed in it before; he'd never doubt its importance again. He also didn't think he'd ever be able to let Sarah out of his sight again. She was his, and he was keeping her close.

She wouldn't like it, of course. She was too independent to meekly accept a possessive attitude from any man for long. But he wasn't just anybody off the street. He was the man who loved her, the man who intended to spend the next fifty years making sure she knew it. Her days of being alone, of fighting her demons alone, were over.

By six-thirty the next morning he was in the kitchen making coffee, satisfied that he had their future all worked out. They'd get married as soon as possible, and then when the school year was over, convince Laura to give over permanent custody of Tory. He didn't fool himself into thinking it would be easy, but Laura wanted Tory's happiness as much as she wanted her own marriage to work. When she saw how important it was to Tory to stay with him, she would have to come around. Then, of course, he would have to sell the house. It was just big enough for the three of them now, but once he and Sarah had children, they would need more room.

His eyes warm at the thought of making babies with Sarah, he turned to get a coffee mug from the cabinet next to the sink and stopped short at the sight of Sarah standing in the doorway. When he'd eased from the bed less than twenty minutes ago, she'd been sound asleep, her face half buried under her hair, her body warm and pliant next to his. Now she stood before him as if braced for a fight, the soft white nightgown she'd worn to bed replaced with jeans and a green and white striped shirt. Even then, he started to smile at her, to cross to her and wish her good morning. But then he spied the small suitcase she'd set just inside the doorway.

His eyes snapped back up to hers. "You going somewhere?"

Wincing at the harshness of his tone, she nodded stiffly. "Home... to Houston."

She saw him stiffen as if she'd struck him and would have done anything short of selling her soul to take the words back, but she couldn't. Not if she was ever going to be the strong, loving woman she needed to be for him. She'd mulled it over for hours before she'd finally gone to sleep last night and had fought the inevitability of it in her dreams. But there was no avoiding the truth. She loved Dugan with all her heart, but until she could allow him to touch her freely, love her freely, fear would always be waiting in the background, looking for the chance to come between them. A future—if there was one in the cards for them—was something they couldn't share until she'd learned to deal with the past. To do that, she had to go back to Houston and face what had happened to her, deal with it, and find a way to put it behind her once and for all.

So she was leaving him, just like that, without a word of warning. A knife twisted in his heart, the pain catching him off guard, stunning him. Damn it, he wouldn't let her do this to him, to them, not when things were finally starting to work out. He'd waited a long time to let a woman into his life again, and he wasn't losing her! "Why?" he demanded tightly, stepping toward her. "There's nothing there for you anymore. Your future is here. With me. Damn it, Sarah, I love you!"

She knew it wasn't the way he'd wanted to tell her; she could see the regret in his eyes. Foolish tears choked her. Did he really think he needed candlelight and roses to tell her how he felt? She'd suspected the first morning she'd awakened in his bed, when he'd unthinkingly scared her by coming down on top of her, then cursed himself in a voice still rough with desire. She'd known for sure when he'd let her make love to him.

"I know you do," she said softly, taking his hands in hers before he could reach for her. If she went into his arms now, she knew she might never find the strength to leave. "I think I must have fallen in love with you that night we danced down by the river. You were so careful with me I wanted to cry. But don't you see, that's why I have to go back to Houston."

"Because I was careful with you?" he retorted incredulously. "Honey, I'm not a monster. I don't want you to be afraid of me."

"But you shouldn't have to worry about the woman you love freezing if you hold her too tightly," she argued. "You shouldn't have to constantly be on guard, questioning your every move before you make it. That wouldn't be fair to either one of us, and I'm afraid that after a while, you wouldn't want to touch me at all rather than touch me the wrong way."

"Sweetheart, that's ridiculous," he began, then realized that he was cavalierly shrugging off her very real fears. Swearing under his breath, he tried again. "You're forgetting that you're not in this alone. I've got a vested interest here, too. I love you. Whatever problems we have, we'll work out together."

If only it were that easy. Her smile heartrending, she shook her head. "*We* don't have a problem. *I* do. And I'm the only one who can fix it."

No! He wanted to yell at her, to shake some sense into her, to drag her into his arms and kiss her until he'd wiped the city of Houston and what had happened to her there right out of her head forever. But the stubborn look in her eye warned him nothing he could say would change her mind. She was going, and if he didn't want to lose her completely, he had to let her go. But doing that was going to be the hardest thing he'd ever done.

His fingers tightened around hers. "I expect you to call me every night," he said gruffly. "If you need me, all you have to do is say the word and I'll be there."

Her tears spilled over then, turning her smile watery. "Every night," she promised thickly. Lifting her mouth to his, she gave him a sweet, poignant, all too brief kiss. Then, unable to manage a word around the lump in her throat, she turned and reached for her suitcase. The front door closed behind her to the accompaniment of Dugan's softly muttered curses.

Houston. It was big and sprawling, the freeways jammed with crazy drivers at all hours of the day and night, the thick, humid air scented with everything from pine and exhaust to oil and natural gas from the refineries. Unlike San Antonio, which had a slower, less hurried pace, time always moved at a fast clip here. Fortunes could be made and lost as quickly as the rise and fall of the price of a barrel of crude.

At one time Sarah had loved the hustle and bustle, the excitement of living in a city that always seemed to be on the edge. But now everywhere she turned, she was hit with images from the night she had spent years trying to forget. The seafood restaurant down at the ship channel that Trent had taken her to just hours before he'd raped her. The hospital she'd gone to afterward. The policeman who'd wanted nothing but the facts and had been so concerned with doing his job that he hadn't seemed to care that her world had just been shattered to bits. Her parents' home, the house she grew up in, the place she'd run to after the ordeal of the hospital rather than return to her apartment and the scene of the crime.

Like water gushing from a faucet with a broken handle, the memories flooded her, swamping her. Once she would have found a way to distract her thoughts, but now she let the emotions come, freeing them from the dark closet in her heart where they'd been locked away, festering, for too long. Pain that cut to the bone, outrage that any man would dare to do such a thing to her, guilt that she hadn't somehow found a way to stop him even though he'd outweighed her by sixty pounds, a deeper, more horrifying guilt that she'd somehow brought it on herself.

She'd felt all those things and more, tortured herself with them, hid from them and let them change not only her life but her. But she was through running. With the loving support of her parents, who were happy to have her home for as long as she needed to stay to work things out, she took a good hard look at the past. Each day she faced a different resentment, a new hurt she hadn't even realized she'd suppressed, agonizing over feelings she should have long since dealt with, until she could finally accept them one by one without justification. And in the acceptance, she found the strength to let them go.

By the time she crawled into bed each night, she was exhausted and emotionally spent. But she never went to sleep without first calling Dugan. Just the sound of his voice steadied her. She would lay in the dark with the phone pressed close to her ear and talk of inconsequential things, silly things, things that had nothing to do with the messages they were really sending to each other—he missed her; he wanted her back in his arms; there was no place she'd rather be; soon, she couldn't stand it if it wasn't soon. Unspoken promises—for now that was all that she could give him.

Then, a week to the day after she'd forced herself to leave him, she came face to face with her past in the Galleria. She and her mother had gone to the mall to shop for shoes when her mother looked up and saw Trent Kingston walking toward them. Sarah saw him almost at the same time and stopped in her tracks, her heart thudding dully.

"Let's go into the card shop," her mother said quickly, grabbing her arm and trying to tug her into the shop they were standing directly in front of. "I need to get an anniversary card for the Nelsons. And it isn't too early to look at the Mother's Day cards. I promise I won't look if you want to pick one out for me."

She was talking a mile a minute, her eyes as desperate as her voice, her gaze jumping to the man rapidly approaching them. Sarah patted her clutching fingers without taking her eyes from Trent. "It's okay, Mother. I'm all right. We don't need to duck into the card shop."

Torn, Margaret Haywood let out her breath in a little huff, the frown linking her brows deepening as shoppers streamed around them the way a current did a jammed log. "Are you sure, sweetheart? You've got nothing to prove to that...worm," she said scathingly. "He hasn't seen us yet. He won't even know you're avoiding him."

"But I would know, and anyway, he's seen us."

As if he'd suddenly caught the scent of danger, Trent Kingston froze, his head coming up like a wild animal caught in the scope of a hunter's rife. From thirty yards away, Sarah knew the exact moment he spotted her. His jaw went slack and his tanned face turned a sickly shade of green.

For what seemed like an eternity, no one moved. The throng of people crowding the mall slipped to the edges of her consciousness and all Sarah saw was the man who had haunted her for longer than she cared to remember. Since that fateful night three years ago, her biggest fear had been that one day when she least expected it, she'd run into him again. Their eyes would meet and just that quickly she would be back in his car, helpless and powerless and hurting.

But now as her gaze locked with his, nothing was as she'd expected. He was the uncomfortable one, the one who was squirming, the one who couldn't quite look her in the eye, the one who was helpless and powerless and pathetically weak. The knowledge that he knew he had wronged her was there in his face, and suddenly she knew why he had accused her of leading him on, of enticing him, then crying rape. She'd thought he was arrogant and cocky and so damn sure that no woman could ever refuse him that he couldn't see what he'd done as anything other than his God given right. But all that time he'd known what he was doing, the coward, and he hadn't been able to face what he was—a rapist. So he'd blamed her.

All this time she'd been afraid of a coward, a worm, as her mother had so aptly named him. Why had it taken her so long to see him for what he really was? He'd hurt her once, put her through a hell that was every woman's worst nightmare, but she'd survived. It hadn't been easy and she hadn't always been as strong as she'd have liked, but she'd handled what fate had thrown at her and found a way not to let it drag her down where he was—in the gutter with the rest of the worms. He and the memory of what he'd done to her could never hurt her again.

"Good," her mother said in satisfaction as he turned abruptly and strode away from them in the opposite direction. "He's slithering off. Probably looking for a dark hole to crawl into. Sweetheart, are you all right?" she asked anxiously when Sarah suddenly broke into laughter. "I know you must be upset—"

Chuckling, Sarah gave her mother a fierce hug. "No, I'm fine. In fact, I'm terrific! I can't begin to tell you what our little shopping spree has done for me!"

The house was dark, the only light that of the television in the den. Slouched in his favorite chair, his eyes trained unseeingly on the television screen, Dugan took a long swig from the bottle of beer he held balanced against his thigh and gave serious consideration to getting drunk. Not just drunk, he amended, taking another pull on the bottle. Plastered.

Who the hell was there to object, anyway? he thought morosely. Tory had gone to Fiesta activities with a girlfriend from school and was going to spend the night at her house. His own house was quiet as a tomb, and he was lonely as hell. It was almost midnight, and Sarah hadn't called yet. Before tonight, she'd always called well before eleven.

God, was he losing her? Was that what her silence was all about? For the last six nights, he'd waited for her to tell him how she was faring with her struggle with her past, but she'd steered the conversation clear of anything serious. And he'd let her. Because he was afraid if he pushed her to tell him about her day, she'd tell him something he didn't want to hear...like she'd had time to put things in perspective, and she was beginning to think that what she felt for him was nothing but a combination of gratitude and lust.

No, damn it! he thought furiously. He didn't care what kind of decisions she came to in Houston, he wasn't letting her end things between them. If he didn't hear from her by tomorrow night, then he'd catch the first commuter flight out the following morning and be at her parents' house in time for breakfast to talk some sense into her. They could be back in S.A. by lunchtime.

He wasn't going to lose her!

The pealing of the doorbell shattered his musings and the brooding silence that crept out from the shadows surrounding him. Scowling at the clock on the VCR, he swore. Who the hell came calling at a quarter to twelve? If it was another of those damn reporters he'd been avoiding for the last week, he was going to haul their carcasses in for harassment! Ever since they'd discovered that Sarah had been staying with him during the time Peters had stalked her, they'd been pestering the hell out of him.

Slamming his half full beer bottle down on the end table, he stood up and stalked barefoot to the door. Jerking it open when the doorbell rang again, he snarled, "Look, buddy, you're pushing your luck—Sarah!"

She waited in the glare of the porch light, her heart thudding painfully at the sight of him. It had only been a week since she'd left him; it felt like ten years. Dressed in cutoffs and a faded T-shirt, his hard jaw shadowed with a day's growth of whiskers and his hair tumbling over his brow, he looked better than her dreams. Dear Lord, how she'd missed him!

Wanting to step into his arms, she forced herself to stay where she was. "Can I come in?" she asked quietly.

He started, suddenly realizing he was still blocking the entrance. "Yes, of course." Damn it, why were they being so formal with each other? Moving aside abruptly, he motioned her inside.

The soft click of the latch sounded unnaturally loud in the darkness that engulfed them with the closing of the door. Surprised by the lack of light and the pervading silence, Sarah glanced up at Dugan and could see only the gleam of his eyes in the thick shadows. "Where's Tory?"

"Spending the night with a girlfriend." Questions tugged at him, ones he'd sworn he wouldn't ask, but one popped out before he could stop it. "Why didn't you tell me last night you were coming back tonight?"

She heard the faint accusation in his tone, the worry and doubts he wouldn't admit to, and knew the past week had been as difficult for him as it had for her. She almost reached for him then, the promise that she would never leave him again there on her tongue, just waiting to be spoken. But first they had to talk, and she couldn't hang onto her thoughts if he was touching her.

"Because I didn't know then," she replied. "Something happened today—"

"If you came all this way just to tell me in person that you've changed your mind about loving me, you can just save it," he cut in fiercely. "I don't believe it. You love me as much as I love you, so you damn well better accept it, because the subject isn't open for debate."

Stunned, Sarah could only stare at him in the darkness, her heart in her eyes and a tender smile tugging at her mouth. "Well," she said in a voice laced with amusement, "I'm certainly glad we got that settled. Now would you like to hear what happened today?"

Expecting an argument, Dugan blinked, then reached over to switch on the entry hall light. At the sight of Sarah's teasing grin and dancing eyes, he did what he'd been dying to do from the moment he'd opened the door. He hauled her into his arms.

She settled against him with a murmur of need, the softness of her breasts pressed against his chest, her hips resting comfortably against his as her arms snaked around his waist. Dugan felt a ragged groan escape his tight throat and did nothing to stop it. God, he'd missed her! Maybe after they'd shared forty or fifty years together, he'd be able to let go of her for longer than five minutes at a stretch, but not anytime soon.

"Okay," he growled, his hands slowly reacquainting themselves with the delicate curves of her body. "I'm listening. Talk."

"I saw Trent Kingston today at the Galleria."

"What the—" Pulling back abruptly, he scowled down at her, confused by the lilting note he heard in her voice. "I never expected to see you smile when you talked about that bastard. What happened?"

She laughed, unable to contain the happiness bubbling up inside her, and lifted her arms to encircle the strong column of his neck. "I realized what a pathetic creature he was."

She told him everything she'd gone through the past week, her soul-searching, the pain of facing memories she'd hidden from the light of day, the exhilaration when she'd finally realized that Trent had never deserved the power she had given him over her in her own mind. "He's a miserable excuse for a man," she concluded. "A worm, as my mother says. When he recognized me, he ran." The surprise of that would stay with her for many years to come. Her eyes, bright with confidence, lifted to Dugan's. "He can't ever hurt me again."

Elation shot through him, urging him to snatch her up and carry her to bed. But he needed her to say the words that acknowledged that she was finally and irrevocably his. "Does this mean you're ready to marry me now?" he asked huskily as his hands settled on her slender shoulders. "Because that's what I want, sweetheart. Complete commitment."

Her smile faltered ever so slightly, but her eyes never left his. "Oh, Dugan, I do, too! But—"

His fingers molded her shoulders, alarm skittering through him. "But what? Damn it, Sarah, you can't still have doubts—"

She cut him off with a kiss. A nip of her teeth, the slow, sensual glide of her tongue, and his thoughts scrambled. Groaning a protest low in his throat when she abruptly pulled back and stepped free of his touch, he reached for her. But she only laughed softly and took his hand. "Ask me again after you make love to me," she said, and pulled him after her into his bedroom.

For the past week he'd dreamed of nothing but having her back in his bed, naked and horizontal, but he hadn't missed her request that *he* make love to *her* this time. Something wasn't quite right here, and he didn't like his suspicions. Standing at the side of his bed, he watched her turn on the lamp on the nightstand, but made no move to touch her. "If you want to test yourself, sweetheart, fine, that's what we'll do. But don't think that whatever happens between us tonight in bed is going to change anything. You're still going to marry me."

Her eyes, big and dark in the glow of the single lamp, entreated him to understand. "I have to know I won't fall apart if you hold me too tight or love me the way we both want you to. Please, Dugan, this is important to me."

She was so earnest, so anxious to please him, to make everything perfect between them. Humbled, he knew if she'd asked him for an engagement ring with a rock the size of Gibraltar just then, he'd have found a way to get it for her. God help him if she ever discovered there was nothing he could ever deny her! "I love you and I'm not letting you go, no matter what," he promised her. "Do you want the light off?"

Her smile broke through, sweet and tender and just a little bit anxious. "No. I don't have anything to hide except a mole on my right hip. How about you?"

His lips twitched. "I'll show you my mole if you'll show me yours. Deal?"

"Deal," she whispered, and stepped into his arms.

He promised himself he was going to build her passion gradually, to take her slowly, luxuriously. There was no hurry; they had all night. And if his patience was all it took to free her of the last of her doubts and inhibitions, he could damn well keep a tight rein on his self-control. Sarah . . . pleasing her . . . loving her . . . driving her to distraction . . . was all that mattered. Every touch would woo, every kiss seduce, until she shattered under him.

But the one thing he hadn't taken into consideration was the hunger. The second his mouth settled possessively on hers and his arms wound tightly around her, it was there, heating his blood, his loins, consuming them both like a fire pushed along by a swirling wind. And Sarah only added fuel to the flames. She was so giving! Her mouth was eager under his, her hands kneading and stroking, ardently moving over him as if she were starved for the feel of him. How could he think about going slow when she moved against him in a way that drove him wild, telling him without words that she wanted him, hungered for him, now? Groaning her name, he gathered her close, but it wasn't nearly close enough. Scattering kisses across the curve of her cheek, the enticing angle of her jaw, the soft tempting skin of her throat, he blindly reached for the buttons of her blouse.

There was a pounding in his head that echoed the pounding beat of his heart, a driving, pagan beat that blocked out everything but his burning desire for the woman in his arms. But then her blouse parted and slipped to the floor. Less than a heartbeat later her bra followed. Dugan sucked in a sharp breath at the sight of her, his fingers trembling as he reached for her. Her bare breasts were magnolia blossom white in the light from the lamp, her nipples a brownish rose and already pouting prettily for him, begging for his touch.

"Sweetheart, this is so much better than making love in the dark," he rasped. "Do you know how beautiful you are?"

She wasn't, she wanted to tell him. She'd always been too tall, too gawky and awkward as a teenager, to ever have any confidence in her looks. And then, later, after the rape, the last thing she'd wanted to be was attractive to a man. But the glow in Dugan's eyes, the trembling of his fingers as they closed around her breasts made her want to be drop-dead gorgeous for him.

Her smile an unconscious siren's call, she murmured, "You make me feel beautiful," and leaned into him trustingly, her mouth lifting to his for another hot, drugging kiss that seemed to go on forever.

Sinking. Dugan could feel himself sinking fast, desire tearing at him with unsheathed claws until his body was keenly sensitive to Sarah's every move. Her hands slid under his shirt and he burned. Her hips settled against him, cradling his hardness, and raw need set his blood boiling. Then her bare breasts rubbed against his chest and her tongue stole into his mouth to tease and dance and seduce, silently whispering to him, "Take me." Control, what he had left of it, snapped.

His clothes went flying, and the rest of hers soon followed. Before she could do more than gasp, they were both bare and in each other's arms, his mouth hard and demanding on hers. He couldn't think and didn't care. He wanted her under him now, and nothing else mattered. Sweeping her up in his arms, he carried her to the bed.

It wasn't until he came down on top of her that sanity returned. Suddenly realizing what he had done, he froze, swearing at himself as he started to jerk away. "I'm sorry, sweetheart! I swore I was going to go slow—"

"No!" she cried, her arms flying around him to hug him close. "Stay!"

He hesitated, hating the thought of her ever again cringing from him in fear. "Honey, I told you it doesn't matter. You don't have to test yourself this way."

"But it's okay," she choked, tears welling in her eyes as he settled uncertainly against her. It was more than okay. It was wonderful! She could feel every inch of him pressing against her, crushing her into the mattress, and not a single twinge of fear stirred to life. "Oh, Dugan, it really is okay! Can't you feel how right this is?"

Love surged in him, his fingers tenderly brushing her hair back from her glowing face. "Yes," he whispered, kissing her gently. He'd felt a rightness with her from the very beginning, a bonding, a sense of destiny with her he'd never felt with any other woman. Drawing back only far enough so he could see her eyes, he grinned wickedly. "Now that I've got you right where I want you, are you going to marry me? You'd better say yes, woman, because I warn you right now, nothing else is acceptable."

Her eyes dancing, she reached up to tangle her fingers in his hair. "Oh, it's not, is it? Then I guess I'd better say yes."

"What was that?" he teased, leaning just a little closer. "I don't believe I heard you."

"Yes," she whispered. Dear Lord, how she loved him! "Yes, yes, yes!"

She was still whispering yeses when his mouth covered hers and he slowly entered her, still whispering yeses when he tumbled with her over the edge into ecstasy moments later. A soft, dreamy smile playing about her kiss-bruised mouth, she hugged him close and floated back to earth, his name a sigh on her lips. If time had ceased to exist at that moment, she doubted that she would have found the strength to care. She held the only thing in the world that mattered to her close to her heart. As long as she had his love, she would never need anything else again.

* * * * *

ᴠINTIMATE MOMENTS®
™ Silhouette

Ever since the appearance of Linda Howard's
incredibly popular MACKENZIE'S MOUNTAIN in 1989,
we've received literally hundreds of letters, all asking
that same question. At last the book we've all been
waiting for is here.

In September, look for MACKENZIE'S MISSION (Intimate
Moments #445), Joe's story as only Linda Howard
could tell it.

And Joe is only the first of an exciting breed here at
Silhouette Intimate Moments. Starting in September,
we'll be bringing you one title every month in our new
American Heroes program. In addition to Linda
Howard, the **American Heroes** lineup will be written
by such stars as Kathleen Eagle, Kathleen Korbel,
Patricia Gardner Evans, Marilyn Pappano, Heather
Graham Pozzessere and more. Don't miss a
single one!

**It's Opening Night in October—
and you're invited!
Take a look at romance with a
brand-new twist, as the stars
of tomorrow make their
debut today!
It's LOVE:
an age-old story—
now, with
*WORLD PREMIERE
APPEARANCES* by:**

Patricia Thayer—Silhouette Romance #895
JUST MAGGIE—Meet the Texas rancher who wins this pretty
teacher's heart...and lose your own heart, too!

Anne Marie Winston—Silhouette Desire #742
BEST KEPT SECRETS—Join old lovers reunited and see what
secret wonders have been hiding...beneath the flames!

Sierra Rydell—Silhouette Special Edition #772
ON MIDDLE GROUND—Drift toward Twilight, Alaska, with this
widowed mother and collide—heart first—into body heat
enough to melt the frozen tundra!

Kyle Carlton—Silhouette Intimate Moments #454
KIDNAPPED!—Dare to look on as a timid wallflower blos-
soms and falls in fearless love—with her gruff, mysterious
kidnapper!

**Don't miss the classics of tomorrow—
premiering today—only from**

PREM

Welcome to Conard County, Wyoming, where the sky spreads bold and blue above men and women who draw their strength from the wild western land and from the bonds of the love they share.

Join author Rachel Lee for a trip to the American West as we all want it to be. In Conard County, Wyoming, she's created a special place where men are men and women are more than a match for them.

In the first book of the miniseries, EXILE'S END (Intimate Moments #449), you'll meet Amanda Grant, whose imagination takes her to worlds of wizards and warlocks in the books she writes, but whose everyday life is gray and forlorn—until Ransom Laird walks onto her land with trouble in his wake and a promise in his heart. Once you meet them, you won't want to stop reading. And once you've finished the book, you'll be looking forward to all the others in the miniseries, starting with CHEROKEE THUNDER, available in December.

EXILE'S END is available this September, only from Silhouette Intimate Moments.

CON1